DOUBLE L
VS
THE CARTEL

Derrick Harper

Self Made Publishing
TARBORO, NC

Double L vs. The Cartel
A Novel By Derrick Harper

Copyright © 2014 by Derrick Harper

Double L vs The Cartel/ Derrick Harper. -- 1st ed.

ISBN 9780692363355

ACKNOWLEDGEMENTS

I would first like to thank my father and mother, Arthur Burton and Carolyn Brown. Without you, there would be no me. I give a special shot out to my babies, Radarius Moody, Alexis Andrews, Tashawn Gunter, Shonderrica Harper, Trenton Harper, and Derrick Harper, Jr. Daddy loves you all! I would like to thank their mothers for giving me beautiful kids. I could never forget my grandmother, Beatrice Holliman. I love you!

I would also like to thank Esteamz Entertainment for giving me a chance to show my skills. My special editor, Tina Nance, thank you for putting up with me and doing a great job. My closest homies, Kentay Knight, Toby Smallwood, Tiyon Cherry, and my brother, Terrance Harper.

R.I.P to Kenny Freeman, Tyrale Knight, Mooky Exam, Wayne Johnson, Qwan Carr, Doanld Hines, Anthony Williams, Scotty Dickens, Laquanta Knight.

Shout out to the special lady in my life.

If I forgot you, charge it to my mind, not to my heart. Shout out to Marion Designs for the book cover. This is just the beginning. I get better every time, so fasten your seat belts!

I love you Aunt Eve!

Connect with me at derrickharper805@yahoo.com or on Facebook: Dayself Harper-el

CHAPTER 1

*D*ayself strolled through the prison yard, glancing periodical-
ly at the men playing basketball. He could tell by the way
they went to the hoop with vengeance that the physical activity
was a method to get away from the pain of being locked up. One
of the men go to the rack to shoot. He's fouled and falls hard to
the pavement. His homies run to the basketball court with knives
already drawn. Just another day behind the wall.

Dayself sped up to get one more lap in. He was enjoying the
sun, on a not so hot day. He walked and thought to himself, *damn,
tomorrow this will be all over with!*

The guards rushed past him to the fight, scared shitless. They
sprayed mace in different directions, some spraying other guards.
Dayself knew the yard was about to close, as more guards rushed
past him. To see brothers hurting each other over a basketball
game bothered him. The five years he had done for robbery had
dramatically changed his outlook on life. He saw many things
from a different point of view than when he was first locked up.
His mind stayed thinking about how he was going to get rich one
day. Dayself watched as the guards regained control of the yard,
carrying each of the inmates to the hole in handcuffs.

Dayself Burton was 24 years old, 5'9", 195 pounds, with olive
colored skin and a close haircut. His wife always told him that
he favored the rapper J. Cole, with muscles. He didn't care about

all that, he just wanted the money J. Cole was playing with. As Dayself entered the prison block, the smell of musk, shit, and weed hit him in the face. He looked around and noticed that everyone was focused on the two televisions sitting high, bolted to the wall beyond reach.

How could these guys sit here like they have no cares in the world, when some have life sentences? Dayself wondered as he took the twenty iron steps two at a time to his room. He closed the door behind him and picked up the designs that he had his friend draw up for him. The plan was to open his own club and studio when he got home. He tried to focus on how and where he was going to get the money, but his mind kept drifting to three people. His wife, Malisa Burton aka Piepie, her two year old daughter, Prokoshia, who was two months old when Dayself met her mother, and his seven year old son, Lil Dee.

Lil Dee's mother was a full-fledged crack head. Nothing could stop her from getting her hit, so she had lost custody of her kids. Lil Dee ended up moving in with one of his aunts, who was very mean to him. Getting his custody of his son was one of the first things he planned to do when his feet touched the ground. He couldn't believe that he let the justice system take him from his family like that, but this time was the last time. That, he could promise.

Dayself let his mind roam all over the place until he dozed off to sleep, waking with barely enough time to take his shower. He stepped in the shower and let out a loud breath of air. "Damn, I'll be able to wear street clothes tomorrow and not these half clean clothes in this motherfucker," he said to no one in particular as he carefully laid his wash cloth, soap, and towel. One's mind can only wonder what went down in prison showers.

After his shower, Dayself dried off and stepped back into his room. He closed the door and lit up his last blunt of OG Kush, letting the smoke from the weed take his mind on another ride. Every time he inhaled the smoke in his lungs, a different thought came to him of how he was going to get rich.

The door to the block opened, and one of the inmates yelled,

"Man in the block!"

Dayself took two more pulls and threw the blunt in the toilet. The officer made rounds, checking each room carefully; making sure no one had hung themselves, been beaten up, or killed. He got to Dayself's cell, looked at him strange, and then walked off, smelling the weed smoke.

Dayself just shook his head, thinking, *How can a man that makes so little, take his job so serious?*

"Chill out with that bullshit, y'all," Dayself heard an inmate yell at two homosexuals who were fighting in their room. Probably over another man.

He walked from the window, laid on his bed and let out a loud scream. Being around this for five long years had made him look at life so much differently. As Dayself dozed back off to sleep, he decided to cherish everything in the free world, even the smell of pussy. The bed was so small, he kept tossing and turning, hitting his knees and elbows on the wall that the bed was bolted against.

Finally, Dayself decided at four in the morning that he wasn't going to get any sleep. He got up and did his every morning one hundred push-ups. The closer he got to one hundred, the tighter his muscles became with every push. He pictured himself sliding in and out of Piepie as he reached the home stretch. The sound of the inmate next door peeing and then passing gas took him out of his trance.

He tried hard to focus, but his mind was on one thing, getting the hell out of prison and staying out. Restless, Dayself paced the small room until morning shift came to let him out. His property had been packed five days ago, so waiting was all he had left to do. Dayself entered the dining hall where everybody had mean mugs on their faces. Inmates were still tripping over what happened on the basketball court, and Dayself knew that something could jump off with them at any minute. He drank his watered down apple juice and left the dining hall.

On the way back to his block, he heard his name called over the intercom. "Dayself Burton, report to the administration building."

An officer was already standing at Dayself's door, waiting for him to get his property. He gave all of his boys dap and a brother-ly hug before he left. Dayself entered the administration building and the assistant superintendent, Miller, stood up at his desk with both hands on his belt buckle, watching him. Miller was an older white guy, around Dayself's height with blue eyes, white hair, a white beard and a big belly. He could easily play Santa Claus.

"I know your wife was bringing you muscle pills, watches, and cell phones in my prison, but I couldn't catch her black sneaky ass." He stated as the back of his neck turned red.

"I have no idea what you're talking about, Miller. I'm here to go home, not to hear this shit!"

"That's mister to you."

"Sounds too much like master to me."

"You think you smart, don't you, boy?" Miller said angrily.

"No boys here, I'm an original man. Who are you?" Dayself smirked.

"Sign these papers so you can get the hell out of here. I'll see you again. Your kind always commits crimes."

"And who did my kind adopt it from?"

After signing the papers, Dayself went to the conference room to wait for his probation officer. He took his time getting there. Around four o'clock that afternoon, he finally walked through the door. Dayself stared him down, shaking his head. The probation officer was white, about 45 years old, tall, with a long nose, brown eyes, and sandy brown hair. All of his facial hairs were shaved off. Dayself recognized him immediately, he was one of the sheriffs that had arrested him for the robbery. He had tried to get his partner to take Dayself in the woods to beat him.

"My name is Mr. Moore, I'll be your PO, and will be supervising you for the next six months. You can play by the rules and get off early, or you can keep your ass here. It really doesn't matter to me!" the PO said, staring Dayself down. "Now, let's go, so I can drop you off and get home to my family."

Dayself heard him, but the only thing on his mind was getting home to his family. He said nothing as they walked to the car.

"I want you home at seven o'clock," Moore said, taking Dayself out of his thoughts.

"Man, I want to see my son. Can I at least get a full day today, and start being home tomorrow at seven?" Dayself asked, trying not to raise his voice.

"No, you can see him tomorrow. One more day won't hurt."

Dayself stared at him and then turned his head. It had been five long years since he had rode in the front seat. The sun was shining hot. Trucks pulling boats rode past them, headed for the beach. Dayself made it his duty to try to see everyone in the passing cars. He admired a 2014 yellow Camaro that rode up beside them. What blew his mind were the yellow deep lip rims to match. He watched the people sitting on porches as they rode by. Little kids running, diving on their slip and slides, and girls coming out of stores with short skirts on.

A country song came on the radio about a John Deere tractor, and the PO began to bob his head as he turned the music up. Dayself shook his head. To block that out, he leaned his seat back a little to let his mind travel. The PO looked at him, but he didn't care. Dayself was already deep into a daydream about his queen.

Piepie had showed up to visit one day with a short skirt on, and no panties. She and Dayself usually would sneak off to the bathroom, but someone had beat them there. His hand stayed in her pussy the whole visit, trying his best to make her cum. Dayself was locked up at an early age, and was never taught what the clit was, but he got her there.

"Dayself, I'm cumming!" Piepie softly moaned while digging her nails into his hand.

The visit was almost over, and Dayself had sat there hard as a rock. His 24 year old, 5'5", 140 pounds, black as night wife, with her fat ass, long hair, and big pretty eyes had him at a point of no return. The need to get inside her would not be ignored. He looked around. One correctional officer was half asleep, and the other one looked back and forth from the window to his watch.

Dayself eased his dick out of his pants, pulled his shirt over it, and walked around the table to hug Piepie. While hugging, he sat her on the edge of the table.

"This is not going to work," Piepie said, with a scared look on her face.

"Dayself squatted, and half of his dick popped into her pussy.

"Oh shit ... Day ... O ... shit!" Piepie said repeatedly as Dayself moved in and out of her. "It feels good. It feels good!" She closed her eyes, moaning softly into his ear.

"Girl, look at that!" one woman said to another that was walking by.

"Stop, they're looking at us," Piepie said breathlessly.

"Dayself looked back at the women, still stroking his wife with his mouth wide open. He closed his eyes tight as cum shot all over her skirt, boots, and the table. She jumped off the table and hauled ass out of the visiting room.

"Man, get your hands off of me!" Dayself screamed at the PO for touching his shoulder, bringing him back to reality.

"Where is the house?" The PO asked.

"I guess it's right there," Dayself said, pointing at the number on the apartment door.

Dayself got out and looked around. The brick apartments looked new, but they had been there for over twenty years. Little kids running in the hot sun, having water fights, grown-ups watching their toddlers play. One guy was putting a sound system in his car as young girls stood around dancing to the music. Dayself knocked on the door with the PO on his heels.

Piepie looked through the peephole, and then she opened the door with a wide grin, wearing a purple see through negligée. She grabbed Dayself and tongued him down right there.

"My baby home ... my baby home!" she shouted, and then noticed the PO. "Oh shit! Excuse me." Horrified, Piepie turned and disappeared into the apartment.

"All right, Mr. Burton. I see that we have the right house," Moore said with a beet red face.

Dayself closed the door and ran to the back room where Piepie was. He pulled his shirt off and threw it backwards. His shoes were left in the hallway. Piepie had taken off her gown, and was laying on the bed rubbing her pussy, with a vibrator turned on in her other hand.

"Come get what's yours, baby," she moaned as she slid her finger in and out of her pussy.

Dayself stood there with his dick about to burst out of his pants. He surveyed the room. It was put together in a frugal, but tasteful way. Everything looked cheap, but it was new. The mirrored piano pictures she had on the wall really brought the black headboard out, with the black and white checkerboard comforter neatly folded back. A black dresser and black night stand to go with the headboard, and a 55"TV sitting on the dresser completed the decor. Dayself could smell her perfume in the air.

"Where's Prokoshia?" Dayself asked as he stared at her pussy getting wetter and wetter with every stroke of her finger.

"She's ... she's ... with my ... mother," Piepie moaned.

Dayself rolled his pants and boxers down his legs at the same time. He crawled up on the bed until his face was inches away from Piepie's pussy. Closing his eyes, he let the perfume and pussy scent travel up his nostrils as his tongue moved around the outside of her pussy hole, causing her to squeeze the sheets. She reached down and opened her pussy lips. A little pink thing that Dayself had found out was the clit slid out.

"Lick it, baby," she moaned.

Dayself moved slowly to it with his tongue out, touching it a little and making her jump. He saw that it turned her on, so he went crazy with his tongue, trying different things on her clit. Dayself picked up the dildo that lay next to Piepie and turned it on. He slid it into her pussy while still licking her clit. Piepie tried to run, but there was nowhere to go. He worked the dildo in and out as she moved her hips in circles. Dayself knew that she was about to cum, so he pulled the vibrator out and slid all nine inches into her moist hole. The more he moved, the wetter her pussy got.

"I love you," Dayself said, stroking her slowly and staring into her eyes.

"I love you too."

Their eyes remained locked on each other as they came together. She soaked the bed. Dayself looked down at the spot on the bed and got right back hard. With his penis still in her pussy, he moved in and out, speeding up with each pump. Piepie met him half way each time.

Dayself grabbed Piepie's big black nipples. He could feel her pussy tighten around his dick, and he kept right on giving it to her. They were fucking hard. The sound of Dayself's dick slamming in super wet pussy filled the room. Dayself put Piepie's legs on his shoulders, giving him access. He stuck her feet into his mouth and sucked on her toes as he pounded her pussy. Dayself fucked her just like she had wrote and told him she wanted it.

He slid out, and Piepie turned over, putting a nasty arch in her back. He slid in and spread her cheeks, watching his dick go in and out. Every time he went in and came out, his dick was wetter. Her wetness had his dick shining like a new marble. He couldn't hold it any longer, and let a load of cum off in her.

Right after he came, she screamed, "Oh … its cumming!"

Dayself kept pumping until Piepie came all over his dick, and dropped to the bed. He slid out of her, and licked the sweat off her back, lifted up her hair, and licked her neck, at the same time, aiming his dick back at her pussy entrance. The doorbell ringing caused Dayself to jump. Being gone for five years had done something to him.

"Bae, it's okay. Get your robe out of the closet and go see who's at the door," Piepie said and walked to the bathroom.

Dayself put his robe on and walked to the door, wondering who it could be. He looked through the peephole, and saw his PO, Mr. Moore.

"What do you want now?" Dayself asked, opening the door.

"Just making sure you're home on time, Mr. Burton."

"Well, you see. Now, please go!"

"All right, but I expect to see you in my office tomorrow morning."

"All right, man. Damn!" Dayself said, closing the door in his face.

Dayself sat down on the couch and checked out his living environment. The couch was dark blue, with yellow and red designs. The walls were bright white, with pictures of flowers that brought the couch and Lazy Boy out. The entertainment system went well with the furniture and light brown carpet.

Piepie came out of the kitchen with a medium sized glass

filled with a brown liquid and ice cubes. She handed the glass to Dayself.

"Baby, you didn't forget," Dayself said, and sipped the Hennessey.

"How could I forget, as much as you used to say that you needed a drink bad?" she said, smiling.

"Come here," Dayself said, pulling his robe back, exposing his dick.

Piepie dropped her robe and straddled him, biting on her bottom lip as she slowly slid down on his dick. Dayself squeezed her nipples, causing her to ride his dick harder. She went up and down, then in circles. She felt herself about to cum, and she leaned her head back, closed her eyes and came all over Dayself's dick. He held her waist and still bounced her on his dick. His dick swelled within her walls, and Piepie knew he was about to cum. She hopped up, turned around, and touched her toes.

Dayself wanted to try anal sex for the first time, but a man just getting out of prison doesn't just ask a woman to do that. He slid in her pussy from the back, watching her ass jump with every stroke. Her pussy muscles squeezed his dick. Dayself fucked her until he heard her moaning again.

"Bae, here it come again. Come with me, oh … shit, come!" she yelled.

"I'm cumin too, bae … oh … shit … damn!" Dayself said, as both of them came together … again.

Piepie turned and stood on her tiptoes to tongue kiss him. Dayself sat back down while she went to fix them some bath water. As he waited, he thought about how he could come up in the game.

Piepie came back in the front room, grabbed his hand, and guided him to the bathroom. The bathroom was very clean, with his and her towels. A new red toothbrush sat in the holder beside hers and Prokoshia's on the sink, and new boxers and a tank lay folded on the closed toilet lid.

Dayself slid down into the water, feeling the bubbles burst, and the hot water squeeze his skin. He laid back to let the soapy water eat at the dirt and sweat on his body. Dayself opened his eyes; Piepie was standing there holding out another glass of Hennessey. She sat on the edge of the tub and washed all of his prison scent away.

CHAPTER 2

The ringing phone woke Dayself up from the first comfortable sleep he'd had in five years.

"Hello," he answered.

"Boy, get up and open the door!" Dayself's friend, Dirty, screamed.

"How did you know I was home?"

"Stop asking questions and come open the door!"

Dayself laughed as he opened the door. Dirty and Trent stood there high and laughing. Trent was one of Dayself's other close friends. He had also just got out of prison after he and his sister had decided that they wanted to rob McDonald's.

Dirty is light skinned, twenty-five years old, 5'8", 190 pounds, bald with a red beard. He favored Eric Simmons, with reddish skin.

Trent is brown skinned, also twenty-five years old, 5'10", 170 pounds, close haircut; he could easily pass for the singer, Mario.

Dayself gave both of them dap and the brotherly hug.

"I need y'all to take me riding. I gotta see some shit today," Dayself said.

"See what, nigga? Your wife back there." Dirty said, pointing at the back room.

"She gone to work. Let's go, I gotta be home by seven."

"You up to some bullshit already, and you just got home," Trent said, laughing.

Dirty handed him a bag. Inside was a pair of Ed Hardy jeans, and a summer Ed Hardy grey and white button up that went with the white Air Ones that Piepie had bought.

"Good looking, man," Dayself said as he went to change into his new gear.

When Dayself walked out of the bathroom, Dirty handed him a cell phone. Dayself thanked Dirty and they headed out. He added sunglasses to his to do list as he walked outside and squinted.

"I like this, Dirty," Dayself said, getting into Dirty's 2014 red Chrysler 300, with 22" Paul Wall rims. "Yo, where the fuck did Trent go?"

"You know that chick, Tonesha, across the street got him fucked up. April is going to kill his ass." Dirty laughed.

"So you're going to leave him over here?" Dayself asked Dirty as he backed out.

"He'll find his way back to the hood. Where you wanna go first?"

"Run me by Shay-Shay crib."

Her mother named her Shameka Willis. She was 22 years old, 5'8", 130 pounds, brown skin, with green eyes, long hair and a baby voice. She was Dayself's girl before he went to prison, but she couldn't keep it real.

When they arrived at her house, Dayself got out and knocked on the door.

A shocked look painted Shay-Shay's face when she answered the door and saw Dayself. "How are you, Dayself?" she asked, giving him a hug.

"You seem shocked to see me." Dayself said, looking her body up and down.

"Would you like to come in?"

"You gone give me some?"

"Do you want it?"

Dayself waved for Dirty to go ahead and leave him. He walked into the house and saw all the expensive furniture. There was a white leather sofa, love seat and recliner, and a 60-inch plasma TV hung on the wall. He knew a nigga had to be kicking out.

Shay-Shay led him straight to her bedroom. Her room was laced too. She had a queen-sized bed with wood-grained posts at each corner. The armoire and dresser matched the bed, and the mirror on the big dresser went to the ceiling.

"We gotta hurry up. My friend will be over in a few," Shay-Shay said.

"You ain't said shit, how do you want it?" Dayself asked, dropping his pants and rolling a condom on his dick.

Dayself heard she was fucking with a nigga getting money in the next town. He didn't care, he just wanted to hit and bounce. She got up on the bed, and got on all fours. Shay-Shay pulled her thong to the side, and looked back at him with those green eyes. Dayself slid a finger in her from the back, and her juices dripped from his finger. He wanted to taste her so bad. Then he thought about how she did him while he was locked up, and went in her pussy with force. She let out a loud moan as he fucked all the hurt that she had caused him out. Every time he went in, he thought about some disrespectful stuff she had said or done, and he fucked her harder, until he heard a gagging noise.

"You all right?" Dayself asked, slowing down.

"I don't know. It's been a while since I've been fucked that hard. It made me feel like I was choking. Go ahead and punish me," Shay-Shay said, pushing her ass back to his dick, holding back tears of regret.

Dayself did as she asked. One thing he couldn't forget, was how good and wet Shay-Shay's pussy was. They came at the same time.

Shay-Shay went to use the bathroom as Dayself pulled the condom off. He put it under Shay-Shay's pillow, spilling cum everywhere. "This for that nigga that kept hanging up on me when I called collect," Dayself said.

After washing up, Shay-Shay drove Dayself to the Double L, which was two big trailer parks with houses on the back side. It's on the outskirts of Tarboro, and it includes about six hundred trailers. The main road is paved, but the yard is rocks and dirt. When it gets dark, people come from everywhere. Cars line the streets, crack heads come from everywhere, girls from town and out of town come out there looking for dick or a trick. Hustlers betting on who can slam who, and dogfights. Any and everything went down in the Double L. Sometimes, they were one hundred deep out there. Any kind of drug could be found. Double L stood out by itself, Lakeside and Long Pine.

Shay-Shay and Dayself rode through the hood. Dayself saw that many things had changed. Some of the new trailers that were there when he left, looked old, and some were gone. Guys stood on the corners that he didn't even know, most of them shooting dice in the middle of the street. Shay-Shay had to blow the horn for them to get out of the way. She rode over broken glass that lay in the street from the night before. One of the guys saw Dayself and hit his fist to his chest.

"How could you have left me out here by myself?" Shay-Shay cried all of a sudden.

"You act like I had a choice!"

"You need to get yourself together so you can take care of your son. He really does need you."

"I don't need you to tell me what he need. What the fuck do you know about need? Where were you when I needed your ass?" Dayself yelled.

"I am sorry for leaving you like that, I really am. I just kept feeling so lonely," she said, shedding tears.

"Just let me out right here!"

Dayself got out and started walking. Shay-Shay drove past him, going about fifty miles per hour. He walked in the yard of the trailer where Lil Dee lived with his aunt and spotted him walking out of the house with his basketball in his hands. It hurt Dayself to see his son in such cheap clothes and shoes.

Lil Dee spotted his daddy. With a huge smile, he ran and jumped in his arms.

"What's good, little me?" Dayself asked, holding Lil Dee in his arms.

"Nothing, Da," Lil Dee said, looking down at the ground.

"When you talk to somebody, you always look them in the eyes," Dayself said, putting Lil Dee on the ground and staring at him. "Where is your mother?"

"She's in jail again," Lil Dee said sadly.

"When I get everything straight, you can come live with me," Dayself said, handing Lil Dee twenty dollars.

"I'll be glad, Da, because Aunt Annett is mean to me."

"Just give me a little time," Dayself said, almost in tears. "I love you, little me."

"I love you too, Da," Lil Dee said and ran off to play with his friends.

Dayself hit the corner in Double L just as Dirty was driving around the corner.

"Dayself, my motherfucking partner!" Dirty said, coming to a stop and rolling his tinted window down.

Dayself got in the car and they rode around so that Dayself could meet different people.

"The streets done changed, dog. Niggas out here think snitching is the shit. A couple of cats getting money, but it's nothing major," Dirty said as they drove.

"Fuck who getting money, I just want to know who snitching. I gotta stay the fuck away from them."

Dirty was running down the names when his phone went off.

"Ride with me to handle some business," Dirty said.

"I'm with you, bruh, let's ride," Dayself said, getting comfortable in his seat.

Dayself realized that they were headed to Princeville to serve some cats. Princeville is a small town owned and ran by blacks. It's the first place blacks went to after slavery ended. Everybody there is black, from the mayor to the store clerks, but you may find an Arab store here and there. Guys were standing around everywhere, chasing money. If they had a true thinker over there, they would be rich, but these were the grimiest, shiestiest niggas around that way.

They pulled up, and Dayself thought to himself, *Damn why is he serving these cats? Some of them hung around the guy that killed his brother, who died in his arms.* Dayself knew Dirty was one of the realest niggas he'd met from the Double L.

Dirty got back into the car counting money.

"You fucking with these niggas over here like that?" Dayself asked.

"I fuck with some of them, not all," Dirty replied.

"If you fuck with some, you might as well fuck with them all. They the same niggas, just got different faces. We are about to get money soon. We can get money over here, it's up to you. But make no mistakes, when you're ready to go to war, it is what it is," Dayself said with a serious look.

"I already know. You don't even have to tell me that."

Just thinking about it made Dayself want to smoke some trees, but the PO was pissing him every week. He decided to dead the subject for now. Dayself and Dirty chopped it up about old times until Dirty dropped him off at home close to seven.

The next morning, Trent came through to pick Dayself up in his girl's 2001 blue Mazda 626. Mashed up French fries, Oreo cookies, and toys were all over the car. His little boy sat in the front seat, Dayself took the back seat. As soon as he sat down, a shit smell hit him in the nose. He looked around everywhere.

"You still got that Yo Gotti CD in the crib?" Trent asked.

"Yeah, I'll go get it," Dayself said, getting out of the car.

Dayself's hand brushed against something soft, mashed flat against his shirt, and he stuck his hand to his nose. "Yo, what the fuck you doing with a shit ball in your back seat?" Dayself asked angrily.

"Where at?" Trent asked.

"On my damn shirt, nigga!" Dayself said, pointing at the shirt.

"It must have fallen out the side of my baby's diaper," Trent said, trying not to laugh.

After changing shirts and going to vacuum the car out, Dayself felt a lot better sitting in the back seat, until his mind started to roam.

"Why you got that look?" Trent asked, studying Dayself in his rear view mirror.

"It's nothing. I'm just tired of wifey paying all the bills by herself. She took care of me my last two and a half years. She'd rather me get a job, but if I decide to hustle, she would give me six months to stack my dough without paying a bill. Dog, I don't even have a connect."

Dayself had fifteen hundred dollars, and it was going fast. His phone rang, interrupting their conversation.

"Hello." Dayself answered.

"Boy, get your butt over here to see me! I'm at your Grandmother Mabee's house!" Dayself's mother said.

"I'm pulling up now."

Dayself smiled as he read the 'Welcome Home Dayself' sign that was posted on the front porch.

"Welcome home, baby, things has been rough around here," Dayself's mother said with tears running down her face. "Doughboy and Tan are on the way."

"Don't cry, Ma, I'm home now. Things will get better, just give me some time," Dayself said, wiping her tears away.

Dayself looked just like his mother. She was beautiful and what people back in the day would call stacked. She was 5'6", 180 pounds, brown skinned, with a short haircut.

"My baby! My baby!" Dayself's grandmother, Mabee, screamed, running out of the house to meet Dayself.

"I'm sorry for leaving you. I will never leave you again," Dayself said, rubbing her jawline.

Mabee's lips trembled as she walked off, cursing at somebody for taking food off the grill. At sixty-six years old, she still looked good, with her small waist and full hips. Even with the streaks of gray in her hair, she could easily pass for fifty.

Some of the guys Dayself had grown up with spotted him.

None of them had held him down when he was locked up, but he knew he couldn't blank. Dayself had learned that you can't make enemies and get money. If you have enemies, eliminate them before they destroy you. So, he gladly gave them the brotherly hug.

"Here you go, my nigga," Dirty said, handing Dayself one thousand dollars. "This Double L nigga know what keeping it real means." Dirty said, looking around at the Double L niggas. "Bruh, it's not much, but I give it to you from the heart."

"That's what's up." Dayself said, and gave Dirty a brotherly hug.

Dirty and Dayself walked off talking. Que, one of the guys who used to chill in Double L, pulled up in the front yard where they were standing. Que was a year older than Dayself, tall and light-skinned with dreads and a mouth full of gold and diamonds. He hopped out of his cream-colored Cadillac truck with 24" chrome rims gleaming, wearing a black, green, and yellow L.R.G short set, with black and red Air Ones. Most guys from the Double L wore a white tee, shorts, or jeans on a daily basis, except club night.

"Dayself, my motherfucking nigga!" Que yelled, drawing attention and showing off his diamonds, with a big smile.

"What's good? You doing it big," Dayself said, pointing at his rims.

"I'm doing all right, just trying to stack some dough, get the fuck out of North Carolina."

"What's good, Que?" Trent said.

Que looked at Trent and frowned. He still felt resentment because Trent took April from him in high school.

"Money, nigga. Something that you don't have. Now would you excuse us?" Que said, still frowning at Trent.

"I got a big gun though, nigga." Trent said, smiling at Que.

Que walked off and got into his truck. He knew that Double L niggas took shit to heart, and Trent was a fucked up in the head nigga.

"Yo, Dayself," Que yelled, calling Dayself to the truck window. "Here you go, my nigga. Welcome home," Que said, handing

Dayself fourteen grams of crack.

"Just throw me a big. I'll re-up with you every week, and then at the end of the month, I'll pay you your three gees I owe, plus an extra gee in interest."

"We cool, but I'm not waiting a month for my money. I already looked out for you. Just come buy from me, and I'll look out," Que said.

The streets had been talking. Dayself knew that Que was sitting on about two or three keys, and about ten pounds of midgrade weed. If he would've thought about it, he could've made twice as much. *You live small, you die small.* Dayself thought to himself. *Cats rather give me small shit than front me big shit. They scared that I'm going to take their shine. I got dreams of selling them keys; they can have the shine.*

A week had passed since Dayself had been home, and he was getting frustrated. He was still on some give it up shit. He just wanted to get money and leave that thug shit alone. Trent had popped up at Dayself's house earlier and handed him seven grams of crack.

"I had to give you something, bruh," Trent had said, smiling.

"Where the hell …"

"Ask me no secrets, I tell you no lies." Trent said, and then turned around walked out the door without saying another word.

Dayself thought to himself, *Four cats done gave me something. I got nineteen hundred dollars in the stash, and twenty-one grams of crack. What the hell have I come home to? That's the shells off the peanuts, to the keys I was buying when I left.*

"Stop counting the money over and over like that. It's not going to change, and stop stressing about what is or ain't going on in them streets. As long as you remember the streets don't love you, nothing can stop you from blowing. Learn to love the people that love you." Piepie said, interrupting his pity party.

"I'm just used to paying my own way. Seeing you pay all them bills by yourself make me feel fucked up, and I do love the people that love me."

"Baby, I've been paying bills all these years by myself. Things will get better for you. Now if you love me, come get this pussy. It'll ease your stress."

Dayself grabbed Piepie's hand, and she walked behind him to the bedroom. Licking his lips, Dayself rolled her lime green boy shorts down her legs. After pulling those off, he stopped at her toes, sucking them one by one, as Piepie rolled her nipples with her manicured fingertips.

"Baby, I need that dick now!" Piepie said, turning over and getting into the doggy style position.

Piepie's pussy lips were shaved bald; nothing was visible but some fat chocolate lips, and hot pink slit. She reached back, rubbed her pussy, and then wiped her wetness on Dayself's lips. He sucked his lips, letting the flavor hit his taste buds. He had to have more. Dayself squatted down behind her and slid his tongue in her pussy, moving in and out. The more he fucked Piepie with his tongue, the wetter her pussy got as she pushed her fat ass back to meet his face.

"Shit … you … make … me … sick!" Piepie moaned, cumming all over his mouth.

Dayself laid on his back and slid between her legs. He raised his head slightly to pull and suck on her clit.

"Damnnnn … Damnnnn!" She moaned.

Dayself slid from under her, stood up, and slid his dick in her pussy. Piepie gripped the sheets, and threw her pussy back on Dayself's dick.

"Bang it, boy! Bang this pussy!" Piepie screamed.

Dayself and Piepie were sweaty and going at it. Piepie's daughter, Prokoshia, walked in the room. Dayself fell over so she wouldn't see him. He was going to buy a lock for the bedroom door first thing in the morning. Prokoshia was getting bigger, and now she would stand up on her little step and open the door. She was an adorable child; she looked just like Raven Symone when she played Olivia on *The Cosby Show*.

"Day … Day, I wanna watch cartoons," Prokoshia said, with her Barbie in her hand.

She loved to watch the Disney channel. Since it was Friday, and because there is actually educational value on the Disney channel, Dayself let her watch it. The little girl would have to tell him what she learned, or she couldn't watch it again, but she always had something to tell him.

Dayself got up the next morning and headed to Double L to get rid of the twenty-one grams of crack. A couple of cats came to the hood to buy grams. Money was slow, so he just broke everything down and sold whatever came. The booming hood he had left was now gone. A sale came through once every thirty minutes. Dayself, not used to being out there in the streets, and with his money low, headed to the mall. By the time he got ready to leave, he had eight hundred dollars, no stash money, and two grams of crack left. On his way out, Dayself bumped into Little and Shay-Shay together.

Shay-Shay couldn't even look Dayself in the face. Dayself knew that Little was getting money before they ended up in prison together.

"Dayself, is that you, my nigga?" Little asked as he and Shay-Shay met up with him.

"Yes, it's me in the flesh," Dayself said, staring at Shay-Shay.

"I'll be in the car." Shay-Shay said and walked away from them.

"I been waiting patiently for that pussy. It better be worth it," Little said, rubbing his dick, watching Shay-Shay walk away. "I've spent over twelve grand on that bitch, and she still hasn't come off the pussy."

"She will in due time," Dayself said, hiding his anger.

"You need to come check me out."

"You straight like that?"

"Not really, but I'm not wanting for nothing."

"Give me your number, I'll get at you."

Dayself had decided after the incident with Que, that he wouldn't ask another man for handouts. Then something formed in his head. He had a plan to move up.

CHAPTER 3

*D*ayself had called Little three times, but he kept giving him the run around.

"I'll be straight tomorrow."

"Don't keep playing with me! I'm trying to be humble with y'all cats, but y'all pushing it for real!" Dayself said angrily.

"I'll call you back in an hour."

Dayself slammed the phone down and laid back to watch *King of New York*. "I can make these soft dudes come up off everything. I'll just sit on dudes for a minute," he said as his phone began to vibrate.

"Yo." Dayself answered.

"Come check me out. I'm at my spot across from the red house in the wooded area in Conetoe," Little said, and then hung up.

Little's spot was in a desolate area with old wooden houses lining the street. A few doors were open to let a little breeze in. Most didn't have central air, so they kept little air conditioners or fans in the windows to keep the rooms cold. Some people were sitting on porches fanning with church fans.

Two trucks pulled up and dropped off a group of blacks and Mexicans. After a hard day in the fields, they were dirty from chest to toe. A few of them even carried the field dirt in their hair. Little kids ran to meet their parents, hoping they brought them a cake or candy from the store.

Dayself got out of the car and noticed a black 500 Benz out front. He knew that Little wasn't stupid enough to buy a Benz and park it right there. Dayself could see someone peeping out of the window. A middle aged Mexican who favored George Lopez stood at the door. They stared each other down until the Mexican broke the stare, and pulled the brown paper bag close to his side. Dayself chuckled a bit at the man's John Wayne getup. He wore a black long sleeved button up opened at the top with three small gold chains showing, blue jeans, and cowboy boots. Clearly, he was either picking up or dropping off.

His thoughts were interrupted when Little came on the porch. "Here you go, my nigga," Little said, handing Dayself seven grams of crack.

Dayself went ahead and took it. He had to earn Little's trust. It was the only way for his plan to work.

Trent dropped Dayself off in the hood so he could set up shop. Sometimes crack sales came through slow, so Dayself bought what Little gave him his self. The faster he paid, the more Little gave him. He made a lot less, because he had to discount the shit. It was stretched so bad, that the fiends complained about it turning black on their crack pipe. Dayself had only made about twenty five hundred dollars in a month.

Little had made it to four and a half keys, thanks to Dayself. He knew that Dayself could out hustle him; all he needed was a connect or enough money to get his own shit. Little knew how to keep Dayself down, and move himself up. He was a weak nigga, of being robbed. He knew by having Dayself on his team, that it would slow niggas down. He still didn't understand what keeping it real meant. Dayself had his back until he handled him one week that he called.

"What's good? Niggas calling for work, and I'm out," Dayself explained.

"Y'all on my time, my money is straight." Little said on speakerphone, with Shay-Shay talking in the back.

"Don't ever come out your mouth like that at me again!" Dayself said angrily and hung up.

Little called his phone straight back.

"Hello!" Dayself answered.

"Call me later, I got you." Little said.

"I'll do that. Peace."

Dayself called back three more times later on in the day, but got no answer. He decided then that he was going to buy his own weight from somebody else.

There wasn't any money coming through the hood, so Trent and Dayself decided to go over to Shay-Shay's house. Her sister, Lagalla, was home from Atlanta. Dayself saw a grey Camry rental in front of Shay-Shay's apartment. He didn't pay it any mind, thinking that the car belonged to Shay-Shay's sister. Little and two of his boys were sitting there when Dayself and Trent walked in. Dayself had been stopping by to see Shay-Shay lately. Little still had no idea about Dayself and Shay-Shay's history.

"Damn, nigga, you following me and shit! I told you that I got you!" Little said with an attitude.

"Nigga, following you?" Dayself yelled, veins popping out the side of his neck." I didn't even know that you were here! If I was following you, I would've been took everything that you have! Why must you test my kill skills? I won't take it there with you, though. I know you're the type that call cops and squeal," Dayself said, grilling Little. Without another word, he walked out the house with Trent behind him.

"Dayself cool, how you going to play him like that?" Shay-Shay asked angrily.

"Why you worried about it? That's probably who condom I found under your pillow," Little said, looking for a lie on her face.

"Nigga, let me speak with you, because you got me really fucked up," Shay-Shay said and walked to her room.

≈

"Yo, Day, fuck that, let's kill them niggas," Trent said, pulling his gun out. "We can make them come off everything!"

"Chill, bruh, we're going to get our weight up."

Trent was hungry. He had three kids by April, and no job. Their car was thirteen years old, and April stayed on him about money and bill problems. Frustrated with their situation, he had started robbing local street corner niggas for what they had.

On the way home, Dayself thought to himself, *Damn, prison done made me soft. I let that nigga handle me in front of Shay-Shay.*

Sensing what was bothering Dayself, Trent said, "Partner, don't sweat that shit, he a nigga that can be dealt with."

"Fuck that, are you trying to handle some shit with Dirty?"

"Yeah, that's my people."

"Hold on, Trent, let me call Shay-Shay." Dayself said as he dialed the number.

"Hello." Shay-Shay answered

"I'll give you five hundred dollars if you call me soon as Little leave."

"You don't have to give me anything, I got you. All I want is you to come back to me, but I'll settle for a kiss soon as this is done," Shay-Shay said, thinking about running her tongue over Dayself's lips.

"All right, I'll give you that kiss. You have my word," Dayself said and hung up.

"You and Dirty go to the nigga house, fuck it up like y'all looking for something. Look around in his room for some shoeboxes.

They should be somewhere in his closet. I saw him stuff rubber bands of money in them. I can't go. I'm already five minutes late getting home."

"We got you, partner."

Trent and Dirty rode in silence all the way to Little's spot. They parked the Mazda in the wooded area and walked the rest of the way. Moving in silence, the two of them circled the house, looking for a way in. They found an unlocked window in the back of the house, and were able to climb in without being detected.

The kitchen door, which separated it from the dining room, was cracked. Trent peeped through the cracked door and saw two of Little's boys, Tim and Rock, running a train on crack head Shaqwana, in the living room. The strong fuck smell had traveled from the living room through the dining room and right to Trent's nose. *Damn, her pussy smells like raw sewage. These are some nasty niggas,* Trent thought to himself as he wrinkled his nose in disgust.

Tim fucked Shaqwana from the back, while she sucked Rock's dick. Rock's belly jiggled slightly as she deep throated him to the rhythm of Tim's backstrokes slamming into her. At only 5'6" and 130 pounds soaking wet, Tim was handling Shaqwana. His heavy breathing made whistling sounds as it traveled through the space where his missing tooth once was.

"Let's get this over quick," Dirty whispered and aimed his .45 at the back of Tim's head.

A single shot knocked Tim on top of Shaqwana.

She let out a loud scream, almost biting Rock's dick off.

"Hold ... hold ... hold! The shit is under the kitchen sink," Rock said, reaching for his gun on the sofa.

Trent aimed at his face with a .357 and pulled the trigger. Rock flew back to the wall as Shaqwana screamed again and covered her mouth.

"Shut up, bitch!" Dirty yelled. He put the gun to her mouth and pulled the trigger, blowing the front of her face out the back of her head.

"Yo, we gotta get out of here!" Trent said in a panic.

"No, we gotta get this money, and then get out of here. Look under the sink, I got the boxes," Dirty said, walking toward the room.

"Shit, man, we should've held them captive, got the shit, then killed they ass!"

"It's too late," Dirty yelled, finding only one shoebox and dumping the money in the bag as he rushed to the front of the house.

Trent was on his way to meet him with the crack he found under the kitchen sink. They ran out the back door, behind wooden houses as sheriff cars shot past. The two of them kept until they reached the car and jumped in, headed back to Tarboro.

"Damn, y'all had to kill the girl too?" Dayself asked, helping them count the money.

"Leave no witness is the saying right?" Dirty asked, weighing the crack.

"Yo, Day, we done got rusty. We killed them first then got the money," Trent said, peeping out the window.

"Dirty, that shit was backwards. It's thirty five gees." Dayself split the money three ways.

"It's nine and a half ounces," Dirty said as he bagged up the crack.

Dayself's phone rang. Everyone stopped talking and stared at the phone.

"Hello." Dayself answered.

"They just walked out the door. I want my kiss, after I curse your ass out," Shay-Shay said angrily.

"That's peace, come get your kiss." Dayself said, thinking

about how good Shay-Shay's pussy is.

"I'm on my way," she said and hung up.

Fifteen minutes later, Dayself received a text from Shay-Shay. I'm around the corner. Come out.

Shay-Shay pulled around the corner from Piepie's apartment in her black 2010, 350Z, and Dayself hopped in the front seat.

"Nigga, how the fuck y'all gon' kill three people? You come home still on that murder shit! What the fuck is wrong with you? You better not leave me again!" Shay-Shay said, tearing up. "Here."

She handed Dayself a bag with four guns in it. "You left them at my house when you got locked up the last time. You may need them."

"Listen to this," Dayself said, pulling out his phone. He let her hear the recording of herself saying she would help with Little, and her calling back saying he left.

"That's fucked up, Dayself." Shay-Shay said, poking out her little lips.

"If you ever mention this to anybody, just remember, you played a part in it," Dayself said, and reached under her skirt. He pulled her thong to the side and slid his finger in her pussy, hard and fast.

"Ooh ... ooh shit, boy!" She moaned. "When are you going to fuck me again?"

"We'll get up soon," Dayself said, licking her wetness off his fingers. "What's up with you and Little?"

"Nothing anymore. I was about to give him some. He had ate my pussy and everything. He was putting his gun under my pillow, and found a used condom. I know you did that shit."

"He had no business trying to get my pussy," Dayself said, rubbing her clit through her panties.

"Excuse you, but you have a wife," Shay-Shay said, pushing his hand away. "As a matter of fact, get out of my shit. And if you're not over my house tonight in this cake, I'm calling your wife, since you fucked my shit up."

"I'll be over there, not because your ass blackmailing me, but because I miss this," Dayself said and slapped her on her pussy.

Little called Dayself's phone about an hour later.

"Yo, Dayself, niggas ran in my spot and killed my people!" Little said, almost in tears. "I'm on the run. The police found a key under the house, and twenty thousand dollars in a shoebox. It was thirty five thousand in the other one, and they didn't say shit about that."

"So why the fuck are you on the run?"

"The house was in my name, so that's my shit they found. Where are you at now?" Little asked

"I'm at my grandmother's crib," Dayself said without thinking. His mind was on the fact that Dirty had left the twenty gees behind.

"I gotta bounce for a while. If you see my cousin, Que, tell him he know how to find me."

"All right, peace." Dayself said and hung up.

The next day, when Dayself went to visit his grandmother, police came from everywhere with guns drawn as Trent drove into the yard. Mabee came outside cursing. Dayself knew that Little had sent the police to his grandmother's house. He got out of the car and laid on the ground.

"Mr. Burton, we need to talk with you downtown," a detective said, after cuffing Dayself.

"For what, man? I didn't do anything."

"If you didn't do anything, you will be released," the detective said.

Not wanting to cause any drama at his grandmother's house, Dayself didn't put up a fight. The detectives placed him in the car and took him downtown to police headquarters.

After answering the same questions over and over, Dayself remembered something. "Detective, what time did you say those people were killed?"

"Between seven and eight thirty."

"I was home. I gotta be home at seven, and my PO came to piss me around seven thirty, then I showed him the applications that I had to fill out. He sat down and read over each one, trying to catch me in a lie. He'll verify that."

The detective stared at Dayself for what seemed like forever, then he picked up the phone and called his PO. After asking several questions, he slammed the phone down.

"I can feel that you had something to do with this, but I can't prove it. You'll slip up somewhere," the detective said, his face turning fruit punch red.

Dayself walked out of the sheriff station, and Trent was out front in the car asleep with Yo Gotti's "All White Bricks" playing.

A couple of days later, Dayself went to buy a Lexus off the car lot. He decided on an all-black 2009 LS 450 with grey leather interior. He put a four thousand dollar down payment on the car, and spent the rest in powder. Things didn't go as planned. People thought Dayself had bullshit coke, because all the bullshit Little had him selling had fucked up his clientele. The coke went very slow.

Dayself called Dirty to see if he was having any better luck.

"How is shit moving over there?" Dayself asked.

"It's slow. We need some of that volume two."

"Man, what are you talking about?"

"You know, that untouched."

"You're just like Jeezy, you got a name for everything."

"We can't build our clientele back up unless we get it. We can holla at my uncle, Yellow, in New York. He can get it from the Columbians. A runner will bring it for one hundred dollars an ounce."

"If he let us get a half of brick for eighty five hundred, including the runner fee, I'll fuck with him."

"We might as well get a key and a half."

"Yeah, let's do that."

Yellow came through for them on the coke, and they decided to cook straight drop. Money started coming in like water. Before they knew it, they were buying four keys. The twenty sales were kind of slow, so Dayself tried his hand at another avenue.

CHAPTER 4

A white woman dressed in a grey Chanel pinstriped business suit and off white Jimmy Choos, waited to speak to the secretary at the PO's office. She was a stunning beauty, looking to be about 35 years old, she was roughly 5'7", 140 pounds, with jet black hair, a small nose, and light brown eyes. Dayself just couldn't stop watching her beauty. He was intrigued by the fact that she kept playing with her nose. Either she had the biggest booger he had ever seen, or she was on something. After she talked to the secretary, Dayself followed her out of the door and watched her get in a silver 500 Benz coupe. She checked her nose in the mirror, put her Chanel shades on, and pulled off. Dayself watched until her car disappeared.

The following day, Dayself showed up at the courthouse to pay his probation fees. On his way out, he bumped into the white woman again. This time, she was wearing a white suit with pink pinstripes, white Liz Claiborne open toe heels, with pink toe nail polish on her toes. Dayself rushed to his Lexus and mixed the powders together. Satisfied with the results, he walked around until he found the white lady's car. He checked the doors, but they were locked. Dayself looked at her tire and smiled. He sat the powder on top of her car tire, and then rushed back to the courthouse. He needed to be in front before she came out.

"Excuse me, are you a lawyer?" Dayself asked the white lady as she exited the courthouse.

"Yes, I am Becky Chance, attorney at law," she said, handing Dayself her card.

Dayself reached for his nose to see if she would grab hers. That was his way of telling if a person really get high. She immediately reached for her nose with one hand, her purse with the other hand, and pulled out a small compact mirror. Becky looked at her nose to see if there was any residue lingering around her nostrils.

"I got the best in town," Dayself whispered to her.

"I don't know what you're talking about." Becky said, putting on her courtroom face.

Dayself handed her a piece of paper and walked away. Becky read the paper, rushed to her car, and checked the tires. There sat a small bag of powder. Becky thought it was a set up or something, so she called her husband, Tom. The cocaine they had been getting lately was cut bad, burning their noses. Becky was skeptical about the package, but even more afraid of passing up the opportunity to get some good candy.

"Hello," Tom answered.

"I just met this black guy. He knew by looking at me that I do cocaine! He gave me a piece of paper with his name, number, and instructions to look on top of my car tire. I go to look, and it's a ball of white powder here! This could be a set-up. Should I call the police?" Becky asked, getting scared as she recounted the events.

"No, don't call the cops. Come by the office and let me check it out first," Tom said, hoping it was some good shit.

Tom paced the floor in his blue Wrangler jeans, penny loafers, tight black t-shirt, with his hair slicked back, until Becky arrived. She handed him the small bag, and he poured the powder on a small mirror, making six lines.

"Go ahead, try it," Tom said, handing her the mirror.

"Why do I have to try it first?"

"Because he gave it to you, not me," Tom said, irritated.

Becky snatched a line, and then set the mirror back on the

desk. She leaned her head back and closed her eyes. Immediately, her eyes flew open and she shot to the window.

"How is it?" Tom asked.

She seemed not to have heard anything he said. Once Tom saw that it wasn't going to kill her, he went to the table to try it. He sniffed two lines and raised his head.

Becky got on her knees, unzipped Tom's pants, and started sucking his dick. She never touched his dick unless she was putting it in her pussy. Becky sucked and jacked his dick with one hand, and handed him the powder with the other. Tom took one more sniff and started to get hard. He usually had to take Viagra to get an erection, due to a car accident when he was a child. Tom watched his wife go to work on his six-inch dick. Little did they know, the powder was a coke and crushed ecstasy pill mixture. At that moment, the couple couldn't care less what it was. They just wanted more of it.

Becky got off her knees and went to get her purse from the chair. As she bent over to find Dayself's phone number, Tom walked up behind her, pulled up her skirt and snatched off her thong. He slammed his still hard dick into her wetness as Becky called Dayself to place an order.

"Dayself ooh … oh … do … you have … more?" Becky moaned over the phone with every stroke Tom put to her.

Dayself heard Tom in the background howling like a wounded dog. Then Becky was back to her normal speaking voice.

"I want an ounce and a half, if you have it," Becky said in a sexy voice.

"Yeah, I got it, but I charge fifteen hundred for an ounce, and seven fifty for a half. I can get you an ounce and a half of some all right shit for fifteen hundred."

"What did you give me the first time?"

"Love and Sex."

"Bring me two ounces of that. I have some friends who may want some too. They'll go through me."

"That's cool."

"My address is 813 Washington Ave."

"See you in an hour," Dayself said and hung up the phone.

He mixed an ounce and a half of coke with a half-ounce of crushed ecstasy pills, and headed to Becky's house.

"You're Dayself right?" Becky asked, staring at his dick print.

"In the flesh," Dayself said, handing her the powder, and at the same time, taking the money from her.

Becky held on to the money for a few seconds longer. She was stuck on Dayself's dick print. Dayself pulled the money out her hand, smiled, and walked back to the car, shaking his head at his new customers.

Becky watched him until he got into the car and drove off.

Dayself decided to stop by Mabee's house to see how she was doing. Before he pulled in the yard, he saw her out there talking to Jehovah's Witnesses. He decided to go in Double L to set up shop. Things were starting to look good for them, and Dayself knew that bad always traveled with that.

CHAPTER 5

*D*ayself's PO took the seven o'clock curfew off of him for good behavior. He left home at nine o'clock every morning and returned between two and four the following morning. Piepie was stressing because of his absence, so she called the phone more and he hit the streets more.

Dirty, Trent, and Dayself were a three man team. So much money started coming in, they had to get some of the Double L crew to help. Dayself brought in his protégés, Boybaby and Castro. Boybaby was eighteen years old, and he mainly picked up the money and dropped the work off. Castro was twenty-two years old, and he sold powder all over. Dirty brought in Dick and Lambo. Dick was twenty-eight years old, about 6'1" and dark skinned. They called him Dick because by the age of fifteen, the boy had an eleven-inch dick. He did the dirty work. Lambo was twenty-four years old, and a little shorter than Dick, with a slight build and a bald head. He was a straight killer.

Moot-Moot and Lil Man, Trent's boys, rounded out the team. Moot-Moot was twenty-seven, 6'1", 160 pounds, and brown skinned. He set-up shop in Southern Terrace, a big section of Princeville that consists of brick houses and trailers. Most guys around that way went to school, but the ones that didn't, had money. Money came through nonstop, and the Double L crew made sure that Moot-Moot had Volume Two for the taking. Lil

Man was brown skinned with dreads and a cut on the side of his face. He ran the spot in east Tarboro that was a gold mine. This is where Que had set up shop.

In four months, the Double L crew had most of the town on lock, but things on the homefront were a bit shaky. Dayself wasn't paying his wife the attention she wanted. He was busy trying to get money so they could live a good life. He always kept Piepie off track. Dayself only kept six thousand dollars in the house, so she would think he was still moving up slow. The less she knew, the better. Dayself saw a lot of hustlers mess up by telling their woman all of their business. He didn't want to make the same mistakes.

"You left something in your money drawer," Piepie said, with a smile on her face.

Dayself went to check, and found a positive pregnancy test. He ran in the front room, tongued her down, until they ended up in the bed naked.

About two weeks later, Dayself took Piepie to the doctor because of stomach and head pain. They both knew something wasn't right, but they hoped for the best. Impatiently, they waited until the doctor came into the room.

"Mrs. Burton, I'm sorry. You had a miscarriage," the doctor said sadly.

"No ... no ... I want my baby!" Piepie screamed, holding her stomach.

Dayself held her tight, kissing the top of her head and rocking her back and forth as his tears dropped in her hair.

When they got home, Dayself tucked Piepie into bed. It was the first time that he had seen her hurt, and he couldn't do any-thing about it. He grabbed his keys and went for a long ride, and rode until the gas light came on. With no energy to stop and refill, he headed back home.

He let himself in the house, and quietly got dressed in the dark to keep from waking his heartbroken wife.

"I'm sorry, baby!" Piepie cried in the dark. "I'm sorry I let you down."

"Baby, you didn't let me down. None of this is your fault. We'll just keep trying," he said, and softly kissed her lips.

"Yes, I love you, Day."

"I love you too."

Piepie cried herself to sleep in his arms. In the middle of the night, she woke up screaming that she wanted her baby. All Dayself could do was hold her and let her know that everything would be all right.

CHAPTER 6

*D*ayself was walking out the door when his phone rang. A month had gone by, and things were going well for the crew.

"Niggas caught me slipping last night! Three niggas ran in the spot and took the money, hard, and my chain," Trent said angrily.

"Do you know who it was?" Dayself asked.

"If I did, they wouldn't be breathing! I think the lady across the street saw something. When I ran out the door with my gun, she was sitting in her window drinking a beer."

"It's time for us to get back on some gangster shit. Niggas be taking our humbleness as being soft."

"I'm down with that."

"Dirty and I will be through there in about ten minutes."

Dayself pulled up to Dirty and Laquanda's house. Dirty jumped in the car with two guns. After Dayself told him what happened, he just sat there quiet. Since his brother, T.K., died in his arms, Dirty had basically been in his own world. He was quiet most of the time.

Trent met Dayself and Dirty getting out of the car. They

walked over and knocked on Ms. Hinton's door.

"Ms. Hinton, did you see anything last night?" Dayself asked.

"It was a blue Camry that's missing a chrome wheel on the side," Ms. Hinton said.

"Yo, I saw that car in Rocky Mount, turning into a yard in Meadowbrook," Dirty added.

"Thank you, Ms. Hinton, your rent and light bill will be paid by us for the next three months," Dayself said, kissing her hand and making her blush.

When night fell, Dirty, Trent, and Dayself sat in Dayself's car, as Dick crept into a white man's yard, behind the courthouse and stole a black 88' Honda Accord. They followed Dick back across the bridge entering Princeville, to the graveyard.

Dayself parked his car in the graveyard and they got into the stolen Honda with Dick and drove to Rocky Mount.

Dirty, Trent, Dayself, and Dick parked across from the house in Rocky Mount, where the Camry sat. They rolled the windows down; Dick was smoking some love boat. Trent exited the car, cut the tire on the Camry, and returned.

"Check it out. Somebody is coming out of the house," Dirty said.

They got out of the car, letting the doors close softly. A light-skinned guy tried to get in the car to leave. He got back out of the car, and walked on the other side to look at the flat tire. Dayself crept up behind him and put the gun to the back of his head.

"If you breathe wrong, I'll blow the back of your fucking head off," Dayself said with his hand on the trigger of the Ruger 9.

"Turn around slow, nigga," Trent said, seeing his chain around the man's neck. "This belongs to me."

Trent patted the guy down and found a black .25 with two bullets in the clip. The dude looked like a young Ginuwine.

"Who's in the house?" Dick asked with a crazy look on his face. The boat had him going.

"Man, ain't nobody in there!" the man insisted.

"I'll ask you one more time," Dick said with spit flying out of his mouth.

Before Dick could get it all out, Trent punched the guy in his mouth. He dropped to the ground immediately, holding his face.

"Stand your bitch ass up!" Trent said through clenched teeth. "Who is in the house?"

"My sister and my girlfriend," the man said with blood flowing from his lips.

"Get your ass in the house!" Trent said with anger, holding the back of the guy's collar and guiding him into the house.

"Please, man, I bought the chain from my man!" Speedy said, almost in tears.

"We'll talk about that when we get inside," Dirty said.

Once they made it inside the house, Dayself handcuffed the trembling man, placed tape over his mouth, and taped his legs down to a kitchen chair in the living room.

Trent checked the room at the back of the house, and Dirty checked the room on the left, while Dick checked the one on the right.

In the room on the right, a girl who resembled Tatiana Ali slept in a queen sized bed in a big T-shirt with no panties on. She looked very familiar to Dick. He awoke her by rubbing her hair. She opened her eyes and let out a loud scream before Dick choked her out.

Dirty tiptoed into the other room and opened the door just enough to peep inside. A young woman lay across the bed moaning softly and playing in her pussy. Dirty watched her until the scream from the other room startled them both. She jumped up, pulled her gown down, and ran toward the door, right into the barrel of Dirty's gun.

"Please don't kill me," she begged. In a bloated sort of way, she was pretty. She was definitely mixed, and could've passed for an overweight Mariah Carey with her long wavy hair and full lips.

Dick walked into the room where Dirty was licking his ashy lips. Dirty walked off, telling Dick to bring the girl into the front room. Dick looked over and noticed the wetness that ran down the young woman's leg.

"Have you been playing with your toy?" Dick asked, looking at her legs. The boat had him tripping.

"No … no … that's nothing."

Dick reached down, rubbed the moisture from her inner thigh and licked his fingers. He was about to reach for her pussy when Dirty hit the corner.

"Dick, what is your high ass in here doing? Bring her in the front room!"

Dick escorted the girl to the living room and made her sit beside the other girl, who was just waking up. He quickly hand-cuffed them both and put tape over their mouths.

"What's your name?" Dayself asked, snatching the tape off the guy's mouth.

"Speedy," he said.

Dick kept staring at the girl who seemed so familiar. "Destiny?" Dick shouted.

She turned her head at the sound of her name, wondering how he knew her, and if it was a good or bad thing that he did. All eyes were on them.

"Excuse us, y'all," Dick said, picking Destiny up.

Everyone looked at each other, wondering what the fuck just happened.

In Destiny's room, Dick took the tape and cuffs off Destiny. She shyly looked up at him, and then a smile formed on her face.

"Rashard!" she shouted then jumped to hug Dick.

Destiny knew that Dick wouldn't let anything happen to her. They had met in the sixth grade. The guys at school didn't like Dick because he always wore army fatigues and made good grades. Destiny thought that it was sexy; her dad was in the army before he was killed, and he always wore fatigues. Dick and Destiny were inseparable for two years. They fought for each other, were each other's first kiss, everything. They almost had sex one day, until she saw Dick's package. They decided to wait.

One day, Destiny's mother asked Dick what he wanted to be

when he grew up. Dick said that he wanted to go into the army and become a sniper like his father. Destiny's mother knew how close they were, and she didn't want her daughter to feel the pain that she had endured when the Army took Destiny's father from them. Without warning, she moved Destiny to Wilson, away from Dick. It was devastating to Dick and Destiny, and it took years for them to heal.

"All right, Speedy, I'm going to ask you this once, and if you lie, I'm going to punish you. Where is the money and drugs that y'all took from our trap house," Dayself asked.

"I have no idea what you are talking about," Speedy lied.

Dayself snatched Speedy up and cut his clothes off his body. His sister looked away.

"You little dick ass nigga, if you don't tell us something, I'll shoot that little motherfucker off," Trent said.

"I don't know anything about no drugs and money!" Speedy said in a scared tone.

In the room, Dick told Destiny what was going on and about the life that he lived. To Dick's surprise, she was cool with it. She even made a deal with Dick, that if his friends let her live, she would turn them on to her mother's Mexican husband, who she says has keys. Dick explained to Destiny that she had to go along with the program.

"Are you still scared of this?" Dick asked Destiny, placing her hand on his dick.

"Damn, Rashard, it has gotten bigger," she said with her eyes bucked open.

"Well, you may have to take it tonight, so be ready if that's the only choice."

"It's something that I've dreamed about anyway. Be gentle, okay?" Destiny said in the little girl voice that Dick remembered.

Dick led Destiny to the front room without the cuffs or tape, and told her to sit down beside the other girl. Everyone stared at them. Destiny regained her scared face when she saw Speedy naked.

"How could you rob someone in my shit?" Destiny asked, shooting Speedy a dirty look.

"Nigga, I'm sick of playing, and you are going to talk," Trent said.

"I told you —" Speedy started before he was cut off.

"Fuck it, I'll just kill your bitch first," Trent said and pointed the gun at Destiny.

"Speedy, give them their shit, I'm not dying for your ass!" Destiny shouted.

"Let me handle it from here," Dick said to Trent, stepping in front of the gun before he decided to pull the trigger. "Let me fuck his girl, he may talk," Dick whispered to the crew.

"I don't care what you do, let's just get this over with," Dayself said.

Dick walked up to Destiny, winked at her, and then snatched her shirt off.

"Speedy, please tell them something, nigga you took some little ass shit, got me going through this bullshit! If I get out of this, I'll kill you myself!" We've been together for five years, I give you my virginity and you play me like this. Fuck you, nigga, straight up!" Destiny said, sniffing to hold back her tears. "I'll fuck y'all if I have to, just let me go!"

Speedy's sister was crying and shaking her head no at Destiny. Speedy looked at Destiny like he wanted to kill her.

Dick, being freaky and still feeling the boat a little, pulled out his dick. Destiny's eyes grew big. His dick was eleven and a half inches long, and three inches wide.

"Speedy, help, he's going to kill me!" Destiny yelled.

"I wanted you, but I'll settle for her," Dick said, pointing his dick toward Speedy's sister.

Please don't put it all in me, I want kids someday," Destiny said, as she laid down on her back and closed her eyes.

Dick got between Destiny's legs and pushed six inches into her pussy. Her eyes popped open.

"Ahh … ahh … that's enough … no more … it's too fat … ahh … ahh," Destiny moaned loud, making an 'it hurts' face.

"Damn, you're tight," Dick said, gritting his teeth as he pushed five more inches into Destiny.

Destiny let out a loud scream, and started calling Speedy all types of names. She soon passed out. Once Dick realized that Destiny was out, he slid out of her pussy. The crew was looking at each other like, 'damn, Dick done killed this bitch with his dick.'

"This happens all the time, Dick said.

He went into the kitchen, got some ice out of the refrigerator, flipped Destiny over, and pushed the ice cubes in her pussy from the back. Destiny gained semi-consciousness. After the ice melted, Dick slid back into her pussy from the back. Destiny became fully awake, and started to moan loudly and throw it back a little. She thought about all the years that she had waited for Rashard to come and find her as she felt him in her stomach.

"Oh … fuck me … ohh fuck meeeee!" Destiny moaned.

The crew couldn't believe what they were seeing. This was the first time a woman had ever told Dick to fuck her after he was in the pussy.

"Oh … oh … what you doing?" Destiny moaned as her pussy made a farting sound. Cum dripped out of her onto the floor. "No more, no more!" Destiny screamed and dropped to the floor with her legs closed.

Dick rubbed his dick on her ass. She thought that it was over, until she felt her ass cheeks being spread, followed by a sharp pain in her asshole.

"No, Dick, don't do that!" Destiny whined, out of energy.

"As long as it was Rashard, Destiny really didn't care. She was scared because it was her first time, and Dick was so big. He popped the head of his dick in Destiny's ass, and she screamed out in pain, hitting the floor and trying to slide away. When Dick thought that Destiny had loosened up, he slid about three inches in and out of her ass slowly until Destiny passed out again. This time, Dick picked Destiny up and carried her to the bathroom.

"Are you ready to talk now?" Dayself asked, snatching the tape off Speedy's mouth.

"I didn't take it, but I know y'all are going to kill me anyway." Speedy said.

"You want to die over that little ass shit?" Dayself asked.

Speedy was silent.

"All right, have it your way." Dayself placed the tape back over Speedy's mouth.

Dayself looked at Speedy's sister. She shook her head no and began to cry.

Dirty and Trent stood in the kitchen eating turkey sandwiches and laughing at what was going on.

"Yo, Dick, come here for a minute," Dayself shouted, but Dick didn't answer. "So what's your name?" he asked as he removed the tape from Speedy's sister's mouth.

"Kendra," she said. "Speedy, please tell them. They're going to hurt me!"

Speedy tried to talk through the tape.

"Speedy, you gotta wait your turn now," Dayself said. "Trent, go see what Dick's high ass is doing," Dayself said.

Trent walked to the back of the house, letting his ears follow the moaning sounds. He opened the bathroom door, and Dick was lying between Destiny's legs on the floor, eating her pussy while she rubbed his head. Trent close the door smiling and shaking his head.

"He said that he will be in here in a few minutes," Trent said to Dayself.

"What the fuck is he doing?" Dayself asked and Trent burst out laughing.

Dick came back in the room two minutes later, with Destiny walking naked in front of him with his gun in her hand.

"Speedy, you let this happen to me, now I know what real dick and tongue feels like. I've made up my mind that I'll die for Dick and kill for him," Destiny said as she put the gun to Speedy's head and pulled the trigger repeatedly.

Dick had taken the clip out. He wanted to see if meant what she said about killing for him, while he was eating her pussy.

"Y'all, Dick done fucked this bitch crazy!" Trent said, not believing what he was seeing.

"Can I have the floor for a minute?" Destiny asked Dayself.

"The floor is yours, baby girl," Dayself said, wanting to see what the crazy girl was going to do.

"Shut the fuck up, nigga!" Destiny shouted as Speedy tried to talk through the tape. "Pay back is a bitch! I noticed how your punk ass look at your own sister's ass and breasts. Instead of you telling these guys where their shit at, you let a nigga with a dick the size of my arm fuck me in both holes!" she screamed. "Your missing tooth ass still didn't tell them after I begged you. She walked toward Kendra. "And bitch, I heard you trying to hook Speedy up with your college friend. I was on the other phone!" she said with anger.

"Don't do this! What has gotten into you?" Kendra cried.

"Bitch, you just worry about losing your virginity. Take the cuffs off of that bitch!" Destiny said as she walked into the kitchen.

Destiny came back with a nine inch cucumber that was as big as her wrist and dripping vegetable oil. In her other hand, she held a knife.

"Dick done fucked her up," Dayself said, staring at Destiny.

Destiny pushed Kendra back and put the knife to her throat.

"Bitch, if you move, I'll kill your ass!" Destiny said, forcing a little of the cucumber inside Kendra's pussy.

Destiny felt Kendra's hymen break as Kendra let out a hurt little whine.

Destiny began to fuck Kendra with the cucumber. Every time Destiny pushed the cucumber in, it came out with blood on it. Destiny still didn't stop. Kendra lay there with her eyes shut, trembling all over.

"This bitch starting to like this shit!" Destiny said to the crew. "Dick, come and fuck her just like you did me."

"No ... no ... please ... no!" Kendra begged as Dick stood between her legs.

Kendra started to slide away from Dick as the carpet burned her yellow ass. All of a sudden, Kendra stopped and looked up at Dick.

"If I do this, will you let me and my brother live?" Kendra asked.

"Yeah, yeah. I got y'all," Dick said and pulled his dick out.

Kendra looked Dick in his eyes, bit her bottom lip, and opened her legs slowly. She reached down and spread her pussy lips open.

Dick got between Kendra's legs. He was so turned on, that he slid seven inches in Kendra's pussy slowly, and moved in and out. He wanted to speed up, but Kendra's pussy was gripping his dick. He had to go slow to keep from cumming. After Dick worked about three more inches in, Kendra wrapped her arms around his neck and moved her hips in circles, while moaning like that was the dick she had been waiting for her whole life.

Destiny burned with jealousy because Dick acted like he was loving Kendra's pussy, and she didn't pass out like Destiny did. She felt like she had to react, because Dick had realized that Kendra's pussy was better than hers. Destiny was scared that Dick would kill her and let Kendra live. She got ready to pull Dick off of Kendra, but before she could make her move, Dick pulled out of Kendra's pussy and came all over her stomach.

Kendra rubbed the cum in with one hand and reached for Dick with the other.

"That's enough, Dick!" Destiny said with anger and jealousy in her voice. "I know your friends probably will shoot me, but if you put your dick back in her, I'll stab you in your neck with this knife."

Dick looked back at the Double L crew for help.

"Mr. Marcus, you're on your own," Dirty said and they all laughed.

Dick pulled up his pants and handed Destiny his gun. "Do what you're supposed to do, then."

Destiny stared Dick directly in his eyes and took the gun out of his hand. She then snatched the tape off of Speedy's mouth.

"It was Shawn and Tony from East Tarboro that robbed y'all. Little and Que paid them to do it. They told us to keep everything, that they just want us to keep hitting y'all spots," Speedy said, speaking faster than ever.

"Oh motherfucker, now you want to tell them!" Destiny shouted.

Destiny aimed Dick's .45 at Speedy's face and pulled the trigger four times, then unloaded four shots in his chest. Blood splattered all over her naked body.

Kendra released a loud scream and tried to crawl away. Destiny shot her four times in the back. She then walked up behind Kendra, bent down and put the gun in her pussy from the back, and pulled the trigger until Dick took the gun out of her hand.

Trent, Dirty, and Dayself stood there with their mouths wide open.

"Baby, you did good," Dick said, patting Destiny on the ass.

"I just killed two people in my house. What am I going to do?" Destiny asked as reality set in.

"Don't worry, we'll help you clean it up," Dick said, still shocked that she had actually done it. "Do anybody live next door?"

"One house is empty, and the people on the other side of me are out of town. I'm supposed to be keeping an eye on their house for them."

"Dayself, before we get started, can I speak with you in private?" Dick asked.

Dick walked into Destiny's room with Dayself behind him. Destiny's room was well laced out with a queen sized bed, matching polished oak headboard, dresser and nightstands, a 50" LED smart TV hung on the wall, and two paintings of black newborn babies rounded out the décor.

Dayself stood in front of the bed with his arms folded.

"We can't kill Destiny," Dick said, watching Dayself closely, checking for his reaction.

"Nigga are you crazy?" Dayself half screamed.

"No, I'm not crazy, her and I go way back. I owe her this much. She helped me out a lot as a kid. She's very special to me," Dick said in a tone that Dayself had never heard him use before.

"If we let her live, she may talk."

"Who is she going to tell on, herself?" Dick asked. "Her mother is married to a Mexican with plenty of money and keys of coke. That may come in handy."

"You know that we don't usually do this. I'm going to hold you to what you're saying. If anything goes wrong, I'll kill both of you. I'm not going back to prison," Dayself said, thinking about the Mexican and their goals.

"All right, I'll take full responsibility."

"Keep a close eye on her. You're right, we just might need her."

The two men exchanged dap and walked back into the living room. Trent and Dirty had already wrapped Speedy and Kendra's bodies in plastic and loaded them into the Camry.

"Thank you for letting me live," Destiny said to Dayself as they cleaned up the blood.

"It was Dick's decision to let you live," Dayself said.

"Am I part of the team now?"

"Yeah, we gotta put you down. You showed how Double L used to do it."

"All you gotta do is say the word. I'll put in that work for you."

"That's a good thing. We are a family and hold loyalty to the heart, but for the record, it's not what I say, it's what we say. You can handle the rest from here, right?" Dayself asked, removing the gloves and bleached rag from his hands.

"Yeah, I got it," Destiny said innocently.

"We gotta pull up outta here. In an hour, call the cops and tell them that your boyfriend and his sister left to go get something to eat four hours ago, and has not returned. They will tell you to come and make a missing persons report after twenty-four hours. Go and handle that. Dick will stay here and keep you company," Dayself said as Destiny began to smile.

"You are good people for real," Destiny said, still smiling because Dick was staying.

"I'll call and check on y'all tomorrow." Dayself said and walked out of the house.

Outside, Dick tightened the last bolt on the Camry, replacing the flat tire with the spare, then released the jack, bringing the car to the ground. Dick stood up and wiped the sweat off his face with his shirt, not realizing that he had just smeared blood on his face. His mind kept going back to the fact that he had Destiny in his life again. When they were kids, they had promised each other that they would die together. Dick made up in his mind that he would never let her go again. She was the love of his life. Dick walked back into the house to take a much needed shower.

"Drive the Camry," Dayself said to Trent.

"Why do I gotta drive the Camry?" Trent asked.

"Fuck it, I'll drive the shit!" Dirty said, growing impatient.

"No, this nigga the one that got caught slipping. You let them lame ass niggas rob you! You can't live like that, bruh. They could've killed your ass," Dayself said, upset at the thought of Trent being killed.

Without another word, Trent got in the Camry and Dirty and Dayself got in the Honda. Both cars pulled out into the night.

"Yo, can you believe them niggas, Que and Little would get together and try some shit like that?" Dirty couldn't believe that they had actually tried Double L.

"Bruh, we shortened their money. You'll be surprised what a nigga will do when you come between him and his money," Dayself said. "But, I have a surprise for them. We'll act like we don't even know right now."

They discussed strategy and the future as they drove back to the Princeville graveyard. After burying Speedy and Kendra, Trent took the Camry and Dirty took the Honda down 258 road and set the cars on fire.

An hour later, Dayself dropped both of them off at home, tired and dirty.

CHAPTER 7

*D*ayself opened his front door and noticed Piepie sitting on the couch with her leg propped up.

"Bae, what are you still doing up?"

"I've been waiting on you, and why are you so dirty?" Piepie asked, frowning at his clothes.

"Oh, it's like that down there? Let me go take a shower first," Dayself said, reaching for Piepie's pussy.

"No, I need to talk to you," Piepie said as she pushed his hand away.

Dayself went to the kitchen, got a garbage bag, stripped in front of Piepie, placed all of the clothes, including the boxers in a bag, and set them beside the door. He walked down the hall to the shower and glanced back at Piepie, who was staring at his ass.

"I thought you didn't want any," Dayself asked with a smile.

"Boy, just take your shower." Piepie said, still staring.

Piepie was sitting in the same spot when Dayself came out of the bathroom clean and refreshed.

"Are you ready? What position can I have tonight?" Dayself asked, rubbing his shaved nuts.

"No, Day, I wanted you to know we're having a baby," Piepie said in a serious tone.

Dayself ran, picked her up, and kissed her real nasty.

"Put me down!" Piepie screamed.

"We're having a baby, we're having a baby!" Dayself screamed, running up and down the hallway with Piepie in his arms. He lowered her to the floor.

Piepie walked away to the bedroom, and lay down.

"What's wrong, baby?" Dayself asked with concern.

"I'm happy, I just want you home," Piepie said sadly.

"Give me time to get a little more money. Then I can buy you that house that you always stare at when we drive by."

"None of that is important to me. I just want you to stay home sometimes."

"Can we talk about this later?" Dayself said in a tired tone.

Piepie smacked her lips and turned her back on him.

Dayself had been fucking Shay-Shay ever since he had been home, but he didn't want to get close to her. She had turned her back on him when he needed her the most. Shay-Shay was a hard person not to care for. To keep from getting close to her, Dayself would sometimes ignore her calls. On this day, she kept calling back to back. Dayself knew he had to answer because he kept a safe there.

"Hello." Dayself answered.

"Could you come by? I really do need to talk with you."

"Yeah, I'm on my way."

Thirty minutes later, Dayself knocked on Shay-Shay's door. She pulled the door open and got on her knees. He walked close to her, and she unzipped his pants, pulled his dick out, and sucked him just like he had taught her years ago. At the same time, Shay-Shay stared up at him with those pretty green eyes. Dayself couldn't hold on much longer, she had such a wet, hot mouth. As she swallowed every drop, Shay-Shay kept right on sucking, as if she was begging the dick to give her more. When she finally let go, Dayself had to stagger, weak legged to the couch to sit down.

"Day, we are having a baby." Shay-Shay said, sitting beside Dayself waiting for a reaction.

"What did you say?" Dayself asked, nearly passing out.

"We are having a baby," Shay-Shay said again. "I know that you're married, but this baby is a gift to us. I promise to never turn my back on you again." Shay-Shay said with sincerity.

"Shit, you said that last time, and look what happened. I'll be right back." Dayself got up and went to the car to get the money for the safe.

"I have to go pick my mother up from bingo. Her car is in the shop," Shay-Shay said after Dayself returned to the house.

Dayself walked out of Shay-Shay's house mumbling to himself. "Damn, Piepie is going to kill me!"

The whole team went on the grind for a month with no problems. Dayself just sold weight to people he knew. The money kept coming in, but enough was never enough. They bought a stash house and a hiding spot. Dayself bought a house they called the chill spot. No drugs were allowed there, except for personal use.

"What are you getting into tonight?" Dayself asked Trent as they sat in Mabee's yard.

"Shakes After Dark in Rocky Mount supposed to be jumping."

"I'm going to call the team up. We're going to party there tonight."

Dayself pulled up to the club in his Lexus. Cars were everywhere. It was his first time going to a casual club. He was eighteen when he was locked up, and you had to be twenty-one to get in the clubs. Dayself stepped out of his shined up Lexus. No rims and no tint was how he liked it. He was wearing a black and white silk Coogie button up, blue Coogie jeans, black and white hiking Timberlands, and a special made bracelet with the Double L sign on it to match his grill.

Dayself strolled into the club checking all the queens out. There were three women for every man. He even bumped into some old classmates from school that he hadn't seen in years. Dirty was the first person he spotted. He was wearing a red and white plaid Marco Polo button up with blue Polo jeans and white Columbia boots trimmed in red. The rest of the team was there as well. It was about thirty of them. Dayself walked over to Dirty. They just looked at each other and smiled.

"What's good, bruh?" Dayself asked over the music.

"Nothing, just checking out them niggas mean mugging us over there," Dirty said, staring back at two guys. They turned to watch a chick with a buffy the body ass, and when they turned back, the two guys were gone.

On the other side of the club, two men were indeed watching the Double L crew.

"Ain't that the nigga we robbed?" Shawn asked Tony as soon as he spotted Trent.

Shawn is about 30 years old, short, stout, light skinned with a big ass head; he could pass for Jay Z when he was young.

Tony is two years older than Shawn, the same height, with a slightly slimmer build, brown skin, little twists in his head, with a full beard.

"Yeah, that's him," Tony said, watching Trent go over to where the Double L crew was.

"How the fuck did he get his chain back?" Shawn asked in a scared tone. "Speedy and his sister are missing, and this nigga pops back up with his chain. Yo, let's get the fuck out of here," Shawn said, walking towards the door.

"I know Speedy scary ass gave our names up," Tony said, walking behind Shawn.

They bumped into Destiny on their way out the club. They

wanted to drill her about the whereabouts of Speedy and his sister, but she had that crazy nigga, Dick, with her. They kept it moving fast.

Dick walked up to the table with his date, Destiny. She wore a white Prada cat suit with orange Prada logo, orange Prada heels, and an orange and white Prada purse. Dick had on a black and grey Gucci button up, white dress pants, with a black and grey Gucci belt, and white and grey Gucci dress shoes. He knew the crew was going to clown him since he never strayed from his assorted camouflage gear.

"Did y'all see them east niggas, Tony and Shawn?" Destiny asked before they got a chance to clown Dick.

"That's them niggas that was staring at us," Trent said, getting ready to go after them.

"Let's party tonight, we'll get them later." Dayself said, grabbing Trent's arm. "I'm headed to the bar. Y'all want anything?"

"Bring back two pints of Patron and two bottles of Cristal," Dirty said.

"You always want the highest shit, but you don't ever spend any money. Your tight ass," Dayself said to Dirty.

"What's good, Dayself?" a familiar voice said.

Dayself turned around and saw Que. "I'm good, just trying to live," Dayself said, not letting Que know what was on his mind.

"I'm feeling that shirt. I started to get the brown and white one."

"I got that one too," Dayself said in an arrogant tone.

"Look over there, both of them are eatable," Que said to change the subject.

Dayself walked off from Que and walked past the chicks that Que was talking about. They both had the looks that men yearned for. The brown-skinned one had a small waist and a fat ass. She was wearing tight pink jeans and a white top from Nicki Minaj's new line, some pink wrap around heels by Jessica Simpson, and the biggest X and O chain he had ever seen. She topped it off with four gold bangles and pink and white nails to match. She was standing with another bad chick who had on a half white tee with "eat it" written on the front, a navel ring that said cotton in diamonds, blue Seven jeans, and white open toe six inch heels on the smallest feet.

As Dayself passed them to go to the bathroom, the one in the tee-shirt stared him down. After coming out of the bathroom, Dayself headed straight for the bar, jumping in front of everybody. He ended up in front of the chick with the Nicki Minaj gear on.

"Excuse you," she said, batting her long eyelashes, causing Dayself to turn around and lick his lips. "Oh nigga, you gotta pay to play."

"You ain't said nothing, what are you drinking?" Dayself asked, looking at her lips.

"Martini." She stared back at Dayself like she had known him all her life.

Dayself ordered the drinks and handed her the Martini when it came up.

"Thanks." She reached for the glass, giving Dayself the prettiest smile.

"I'll be back. Let me take these drinks to my table," Dayself said, turning to walk away. "I'll tell you what, just give me your number, and I'll get up with you after we leave the club."

"My name is Muffin. I'll program my number in your phone," Muffin said, taking Dayself's phone off his side and typing her number in. "Make sure you call me."

They went their separate ways and partied the night away. By the time the club was over, Dayself was feeling nice. He decided to call and see what the deal was with Muffin.

"Hello." Muffin answered on the third ring.

"What's good, Ms. Muffin?"

"Who is this?"

"It's Dayself. Damn, that many niggas call that you can't remember voices? I think I got the wrong number," Dayself said and hung up.

Muffin called straight back.

"Hello," he answered over the music.

"I'm sorry, how could I forget a voice like that? You never gave me your name though, right?"

"Dayself, that's the name my mother gave me. What's good? I'm trying to see you tonight."

"I'm at the Red Roof Inn in Rocky Mount. Come on through."

"Man, don't go. They some strippers, they going to rob us!" Lil Man drunkenly yelled over the music.

"Your drunk ass tripping. I should've let you ride back with Boybaby and them," Dayself said as he headed to the motel. He called Muffin back as he was pulling up.

"Hello."

"What's the number?" Dayself asked, getting out of the car.

"I'm sorry. It took you too long. My cousin and I are on our way to another club. I guess I'm going to have to see you another time. I'm sorry that I missed you."

"Yeah, me too, bye." Dayself said. He hung up and deleted her number out of his phone. "Fuck it. I'm going home to my wife," Dayself said as he pulled off from the motel.

Piepie was curled up sleep on the bed when Dayself got home, drunk as fuck. He laid down and stared in her face until he dozed off to sleep.

He woke up the next morning with his boxers down to his ankles, dick sticking straight up in the air, and the look of dried cum on it.

"Call the police, I been raped!" Dayself yelled.

"Stop playing, boy. I just wanted to try it. It was good too. I rode you for about an hour, and you never knew it. You must have been fucked up last night," Piepie yelled from the bathroom.

"Yeah, I was pretty fucked up," Dayself said as his phone rang.

"Hello." Dayself answered.

"Radio." Dirty said.

"What's good?"

"I need you to meet me at Abrams restaurant."

"I'll be there. Food on you today, anyway."

"That's peace," he said and hung up.

"Dayself, come here!" Piepie screamed.

Dayself jumped up, thinking somebody had broken into the house. He grabbed his gun out the drawer, and hit corners like he was Tarboro police swat team, until he made it to the bathroom. Dayself pushed the door open slowly. Piepie sat on the toilet crying, holding something in tissue. Dayself dropped his gun and ran to her side.

"What's wrong, baby?" Dayself asked. "What's that in your hand?"

"It's our baby!" Piepie cried, handing him the tissue.

Dayself held their baby in his hands. It was tiny and pink, with legs, arms, and a head. He stood there staring at the baby in the tissue until he felt light headed. Dayself handed the tissue back, and walked outside. Piepie took the baby and rocked it like she was rocking it to sleep.

Dayself sat on the stairs, letting the tears fall. "Why this keeps happening to us? Why are we being punished?" he questioned.

Dayself stood and prepared to walk back into the house. He could see Piepie sitting on the couch with that look of hurt again. Placing one hand on the brick wall beside the door, he dropped his head and let out a tortured whine, then broke down crying. Dayself stood there for several minutes until he got himself together.

"I'll be back in a few," Dayself said, sticking his head in the door.

"All right," Piepie said sadly, and turned back to watch TV.

Dayself rode around until it was time to meet Dirty at Abrams.

"What's good?" Dirty asked as Dayself walked up to the table.

"Nothing, same shit." Dayself said and took a seat.

"What's wrong, bruh?" Dirty asked again with concern.

"It's nothing. What's this meeting about?"

"My uncle, Yellow, just got out of the Feds, about seven months ago. A couple of guys don't want to come off his block or cop from him. You know that's not how they do it in Brooklyn."

"Call him and let him know that were coming through around Tuesday."

"Bet."

Dayself and Dirty ordered their food to go, and headed to their spots. They made some drop offs and pickups, making sure everything was straight. After dropping the money off at the stash spot, Dayself rode around thinking. All he could do was picture his baby in that tissue. Every time a tear, came to the corner of his eye, he wiped it away. Dayself, phone started ringing.

"Hello," Dayself answered.

"Last night was crazy. The Double L chicks do it all and take it all," Castro said.

"You better slow down, nigga," Dayself said.

"Look who's talking. Oh, how about the other day I was about to fuck Tasha."

"Tasha who?" Dayself asked, thinking about his first love.

"Tasha from Princeville, the one with the gay brother that call himself Strawberry."

"I know who you talking about," Dayself said.

"I was about to fuck her, right. I couldn't get hard. How about she stuck her whole hand to the wrist in her pussy, and going to ask me, do that make me hard. I hauled ass up out of there."

"You're crazy as hell," Dayself said, laughing at his man.

"I gotta go, bruh, pussy beeping in."

"All right, peace," Dayself said and hung up as he pulled into Mabee's yard.

"Hey, Mabee, what have you been up to?" Dayself asked, getting out of the car.

"Nothing, just waiting on a fine man to recognize what he has been missing. He got to have a job though. Both of us on disability won't work."

"You're too old to be looking for a man."

"As long as I got these hips, I'm never too old." Mabee said, doing a dance one of her granddaughters had showed her.

"Here's some money to pay the bills. Don't go down there and play it up in numbers, then be calling me talking about you left your purse on the church van, and when you got it back all your money was gone."

"That is what happened," Mabee said innocently.

"Well, why did the number man, Earl, say you played three hundred dollars' worth of numbers, and only won seventy five dollars?"

"Earl telling a got damn lie! I'm going to get his ass when I see him."

"I love you, I'm gone," Dayself said, kissing her on the cheek. As soon as Dayself got into his car, his phone rang.

"Hello," Dayself answered, not recognizing the number.

"Are you trying to see me before I go back?"

"Who is this, and where are you going back to?

"This is Muffin. I'm going back to Winston-Salem where I live."

"That's what's up. I'll meet you in Rocky Mount, at the McDonald's that has the fuel dock hooked to it, across from Hardees. Around seven thirty," Dayself said, looking at his G-shock watch. "Is your friend with you?"

"Yes, I'll see you then."

Dayself rode around, picked up and dropped off until it was close to seven. When he got ready to go to Rocky Mount, he decided to call Castro to go with him.

"Hello," Castro answered.

"You trying to ride with me to go check these chicks out I met last night?"

"Shit, hell yeah. I need some new pussy."

"What's good, y'all?" Dayself asked, pulling up beside Muffin's car.

"Nothing, just waiting on you," Muffin said with that pretty smile.

"Follow me, then," Dayself said and pulled off.

A few minutes later, they pulled up in Howell's Inn. Muffin and Cotton had scared looks on their faces. Dayself could tell that they weren't used to going to the hood motels. Muffin was wearing brown khaki shorts, a pink tank top, and pink flip-flops. Cotton was wearing a short skirt, white tank top, and white pro keds. Dayself and Castro wore their usual, white tee, blue jeans, Air Ones or Timb's.

"Are we going in there?" Muffin asked.

"Are you staying the night?" Dayself countered.

"No, I got to get home to Shyleek," Muffin said.

"We're going in here then, and who is Shyleek?" Dayself asked.

"That's my son, he's two years old." Muffin said, smiling.

Once inside the room, the girls got comfortable. The inside looked two times better than the outside. Everyone began talking. Muffin and Dayself realized that they had a lot in common, until Dayself decided to tell her he was married.

"You're married!" Muffin said. "I'm not trying to come between you and your wife. I'm about to graduate from Winston-Salem State, I have goals."

"Don't get me wrong, I love her, but life just won't complete itself for us, and that's causing a strain on our relationship." Dayself said, speaking from the heart.

They talked a little more, and smoke two cigarillos of white widow weed. Cotton, Muffin's friend, was just sitting there acting all stuck up. Castro kept trying to talk to her, but she was one of those chicks, who wouldn't fuck with a nigga if she thought he didn't have any money. Boy, she was sadly mistaken. They were the type of chicks Double L would give a little money, fuck, and leave her begging for more. Castro's phone ringing brought Dayself out of his thoughts about Cotton.

"I'll be over there," Castro said, and then hung up. "Yo, I need to make a run. Call me when you're ready," he said, grabbing the keys off the table and heading for the door.

"All right, give me that liquor out of the car," Dayself said.

"Y'all want some of this?" Dayself asked Muffin and Cotton, knowing that it was mixed with ecstasy.

"No, I'm good. I gotta drive back," Muffin said.

"Yeah, let me get some of that." Cotton said, filling her cup halfway.

Cotton drank most of what she had poured in the cup. About ten minutes later, she kept cutting her eyes at Dayself.

"It's hot in this motherfucker!" she said, a little too loud, and turned the air conditioner up.

"Girl, your ass is high!" Muffin said, laughing.

The ecstasy had kicked in, and Castro was gone.

"I gotta pee," Muffin said. She got up and went to the bathroom, closing the door behind her.

"Dayself … Dayself … Dayself …" Cotton moaned softly, with her skirt up, thong to the side, fingering her pussy, while pulling on her pierced clit.

The toilet flushed, and Muffin came back out of the bathroom. Cotton acted like she was asleep. Dayself stood up, walked up to Muffin and kissed her hard. He slid his tongue out of her mouth, and sucked on her bottom lip.

"Take these off," Muffin said, grabbing the button on Dayself's pants.

Dayself and Muffin stripped at the same time, watching each other remove piece by piece. Dayself laid Muffin down on the bed. Her breasts felt so nice and warm to his chest. He kissed her slow and nasty, then led his tongue down to her breast. After sucking on her second breast, Muffin's legs started to tremble. Cumming on herself, she reached for his dick.

Dayself slid out of reach, and down to her pussy. The closer he got, the stronger the strawberry smell hit his nostrils. Dayself spread her pussy lips open, making her clit slide out of hiding. He licked her clit in circular motions. Muffin moaned softly, so Cotton couldn't hear her.

Every time Dayself flicked his tongue on her clit, Muffin's legs would jump, making her feel like she was cumming back to back. Dayself stopped and pushed her legs back, ramming his tongue deep into her pussy. She let out a long moan. He continued to go in and out of her pussy with his tongue, playing with her clit at the same time with his pointer finger. Dayself cut his eyes at Cotton. She had slipped her hand between her legs, fingering herself. Muffin's pussy muscles tightened around Dayself's tongue. She grabbed his head, pulled it close to her pussy, and came all over his face.

"Damn, you got that water!" Dayself said, licking most of her cum up.

Dayself slipped a condom on and slid slowly into Muffin. Before he could get it all in, she started rotating her hips.

"Ah … Day … ah … ah …!" Muffin moaned repeatedly in his hear.

Dayself placed a hand on each breast, squeezing her nipples. He slid out of her pussy, went down, and sucked each nipple like a hungry baby. At the same time, Dayself rubbed his dick up and down the slit of her pussy, letting the head go in a little. Once her nipples became hard, she gripped Dayself around his neck and came on the tip of his dick. Dayself slid back in Muffin's wet pussy and worked her for about five minutes in that position, then placed her legs on his shoulders and moved in circles, making sure his dick touched every piece of meat inside her pussy.

Muffin felt herself cumming again. She threw her pussy back to him with every stroke. "Baby, take that rubber off, let me feel it," she moaned, still throwing it back.

Dayself didn't think twice. He slid the condom off and placed his dick head at her entrance. He could feel Muffin's pulse beating through her pussy. Dayself went back into her an inch at a time. He pushed the rest of his dick in, and Muffin's juices splashed all over his dick hairs.

"Ah … ah … I … never … came … like … ah … this!" Muffin moaned, coating Dayself's dick with her juices, while digging her nails into his back.

"You like that, baby?" Dayself asked, sliding out of her pussy, dick still hard.

"Hell yeah!"

"Turn over, let me try something," Dayself said, lifting up off her. He spread her ass cheeks and licked her ass hole.

"That tickles!" Muffin said, jumping with every lick.

Dayself put his hand underneath Muffin and played with her clit while licking her ass. Dayself pushed his tongue in her ass, and she moaned louder. He slid his tongue in and out at a fast pace, still playing with Muffin's clit.

"Oh ... God ... Oh ... Oh ... God! What ... are ... you ... doing to ... o ... to ... me? Oh ... Oh ... God ... it ... feels ... so ... ah ... ah ...!" Muffin moaned, coming again and dropping to the bed.

Dayself pulled Muffin's ass back in the air, slid his dick in her pussy, and fucked her in a medium rhythm for three more minutes. He sped up, looking over at Cotton. She had her eyes closed, sucking her wetness off her fingers.

Cotton watched Dayself as she slid her fingers in and out of her mouth.

Dayself let off deep in Muffin's pussy, with his eyes closed, mouth wide open. She lay there for a minute, still moaning. Then, Muffin got up and went to wash off.

Cotton just lay there staring at the big circle of cum that Dayself and Muffin had just left on the bed.

"Why did you do that?" Muffin asked, coming out of the bathroom.

"I'm your protector now. I can see it on your face that you need a man to love you right, and that was a start. Will you let me love you the way that you should be loved?" Dayself asked while rubbing her lips with his thumb. "I can't promise anything, but I can love you," Dayself said, catching her tears before they fell out of the corner of her eye.

They got dressed and Muffin prepared to leave. She had a two and a half hour drive ahead.

Castro pulled up as the ladies were leaving.

Dayself washed off and headed home.

Piepie was lying down, staring at the wall when Dayself entered the room. The pictures of their prison wedding lay beside her. Dayself sat there mesmerized as he flipped through the pictures. He said to himself, *Damn, I keep hurting her. I can't keep my dick in my pants.*

Dayself rubbed Piepie's shoulders and held her until they both fell asleep.

The next morning, Dayself made his rounds, collecting and dropping off. He left the spot and went to Mabee's house. While sitting on the hood of his car, his phone rang.

"Hello," Dayself answered to someone crying on the phone. He said "hello," about three more times, to nothing but crying. He hung up the phone and they called right back.

"Hello," Dayself answered, getting irritated.

"I need to talk to you," Muffin said, sniffing.

"Did you just call?" Dayself asked.

"Yeah, I'm calling from my house phone."

"What's wrong?"

"I'm really feeling you, and I don't want you to think I'm a whore because I gave it to you on the first night. I've never done that before. I just felt so loved and free with you."

"I don't think that of you. Besides, it was the second night, not the first," Dayself said, trying to make her feel better.

"I felt so free with you."

"There's more where that came from," Dayself said, watching Dirty get out of his car. "Well, I gotta talk to my man, Dirty. I'll speak with you later."

"All right, bye Day."

"Bye, Ms. Pay to Play," Dayself said, repeating what Muffin had said at the bar.

"You know we got to handle that in New York tomorrow," Dirty said.

"Yeah, we'll pull out to do that early."

"All right, partner, let me get back to the spot. That new shit we got is booming."

"That's peace, partner."

"Peace," Dirty said, getting in his car to leave.

CHAPTER 8

$\mathcal{D}$irty, Trent, and Dayself made it to Brooklyn late the next afternoon. Yellow hopped out of a black 2014 Suburban with tinted windows and factory rims.

"What's good, country boys?" Yellow said, getting into the truck with them. "Turn around this way, and make a right by the navy yard, then make a left." Yellow said, giving directions to one of his hideouts.

Five minutes later, they were all inside, and Yellow went straight to the bar and fixed four cups of rain, no ice.

"Y'all, these boys keep short stopping my money," Yellow said, passing out glasses. "I asked them nicely to either join me or cop from me. They seem not to respect my gangster. I put in work out there before these boys were born. I earned that block!" Yellow yelled. "There's so much blood on my hands, I can see it and smell it from going to war over that block," he mumbled, looking at his hands.

"Unc, I know that you're still on probation from the fed time you done. Just point them out, and we'll handle the rest," Dirty said, hating to see cats trying to play his family.

"Just give us the heat, and it is done. Let's talk cash," Trent said, rubbing his hands together.

"The cash is not a problem. I would've gotten one of my people to do it, but I don't want the heat to fall back on me. I'll give y'all thirty thousand for all three."

"You got yourself a deal, old man," Dayself said, shaking Yellow's hand.

∽

The next morning, Dayself, Trent, and Dirty rode through the block, in a 1989 black Ford Taurus with tinted windows. Yellow had his little lookout to point out the three guys and their bar to Dayself and his crew. When night hit, Dayself, Dirty, and Trent, pulled up to the bar. Cars came and went all night long.

"Don't forget, Yellow said don't shoot the real light skinned one in the face," Trent said, loading his gun.

Around nine thirty, they saw five different strippers come out of the club. Then around twelve, four men walked out.

"That's them right there!" Dirty said, pulling out his gun and putting his ski mask on.

The three men got close to the car, and Dirty, Dayself, and Trent jumped out with their guns drawn.

"Yo, lay the fuck down, nigga!" Dayself yelled.

"Yo, son, y'all got that. Take it all!" one of the men said in a strong New York accent, handing over the money bag and jewels.

"Really, son, if I ever find out who y'all are, I'm a murder y'all niggas!" the light skinned one said, reaching for his gun.

"Put your fucking hands up!" Dirty yelled. "Nigga, you on the wrong end of the gun to be talking shit!" Dirty shot him between his eyes with his .45.

The other two tried to run away, but Dayself and Trent took aim, giving them both shots to the back of the head and body. Trent walked over to them and filled both of their faces with lead. Yellow had given them orders not to shoot the light-skinned one in the face. Yellow went way back with his father. He wanted him to have an open casket funeral. Dirty didn't listen, he still put two more in his face.

They took the car to the chop shop that Yellow's friend owned, then got rid of the guns and clothes. Finally, they jumped into Trent's Expedition and went to meet Yellow at White Castle.

"I thought I told y'all not to shoot the light skinned one in the face," Yellow said, getting into the truck with a big smile on his face.

"It was night, Unc. They all looked dark, so I made sure that they were gone." Dirty said, rubbing his red beard.

"Boy, you're just like I was in my younger days. Here's the money. I threw in a little something extra," Yellow said, giving everybody dap, and hopping out of the truck.

Trent opened the tote bag; it was a QP of blueberry Kush, and about fifty ecstasy pills.

Piepie was in the kitchen, cooking when Dayself made it home the next evening.

"Hey Piepie," Dayself said, speaking to Piepie but being ignored. Dayself tried to talk to her three more times, but she still ignored him." So, you're not going to talk to me?"

"Go where the fuck you were the last two days," Piepie said angrily.

"Who are you talking to like that?" Dayself asked, walking up behind her.

"I'm talking to your sorry ass!" she yelled, slamming the dishcloth into the water.

Dayself reached around, unbuttoned Piepie's pants, pulled them and her thong to her ankles. He dropped his pants and boxers, and slid in her pussy from the back. With his hands on her shoulders, Dayself bounced her on his dick for five minutes. Piepie's pussy tightened around his dick, and he had to fuck her slow to keep from cumming. She tightened and released her pussy muscles over and over, as Dayself slid in and out. Piepie came all over his dick, squeezing the countertop. Dayself got about two more strokes in, and came deep inside her pussy.

After cumming, Dayself pulled his pants up to go take a shower.

"Oh, nigga, you still in the dog house. Just because you got some pussy don't mean shit. Your pillow will still be on the couch tonight," Piepie said, stepping out of her clothes and following him to the bathroom.

The next evening, Dayself took Piepie to Golden East Crossing mall in Rocky Mount, trying to get off the couch. He bought her everything she wanted. Dayself even snuck off and bought Piepie a diamond bracelet. She had the biggest smile on her face, and Dayself knew that he was off the couch.

"Baby, you been in the game long enough. It's time to quit," Piepie said.

"Not yet, it won't be long though." Dayself said, taking Piepie's hand, and walking with her to the food court to get some Stromboli's.

Dayself set their bags and his phone down, and went to the counter to order.

As Piepie waited for Dayself to bring their food, his phone started beeping. Piepie ignored it until it beeped again. She picked the phone up and checked it. It was a picture text of a pussy spread open with the words, *come get it,* at the bottom. Piepie called the number back, but there was no answer.

Dayself walked back to the table with a tray full of food. "What's wrong now?" Dayself asked, seeing the hurt look on Piepie's face.

"Take me the fuck home now!" Piepie yelled, and then broke down in tears.

"What's wrong with you?" Dayself asked, catching Piepie looking down at his phone. He grabbed the phone and saw the picture text on the screen.

"Hell naw!" Dayself said, shocked at what he'd found. Dayself had just met the girl earlier that day. She was on her way to church, and had stopped at the store in Double L. She acted shy, so he gave her his number. "B,aby let me explain!"

Piepie just got up and walked off.

Dayself followed her out of the mall, hands full with bags, and food. Their drive back home was very quiet. Dayself tried to talk, but Piepie just stared ahead. Finally, he stopped wasting his and her time, trying to explain. He was caught red handed.

"Pack your shit and get the fuck out!" Piepie yelled, walking into the house. "Come back when you get your shit together."

Wiping away tears and trying to be strong, Dayself packed his bags. He headed to the chill spot, and went straight to bed. Rest was what he needed.

Two weeks later, Dayself was watching Maury at Piepie's house when she walked in with a bucket of KFC chicken in her hand and gave him and evil look. She threw the chicken box right at his head. Chicken grease ran down Dayself's face.

"Girl, what the fuck is wrong with you?" Dayself asked, jumping up.

"Why the fuck you didn't tell me that Shay-Shay was pregnant!" Piepie yelled.

"That shit happened when you kicked me out! I didn't tell you, because she said it wasn't mine," Dayself said, trying to lie his way out of it.

Piepie broke down crying, and started fighting Dayself. She stopped all of a sudden, grabbed her stomach, and dropped to the floor.

Dayself didn't know what to do. He looked down, and saw her crying, rocking back and forth, and holding her stomach. Dayself picked Piepie up, ran out the door, and rushed her to the hospital. They pulled up to the emergency department and Dayself threw the car in park, opened her door, and ran with Piepie into the emergency room.

"Help her, somebody!" he screamed.

A nurse ran over to assist them. They put Piepie in a wheelchair and rushed her to the back. Dayself sat in the waiting room for thirty minutes before a doctor came out to see him.

"Your wife will be fine, but she lost the baby," the doctor said sadly.

"Can I see her?" Dayself asked.

"Sure, she's signing herself out. I told her to spend the night so we can run some tests, but she refused."

Dayself went to Piepie's room. "Why didn't you tell me that you were pregnant?"

"Because I didn't want to disappoint you."

"Baby, you couldn't disappoint me. I may hardly be home, and do crazy shit, but you could never disappoint me for something like that."

"Are you ready?" Piepie asked, walking out past him.

They rode in silence once again back to the house.

"Just leave, I wanna be alone," Piepie said.

"Bae, I can't leave you here like this."

"You left the second day you were here, and haven't come back yet."

"Listen baby, come here," Dayself said, calling her to sit down. "Neither one of us are happy. Maybe it's time we go our separate ways," Dayself said.

"I'm sorry, please don't go," Piepie cried.

"It's not you. I just can't do right by you, and I'm tired of hurting you," Dayself said, dropping his head and walking out.

He headed to the chill spot to give himself some time to be alone with his thoughts. Some called it going to the mountaintop.

CHAPTER 9

$\mathcal{A}$nother month had gone by, and money was still coming in. Dayself was going back and forth to different women. Shay-Shay was showing a little, and she constantly called to fuss about him not spending time with her. Muffin was driving back and forth from Winston-Salem to Tarboro every weekend. Piepie only called for sex then kicked him out. Dayself was contemplating hard on changing his life, when his phone went off.

"Hello," Dayself answered.

"Come to the hiding spot," Trent said.

"What is it?"

"Man, just come and wear your gloves. I have a surprise for you."

Dayself pulled up around the back of the house and put his mask on. He went straight to the basement. There were four men handcuffed with tape over their mouths, blindfolded. Two of them Dayself recognized. One was Que. He was dead, with two holes in his chest. The other one was Little; he had pissed all over his self.

"Damn, y'all started without me," Dayself said, pointing at Que.

"This guy said Que smiled at him, so he shot him." Trent said, pointing at Dirty. "He got issues."

"Tell Day how we got Little and Que here," Dirty said.

"We kidnapped Tony and Shawn last night. We had them call and say that they had you and Dirty tied up here, and they came right to the back door," Trent said, smiling.

"Is that right?" Dayself asked, pulling out his gun and shooting Little in the chest two times. "We're even now, nigga," Dayself said, smiling through his mask at Dirty. "So this is Mr. Tony and Mr. Shawn," he said, snatching the tape off the other two men's mouths.

"What we do? Why y'all got us handcuffed and tied down like this?" Tony asked.

"That's not important. Just know y'all done fucked up. To make sure y'all don't make the same mistakes again, I have a special treat for y'all," Dayself said and picked up the phone to call Tasha's house.

"Hello," Tasha answered.

"Yo, Tasha."

"What boy, have you seen lying ass Castro?" she asked before he could tell her what he wanted.

"No, let me speak to your brother," Dayself said, laughing as he pictured Tasha sticking her whole hand in her pussy.

"What's so funny?"

"Nothing."

"Strawberry, telephone!" Tasha yelled.

"I got it," Strawberry said in a female voice. "Hello."

"Bobbi, check this out. I need you to handle something for me, and I'll drop you a gee."

"Why you can't call me Strawberry like everybody else?"

"Gone with that, you know I don't be doing that shit. You want the job or not?"

"Yeah, cause I do need the money," Strawberry said, twisting the hair on the end of his wig.

"How fast can you get to Conetoe?"

"I'll be there in five minutes."

"It's the only white house, with three black rocking chairs on the front porch. The fourth house on the left."

Strawberry walked in the house wearing a tight mini skirt, some cheap heels, and a wig Tasha had just made for him. Trent playfully pointed his gun at him. Strawberry screamed like a woman, then begged in a man's voice. Dirty just sat there shaking his head.

"I'll let y'all get your last piece of ass before I give y'all the next treat," Dayself said, walking down the basement stairs.

"What type of game is this? Y'all bring us here, kill Little and Que, tie us up, so we can fuck a bitch?" Tony's voice shook as he spoke.

"It turns her on," Dayself said, kicking their clothes toward the door.

"You can go in now," Dayself said to Strawberry.

"Thank you for calling me, I haven't had fun like this in a long time," Strawberry said.

"I don't want to hear that shit. Just do whatever you do, all right?" Dayself said, pointing to the basement.

"Who's first?" Strawberry asked as he closed the door behind him.

Tony and Shawn looked at each other, and screamed for dear life.

Thirty minutes later, Strawberry walked out of the basement smiling. "They're all yours now," Strawberry said. "That was a pleasure. Call me if y'all need me again." Taking his money out of Trent hand, he walked toward the door.

"Get the fuck out of here!" Trent screamed, kicking Strawberry up his ass.

Strawberry let out a loud feminine scream and hauled ass out of the house.

Trent, Dirty, and Dayself walked back into the basement with their masks and gloves on. The room smelled like straight shit.

Tony and Shawn sat there, butt ass naked and crying. Dirty fell out laughing, until he could hardly breathe.

"Y'all walking dead now," Dayself said.

"Man, what are you talking about? How could you let him rape us?" Shawn yelled, beginning to cry again.

"There's more where that came from, so don't cry yet. See, that dude has full blown AIDS, so that means ..."

"Man, just kill us. I can't live like this!" Tony screamed, crying harder.

"I was going to kill y'all, but Dirty had another idea." Dayself said, pulling the edgers from behind his back.

"What are you going to do with those big ass scissors?" Shawn screamed, his eyes big as saucers.

"Cut y'all dicks off, so y'all won't pass that shit to any of my sisters," Dayself said.

"God no ... God no ... why have thou forsaken me?" Shawn yelled in tears, as he looked up at the ceiling.

Trent spit green tea all over the wall laughing.

Dayself walked up to each man and chopped their dicks off with the scissors. They both passed out from the torture. He shot them with a needle of coke and sleeping pills to ease the pain. Their socks and shoes were the only thing on when they woke up. Tony and Shawn felt the bandages on their hands and feet. They were so high from the needle, they couldn't hold their heads up.

"Let me guess, y'all are wondering about the bandages on your hands and feet, right?" Dayself asked.

They shook their heads again. Dayself stuck his hand in their pit bull dog food bowl, and threw their dicks, toes, fingers, and tongues at their feet. "Your toes are gone, so y'all won't run to the cops, your tongue, so you won't tell the cops, and your fingers, so y'all won't fuck with nobody else's shit. Y'all already know why your dicks are gone. Any more questions, gentlemen?"

They both sat there crying with snot running out their noses.

Dayself dialed Dick's number.

"Hello," Dick answered.

"It's about to be dark in an hour. I need you to come to the hiding spot and drop a package off over east. Leave a letter that says, 'the hand cuff key is in my pants.'"

"I'll be there in about forty minutes."

The next morning, it was in the newspaper. The headline read, TWO MEN FOUND WITH THEIR BODY PARTS AMPUTATED in big bold letters. The article detailed the gruesome condition of the two men and identified the victims. At the end, it said, "If you have any information about this crime, contact Tarboro police department at (252)641-9911.

I've been running ever since I came home from prison, Dayself thought to himself. *It's time I take a vacation.* His ringtone, "Lovers and Friends," by Usher came on, bringing him out of his thoughts.

"Hello," Dayself answered.

"What's up?" Muffin said, sounding down.

"What's the matter?" Dayself asked with concern.

"I'm pregnant," she blurted out, trying to get it out while she still had the strength to do so.

"I don't know what to say," Dayself said. "Are you going to keep it? You know Shay-Shay is pregnant. It's your decision, just think about it and let me know." Dayself was nervous, and the words just spilled from his mouth.

"Slow down, you're talking a mile a minute. I'll give you time to let it sink in," she said and hung up before he could get another word out.

Ten minutes later, Dayself was getting into his car to leave the chill spot, when "Lovers and Friends" started to play again.

"Yeah?" Dayself answered. Stress was evident in his voice.

"I'm going to have my baby. You don't have to be in his or her life, but I can't kill my baby," Muffin said between sniffles.

"Wait, you're misunderstanding me. If you have the baby, I'm behind you one hundred percent. I just thought with your goals, me being married, and an outside child on the way, that you didn't want to have my child."

"I didn't want to get pregnant, but I am, so I'll have to deal with it."

"We'll finish this later. Let me think for a minute," Dayself said, rubbing his temple.

"Don't forget to call me later."

"I won't, bye." Dayself hung up and hit his hand on the steering wheel. "Damn, soon as I'm about to get out the game." He picked up his phone and called Dirty.

"Radio," Dirty answered.

"Is Trent with you?"

"Yeah, we're at Jones' Soul Food, getting some food," Dirty said, sampling one of their homemade apple pies.

"Meet me at Mabee's house."

"That's peace."

Dirty and Trent drove up in Dirty's car, listening to Beenie Segals first mix tape. Dirty pulled up beside Dayself's car and rolled the window down.

"Here, I bought you a chicken dinner," Dirty said, handing Dayself his food through the window.

Dayself got out of his car, took the tray, and got into Dirty's back seat.

"What's the meeting about?" Trent asked.

"Destiny's stepfather. You know Destiny told Dick her mother is married to a Mexican with plenty of keys and money," Dayself said, wiping the chicken grease off his lips.

"Let's go to Destiny's crib and see what's up. I'm trying to retire soon," Dirty said, his eyes red as fire.

Dayself knocked on Destiny's door for about five minutes.

They knew that they were in there, Dick's truck was in the garage, and they could hear H-Town, "Knocking Boots" playing in the house.

"What's good, brothers?" Destiny asked, opening the door and letting them in. She walked to the couch like her pussy was sore.

"Your step daddy," Dirty said, looking at her seriously.

"I'm down with that," Destiny said, and looked back to find Dick standing behind her. "I owe him a little payback anyway. He don't keep drugs in the house, but he got money there. He owns a Mexican club in Wilson, North Carolina, called Megos. Just don't hurt my mother. She and Dick are all that I have left," Destiny said.

"That's our word; we won't harm her," Trent said.

"Y'all have a plan ready by the time I get back," Dayself said, standing up to leave.

"Where are you going, to Africa?" Dick asked, making everybody laugh.

"Real funny, nigga. I don't know, but I need a break from this shit. Did you feed Que and Little, to your uncle's hogs in the country?" Dayself asked.

"Yeah, and enjoyed every minute of it," Dick said with a smile.

"We don't want their bodies to ever be found." Dayself said.

CHAPTER 10

At the chill spot, Dayself lay on the couch in silence, letting his mind travel. The thought of getting away crossed his mind. He hopped up and started dialing numbers.

"Hello," Piepie answered on the first ring.

"Hey Piepie," Dayself seductively said.

"Stop your bitches from calling here and calling my job!" she yelled and hung up the phone in his ear.

Dayself decided to call Shay-Shay; she had been blowing his phone up.

"Hello," she answered in a sweet tone.

"Give me a kiss," Dayself said, trying to make her laugh.

"Motherfucker, now you want to call! I been spotting, trying to call your ass, and you wouldn't answer your phone!" she cried, and then hung up.

Dayself dropped his head, let out a breath of extra stress, then dialed Muffin's number.

"Hello," Muffin answered, sounding stressed.

"Don't hang up on me!" Dayself said somewhat loud.

"Baby daddy, why would I hang up on you?"

"My wife and Shay-Shay seem to have it out for me today."

"Don't feel bad, I'm tired of arguing with Shyleek's father."

"How old his Shyleek?"

"I told you, two. You'll get to meet him."

"Do you want to get away for a couple of days?"

"I graduate from college tomorrow. I have just been promoted to a higher position, but by me graduating, my boss will understand. Are you coming to my graduation?"

"Yeah, I'll be there."

Dayself made it to Winston-Salem that night. His navigation system took him around in circles, but he spotted the hotel on the right, and rode around until he found Muffin's car in the parking lot. Dayself pulled up beside her car and watched her peep out the room window. She opened up the door, ran and jumped into his arms, giving him a big kiss.

"Girl, get down, you done got heavy," Dayself said, kissing her back and carrying her into the motel room. He shut the door with his foot. "I got a surprise for you. What are you going to wear to the graduation?" Dayself asked, as he put her down on the bed and sat beside her.

"Are you asking me what clothes I'm going to wear?" Muffin asked, confused.

"No, I'm asking you to wear this," Dayself said, and pulled out a pink ice bracelet.

"Thank you … thank you!" Muffin screamed jumping into his lap to hug and kiss him.

"Wait, wait, what are you going to wear with it?" Dayself asked as Muffin gave him a confused look. "Wear this with it." He pulled out a pink ice ring surrounded by little diamonds. "You'll get straight diamonds, when you prove to me that you are a diamond."

"You make it so hard for people not to love you!" Muffin said with tears in her eyes. "Oh shit!"

"What is it now?"

"My granddaddy came down for my graduation. I told him that I would bring his food back that he ordered.

"Go ahead. I'm getting ready to get high. I'll probably be sleep when you get back."

Muffin grabbed the key card and walked out

About an hour later, there was a knock at the door. Dayself was high as hell; he wondered who it could be. He looked through the peephole, and Muffin was standing there in a trench coat.

"Girl, what are you doing wearing a trench coat in the summer time?" Dayself said as he opened the door and let Muffin in. He turned around, and she dropped the coat, revealing her naked body with her brown skin gleaming with baby oil. "Bae, you read too many books."

Dayself walked toward Muffin and got on his knees as she sat on the bed. He lifted her feet, going to each toe, sucking them like he was searching for the last drop of water on earth. Muffin lay back and massaged her breast and nipples. Dayself wet his mouth real good, and ran his tongue up the side of her thigh, stopping at her pussy lips. Muffin couldn't keep still. He ran his tongue up her rib cage, reaching down to roll her clit in his hand at the same time.

Muffin let out a loud moan as she reached and grabbed Dayself's dick. She jacked it slowly, letting the pre-cum drip on her hand. Dayself closed his eyes tight, with her clit still between his fingers. He lightly nibbled on her nipples, making her pussy wetter. Dayself's fingers moved the hood on Muffin's clit in an up and down motion, just like she was doing his dick. The faster he went on her clit, the faster she jacked his dick. Muffin came all over Dayself's hand.

Dayself slid up and sucked on her bottom lip. Muffin grabbed Dayself's dick and guided it toward her pussy entrance, grabbed his ass cheeks, and pulled him all the way into her pussy. Muffin rotated her hips, causing her pussy to make a wet splashing sound. She opened her legs like she was doing a split. Dayself fucked her like that for ten minutes; she soon came again on his dick.

Dayself rolled them over so Muffin would be on top. Her cum ran out of her, down his dick, and dripped off his balls on to the sheets. Muffin moved in circles on top of Dayself's dick, like she was playing hula hoop. Dayself rubbed and squeezed Muffin's breast and nipples. Muffin rode Dayself hard and fast. She came again, all over his dick. Feeling Muffin's cum drip off his balls turned Dayself on even more, and he came inside her pussy.

Muffin and Dayself woke up the next morning with her on top of him, and his dick semi hard, still in her pussy.

"Oh shit!" Muffin said, glancing at the clock and jumping up. "I'm going to be late!"

She quickly got dressed and ran to the door. "I'll meet you there!"

Blowing Dayself a kiss, Muffin closed the door behind her.

Dayself got to the graduation just before Muffin walked across the stage. She received her diploma, and nervously looked around for Dayself as she walked off. Muffin spotted him smiling at her. She ran to him and wrapped her arms around his neck.

"I did it, baby … I did it," she screamed with excitement and tears.

"I'm proud of you, baby," Dayself said, pulling her close, feeling the little bump in her stomach.

Muffin's family came over and introduced themselves. Her aunt was being very friendly, but Dayself had his mind on the little short long headed guy standing there with a mean mug on his face. He tapped Muffin on her shoulder and they walked off a distance. Dayself could see him fussing at her. She stood there and took it. He walked off, still mad, and then grilled Dayself like he weighed two hundred and fifty pounds of muscle. Dayself smiled at him; he didn't know any better.

"I'm sorry about that," Muffin said with an embarrassed look on her face.

"It's not that bad. If I would've lost somebody like you, I would feel the same way," he said and kissed her lips.

"Stop … my family is looking at us." Muffin said shyly.

Dayself and Muffin went to Muffin's surprise party, but had to leave early for their flight the next morning.

They woke up early, and headed for the airport in Charlotte, North Carolina.

"I'm sorry for how my son's father acted yesterday," Muffin said, taking a seat beside Dayself on the plane.

"Don't worry about that, just enjoy your trip." Dayself said and rubbed her stomach.

Dayself and Muffin changed planes in Miami before they were able to get a little bit of rest on their last flight. Muffin stared in Dayself face, not knowing he was awake.

"Girl, are you trying to kill me?" Dayself asked playfully.

"No, I just never met anyone like you," she said, laughing.

"And you never will," Dayself responded and closed his eyes.

An hour later, they were landing at Sangster International Airport in Montego Bay, Jamaica. Muffin was literally bouncing in her seat from excitement. They got off the plane, and Muffin grinned and waved like a princess as they walked down the stairs of the plane into the Jamaican sunshine.

"You so unpredictable," Muffin said, after seeing the sign that read, "Welcome to Jamaica."

"It's in the genes. You'll see when you have our baby," Dayself said, walking into the terminal building.

After they went through customs and collected their luggage, they found a Jamaican man outside in front of a cab, holding up a sign that said, "Mr. and Ms. Burton."

"Baby, let's go site seeing first." Muffin said, getting into the cab.

"Let's go change into something cooler first, and then we can do whatever you like."

Muffin lost her breath when she walked in their room. It was more beautiful than anything she'd ever seen. The California King sized bed sat on top of Coral colored tiles, with iridescent gauze streaming from each of the four bedposts. A 52" inch LED television was bolted to the wall over a beautiful white armoire with gold accents. The bathroom had marble countertops, an oversized Jacuzzi tub, and a walk-in rainforest shower. White his and her robes hung on the bathroom door rack. The suite also featured a spacious living area complete with a kitchenette, plush floral patterned furniture, and a desk with fresh roses sitting inside a clear vase. An oversized lanai stretched along the side of the bungalow, overlooking the private beach.

"This is beautiful!" Muffin said, looking around.

"It gives us more space to try different positions," Dayself answered, grabbing Muffin around the waist.

"You're already thinking nasty!" Muffin pulled away from Dayself's grip and walked toward the phone. "Go ahead and shower. I got to let my family know that we arrived safely.

Dayself came out of the shower and watched Muffin take off the rest of her clothes. He could tell that she had gained a little weight. Muffin caught Dayself staring at her, and walked off naked to the shower, making her ass jiggle, while looking back at him and smiling.

Ten minutes later, Muffin came out of the bathroom in about ten minutes with a thin flowered dress on.

"Baby, look in my luggage and hand me a thong," Muffin said.

"You don't need them," Dayself responded, trying to see through her dress.

"Why not?" Muffin asked with a smirk.

"Come here, I'll show you." Dayself lifted Muffin's dress and pushed his middle finger deep in her pussy.

"Why did you do that?" she moaned in a sexy tone," Now I want you to put it in." She reached for his dick.

"Let's go, before our ride leave us," Dayself said as he stepped out of Muffin's reach.

Dayself had arranged for them to spend the day on a private yacht. They were the only passengers besides the crew. The captain gave them a tour. The top deck had a built in swimming pool, a place to cook on the grill, fishing posts all around, with summer chairs and tables everywhere. They got to the bottom deck; the captain showed them the kitchen, the staterooms, and the very elegant dining area.

"This is the master stateroom," the captain said, opening the door.

"This looks better than my room," Muffin said, walking in and admiring the expensive decor. A huge bed with silk curtains around it trimmed in gold fabric was the focal point of the room. The ceiling had been covered with a projection screen, and it seemed to be connected to the 60 inch LED TV on the wall. The dressers were white, trimmed in gold. The carpet was cream, with fresh flowers in gold vases.

"Y'all are welcome to spend the night," the captain said, seeing how taken Muffin was with the room.

"No, thanks, Captain, I got to show her a few more things," Dayself said.

"I'll leave you two alone. Dinner will be ready in an hour. Please enjoy," the captain said, leaving the room.

"I wish things could be like this forever."

"Maybe someday it will, but for the time being …" Dayself's words trailed off as he pushed Muffin on the bed.

"What are you doing?" she whispered.

"Eating breakfast before I eat lunch."

Dayself pulled up Muffin's dress and licked her from her asshole to her clit in slow motion.

"Ah … oh … it … feels … sooo … good!" Muffin moaned.

Dayself sucked on Muffin's clit like she did his dick. He licked around her pussy hole, grabbed her pussy lips with his mouth, sucking them like he was giving them a hickey. Dayself went back to Muffin's clit, letting the tip of his tongue touch the tip of her clit, softly flicking his tongue back and forth.

"I'm cum … oh shit … eat it …oh eat it!" Muffin screamed cumming all over Dayself's tongue. She stood up and reached for Dayself's dick.

"The dinner is served," The captain said over the intercom as

Muffin worked her way down Dayself's shorts.

"It's all right, bae. You'll get to play with him later," Dayself said.

"Let's eat," Muffin said, pulling his dick out and kissing the head.

The room that Dayself and Muffin ate in had one table and two chairs. A candle burned in the middle of the table. This was a different space than the dining area that they had seen earlier. "You Complete Me," by Keyshia Cole played through the speakers. Dayself pulled her chair out, and then pushed it up. Muffin couldn't take the smile off her face. They dined on escovitch snapper with steamed callaloo, mango salsa, rice and peas and plantain fritters for dessert. They ate and laughed until they couldn't eat any more. It was late when they made it back to their hotel.

A local man approached them as they walked to the entrance. "Bless, brethren. Me naa looking for nuh problem. Me haffi de prime ganja on de island, for de best price, seen?"

Dayself bought half an ounce and rolled himself a fat one. Muffin and Dayself walked to the beach, laid their towels down on the sand, and stared at the sky.

"My turn to take care of you," Muffin said, getting on her knees and rolling Dayself's shorts down his legs.

Once Dayself's shorts were off, Muffin licked up his leg to his nut sack. She loved that he kept his balls shaved. Cupping Dayself's balls in her hands, Muffin slowly licked his sack. Dayself's dick grew instantly hard. While licking his balls, Muffin grabbed his dick with the other hand and jacked it. Muffin removed her hand, licking Dayself's dick like an ice cream cone. Her mouth was so wet and warm to him. She slipped just Dayself's dick head in her mouth, sucking on the head without letting her teeth touch it. Still sucking the head, Muffin started back jacking his dick, hard and fast.

Dayself loved the way she did that. He soon couldn't be still, and fucked Muffin's mouth, lying on his back. She felt the vein in his dick swell, and knew he was close to cumming. Muffin lifted up her dress and slid down on Dayself's dick. She rode him hard and fast. Muffin slowed down and whispered in his ear, "Baby tell me when you're cumming."

Dayself shook his head as Muffin's cum ran down his balls, into the sand. She kept riding and riding. The weed had Dayself wanting to go all night.

"Damn, bae ... damn ... here it comes!" Dayself moaned.

Muffin lifted up, slid down, and caught Dayself's cum in her mouth. While swallowing, she massaged his balls, trying to get every drop.

The next morning, Dayself and Muffin woke up early to their private butler preparing breakfast for them. They ate and went to do a little shopping. Muffin picked out a pink and yellow Fendi skirt and top for herself, and some Gucci shorts and a tank top for Dayself.

"Can I get them two pairs of sandals to go with my outfits?" Muffin asked in a spoiled tone.

"Girl, I'm not paying no five hundred dollars for no sandals!"

"Our money is worth more over here, so it's not quite five hundred. Besides, I've seen you wear two different pair of Tom Fords that I know cost about nine hundred a piece," Muffin said, poking out her lips.

"I hustled for the money to buy them too."

"Just buy the sandals, I'll pay you back. I didn't bring anything but my checkbook," she said with attitude.

"Nope, because you got your lips poked out. Give me a kiss on both sides of my jaw, and one on my lips, and I'll buy them for free," Dayself said, licking his lips.

"Honey, kiss he tree times," a heavyset Jamaican woman said.

Muffin kissed both sides of Dayself's jaw, then stuck her tongue out, and licked around his lips.

"Work he now!" The Jamaican woman yelled, causing Dayself and Muffin to bust out laughing.

Dayself paid for the stuff, and the Jamaican woman hugged them on their way out.

The tour guide took them to so many places. Dayself and the Jamaican driver smoke and rode. Muffin caught a contact, and kept laughing at everything. They stopped at an outside restaurant, and ate barbeque goat, fish, steamed cabbage, and jerk chicken, dipped in scotch bonnet pepper sauce. Dayself and Muffin left there, and went to a Beres Hammond concert, before heading back to the resort.

When they entered the open air lobby, the sound of reggae music greeted them. Muffin and Dayself followed the music and found the resort nightclub. Beenie Man's "King of the Dancehall" filled the space. The lights popped on and the DJ said, "The lights stay on for thirty seconds, and go off for twenty minutes."

Dayself saw many women fixing their clothes and men holding tissue in their hands. Super Cat came on, and Dayself pulled Muffin to the dance floor. She grinded on him. The lights went out and Muffin danced nasty against Dayself's dick. He could feel her ass as if she was naked; her dress was so thin. Dayself's dick became super hard. He pulled it out, pulled Muffin's skirt up, and slid into her from the back. She grinded her ass in circles from the back to the beat of the song. They fucked that way for half of the song.

Muffin pulled away and turned to face Dayself. She hopped in his arms and wrapped her legs around his waist, as he slid in her pussy. Dayself bounced her on his dick to the beat. Feeling himself about to cum, with about three minutes left, Dayself lowered Muffin to the floor.

"Baby, did you cum?" Muffin asked.

"No, I didn't want to get it on the floor," he said, with his dick sticking straight out in his shorts.

Muffin reached in Dayself's shorts, pulled his dick out, and jacked it hard and fast, trying to beat the lights.

"I'm cumming, bae … oh shit," Dayself whispered in her ear.

"Ten seconds 'til lights come back on," the DJ said.

The lights came on, and Muffin was looking at Dayself smiling.

"What did you do with that stuff?" Dayself asked, sounding weak.

"I'll show you when we get on the elevator," Muffin said walking out of the club with Dayself behind her.

They got on the elevator, and as soon as the door closed, Muffin opened her hand, looked at Dayself and licked the cum from her palm.

"You're nasty," Dayself said, grabbing his dick.

"And you're not?" Muffin stuck her hand under her skirt in her pussy and rubbed it across Dayself's lips.

The elevator opened. Muffin grabbed Dayself's dick and pulled him all the way to the room. They closed the door, then reopened it and put the do not disturb sign on the door.

The next morning, Muffin woke Dayself up with a kiss to the lips.

"Baby, I want to go feed the horses and goats," Muffin said.

"All right, let me go hop in the shower first," Dayself said, getting out of the bed and heading to the shower.

Muffin and Dayself decided to walk to the farm since it was a half mile away. Muffin saw a man walking a cow on their side of the road. She screamed and ran behind Dayself.

"Girl, come on, that cow is not going to mess with you."

"It's big, bae!" Muffin said, holding on to Dayself's arm.

They arrived at the farm, and the Jamaican that ran the farm showed Dayself and Muffin around. He gave them some food to feed the animals.

"They might bite!" Muffin said, snatching her hand back when the goat tried to eat the berries out of her hand.

"Baby, why did you ask to come then?" Dayself asked.

"I don't know."

A little mix puppy ran up to them barking. Muffin ran behind Dayself, screaming and crying. He put her on his back, and the puppy followed them, barking almost the whole way back.

Later, they rode the jet skis. Muffin wanted to race, but was scared to go fast. Dayself kept trying to make her fall in the water.

"They got guns!" Dayself yelled, tackling Muffin off the Jet Ski into the water.

"That's not funny, boy!" Muffin said, coming up for air.

"They did have guns." Dayself lied with a laugh.

After being in the water for most of the day, Muffin was hungry. They went back to the hotel and ordered room service. Dayself rubbed Muffin's stomach until she fell asleep, snoring.

Dayself and Muffin had to be at the airport by noon. Dayself took his shower and came out of the bathroom.

"Get up, and get in the shower, so we can go to the airport," Dayself said.

"I don't want to leave if we're going to be apart!" Muffin cried.

Dayself planted kisses all over Muffin's face, and continued down to her neck. He kissed her tender breasts lightly, going down to her stomach. Dayself stopped at Muffin's pussy, opened her lips, and kissed the inside of her pinkness. He put his mouth around her pussy hole like he was giving her CPR, and blew hard in her pussy, making it blow air back at him. As the air came out, Dayself flicked his tongue on Muffin's clit.

Muffin arched her back and closed her eyes as her cum ran out of her pussy. Her legs trembled and she closed Dayself's head up between her legs. Muffin laid there until she caught her breath.

"Lay on your back," Muffin said.

Dayself turned over and laid on his back. Muffin climbed on top of Dayself, grabbed his dick, and put the head in her pussy. She bit on her bottom lip and moved down on his dick in circles. Muffin came all the way up off Dayself in circles, grabbed his dick and tried to put it in her ass.

"Girl, what are you doing?" Dayself asked, watching Muffin.

"I saw the lady on a porno do it, and it slipped right in."

"Have you ever tried it before? The porno people have been doing it for years."

"No, but I can handle it." Muffin continued trying to put Dayself's dick in her ass with no luck.

"Bae, try it like this," he said, getting in the doggy style position.

Dayself grabbed the baby oil, put it all over his dick and finger.

"That feels funny!" Muffin said as Dayself slid his finger in her ass.

"Wait until you feel this dick," he said, working his finger in and out of her ass.

"Come on then, don't talk about."

Dayself slid his finger out. He got behind Muffin, sliding inch by inch in, trying not to hurt her.

"Oh … shit … damn!" Muffin screamed, when most of his dick was in. He moved in and out slowly. "Oh … shit … fuck!" Muffin screamed.

"Damn, bae … it … feels good … damn bae!" Dayself moaned in Muffin's ear, turning her on more, causing her to move back to meet his dick. Muffin got wetter and wetter the more Dayself penetrated her.

"Damn … I'm cumming … Damn …oo!" Muffin screamed loud. "Cum in it, bae. Cum in it!" she continued to yell.

"Here it come, bae … here it come … damnnn!" Dayself screamed along with Muffin, busting his load of cum in her ass and fell over on her back.

"Boy, get off me before you hurt my baby!"

It was 11:30 by then, so they washed up and headed to the airport.

"Don't you ever leave me. I know you're in the game, and shit comes with that, but you better not leave me," Muffin said as they fastened their seatbelts.

"I won't leave you. You're my Muffin."

It was bittersweet when Dayself and Muffin finally made it back to Charlotte Airport. They hugged and kissed, got into their cars, and headed in two different directions, to two different lives.

CHAPTER 11

Dirty and Trent were in the chill spot playing the PS3 when Dayself walked in wearing the Gucci shorts and tank top that Muffin had picked out for him, with some Gucci shades on top of his head, and all white Air Ones. He was dressed out of his usual hustling gear of white tee, jeans, and Timbs.

"We thought you were bullshitting about going away." Dirty said, checking out Dayself's attire.

"Yeah, I went to Jamaica. That shit was fun!" Dayself said with excitement. "So, what's been going on around here?"

"You want to hear the small shit or the big shit first?" Trent asked.

"The small shit, and then the big shit," Dayself said.

"While you were gone, Dirty started fucking this chick from Princeville named Sheek. She favors the rapper, Charlie Baltimore. He had hit her off with some soft. She came through two days ago, and gave him the money she owed him. She said she got a new man, and was through hustling. She was in a '82 Bonneville with a sixty five year old man that kept calling her baby!" Trent explained, busting out laughing.

"What's so funny about that, nigga?" Dirty asked, laughing with him.

"I peeped in the car. He had on some green dress pants and a pink butterfly collar shirt, with a bottle of thunderbird between his legs!" Trent said, falling over laughing.

"Y'all niggas are stupid!" Dayself said, laughing with them.

"Man, I'm for real!" Trent said, still laughing. "Oh yeah, Shay-Shay said she was going to fuck you up. She came to Double L, jumped out of the car with some Tweety Bird bedroom slippers on, Tweety Bird pajama pants, a long Tweety Bird shirt, and cotton in one of her ears." Trent said, laughing again. "Day, she had a big ass butcher knife in her hand!" Trent and Dirty burst out laughing again.

"Y'all niggas high," Dayself said. "What's the big shit?"

"I followed Destiny's stepfather, Górmez, the last two days. He led me straight to his stash spot. I couldn't get close because he had cameras. I used the night vision binoculars that I got from a friend. I only saw one bodyguard there," Dirty said.

"How do you know it's a stash spot?" Dayself asked.

"Every time he went there, the Mexican came to the door with a gun, and Gormez always left with a tote bag. Destiny said he has a daughter who he thinks no one knows about. Her mother had a private investigator follow him one Sunday, thinking he was cheating. Destiny went to the house and took pictures of the girl and her address. Her mother has been saving them just in case he wanted a divorce," Dirty said.

"Call Destiny and Dick, tell them to meet us at the hiding spot. I'll call Castro and Lambo so we can get this thing in motion tonight," Dayself said, picking up his cell phone.

Later on that night, Castro followed Gormez to a Mexican whorehouse. Gormez got out of his black 500 Benz in a black cowboy hat, blue wrangler jeans, a black button up shirt, a big buckled belt, and some brown cowboy boots with spikes in the back. The door came open as soon as he stepped on the porch. One of the Mexican whores greeted him with a big hug. Gormez stayed in the house for about twenty minutes. Castro squatted down in his back seat waiting.

Gormez got into his car, smelling like perfume and sex.

"If you make one false move, you're dead!" Castro whispered to Gormez, pressing the barrel of the gun to the back of his head.

Gormez started speaking in Spanish. Castro hit him in the back of the head, opening a small cut. Gormez fell over and then bounced back up like he was never hit.

"You have made a terrible mistake, my friend!" Gormez said in broken English. "Do you know who the fuck I am?"

"Fuck who you are. I'm Double L, bitch!" Castro said with confidence as he choked Gormez out.

Castro got out of the Benz, opened Gormez' door, placed tape and handcuffs on him, threw him in the trunk, and drove the Benz to the hiding spot.

Castro came in the hiding spot dragging Gormez, who was kicking, trying to get away. Lambo walked over, grabbed Gormez, and dragged him to the basement. He slammed Gormez into a chair and tied him down.

"I'm out, y'all, I got money to make," Castro said.

"All right, bruh, we'll get up later," Dayself said, giving Castro dap. "Hold up, I remember seeing Gormez coming out of Little's house one day!"

"Well, he's in your house now," Castro said, walking out of the door.

Dirty, Trent, and Dayself left right after Castro to go to Gormez' stash house.

"What's poppin', amigo?" Lambo said to Gormez. He started speaking in Spanish. "Cut the bullshit, you speak English." Lambo said, staring Gormez down as he continued to speak Spanish.

"Hello, stepfather," Destiny said, walking down the stairs.

"Why are you doing this, Destiny?" Gormez asked in broken English.

"My brothers want what you have. Besides, I owe you anyway. All the times you grabbed my ass when I was a little girl. Then you would hold my face, and stick your nasty tongue in my mouth!" Destiny said. "Well it's payback time for that!"

"This is what you kidnapped me for?" Gormez yelled.

"No, we want the drugs and money that you have," Destiny said.

"You know I don't sell drugs. The money I have is from the club."

"You lying motherfucker!" Destiny yelled. "We have some friends that work at Sprint. We have the names and numbers of all your connects. We also know where your stash house is. I have a little secret to show you. You're not as smart as you think you are." Destiny said with a smirk.

"Destiny, listen to me. I'm a very powerful man, with a powerful family. Please don't put yourself in a position to die," Gormez pleaded.

"You should be saying that to yourself," Destiny said, as Dick walked into the basement.

"You put her up to this!" Gormez yelled at Dick.

"Fuck all this talking, time is money. We need you to tell us where the money at, and call your bodyguard, tell him to go get the package from behind the house," Lambo said calmly.

Gormez spit in Lambo's face and said something in Spanish.

"What did he say, Destiny?" Lambo asked, wiping the spit off with a towel.

"He said that we have to kill him first, and the Gormez Cartel will kill all of us. Then he said, 'y'all niggas will pay.'" Destiny said.

A white family adopted Lambo when he was twelve. His adoptive mother raped him repeatedly while calling him a nigger. The look in Lambo's eyes showed that Gormez had fucked up. Lambo took Gormez' shoes and socks off. He clamped crinkle irons to both of Gormez' feet, and then plugged them into the socket.

"What are you doing?" Gormez asked as sweat popped onto his forehead.

"I'm turning you into a nigger," Lambo said in a serious tone.

Gormez' feet started to burn. The room smelled like burnt flesh and stinky feet. Gormez screamed out Jesus Christ in English, then Spanish, over and over.

"Are you ready to talk now?" Lambo asked, taking the irons off of Gormez' feet.

Gormez yelled something back in Spanish.

"He said, he's the toughest Mexican on the planet, bitch!" Destiny said.

Destiny stared at Lambo to see what he was going to do about it.

"We just got started. Let's get this show on the road," Lambo said smiling as he went in his bag and pulled out a hammer and some big nails.

"Since you like calling on Jesus only when you're in pain, let's see if you can take the pain they say he took."

Lambo put the nail in Gormez' kneecap. He came up high and hit the nail. Gormez' bone gave way, and Lambo hit the nail again. It went all the way through Gormez' leg and stuck into the chair. Lambo put the nail to Gormez' other knee and hit the hammer. This time, Gormez passed out. Lambo hooked the nail to the other end of the hammer and snatched the nails out. Gormez came to, screaming. His legs from the kneecap down, hung on like two rag dolls.

"Are you ready to talk now?" Lambo asked.

Gormez raised his head and dropped it back to his chest.

"I knew you wouldn't play fair, so I brought your little secret to join us," Destiny said.

Dick walked in with Gormez' daughter, Bamena, wearing only her bra and thong. At eighteen years old, she was 5'5", 135 pounds, model face, with a tiny mole on her top lip, and black hair that she kept at shoulder length.

"Don't hurt her, she's only eighteen!" Gormez cried.

"That's about how old I was when you told me you would buy me almost any car I wanted if I let you fuck me!" Destiny yelled.

"Please don't do this, Destiny!" Gormez begged.

"Tell us what we need to know, or she will suffer," Lambo said.

Destiny removed the gag from Bamena's mouth.

"Papi, please help me!" Bamena screamed.

Gormez became quiet.

"All right, have it your way," Destiny said, placing the gag over Gormez' mouth. "I've always wanted to try this. It's a fantasy of mine."

Destiny pulled her shirt over her head and pulled her pants and boy shorts off at the same time. She walked over to Bamena with only a bra and ski mask on. Destiny reached down and ripped Bamena's thong off. Lambo stood there watching and licking his lips.

"Papi, please don't let her do this!" Bamena begged. "Please stop, please!"

"Could you please step out for a minute?" Destiny asked.

Lambo looked at Destiny like she was crazy.

"Lambo," Dick said, nodding toward the door.

On the way out of the basement, Lambo dialed Dayself's number.

"Hello," Dayself answered.

"Everything is in process. Dick and Destiny are in there with them now," Lambo explained.

"Y'all need to hurry up, dog. I'm tired of sitting out here!" Dayself said.

"It'll be in the next twenty minutes."

"All right, peace."

"Peace," Lambo said and hung up.

"You like what you see?" Destiny asked Gormez, who was in tears and shaking his head no.

"Bamena, open your legs. Bear with me, Gormez, I've never done this before," Destiny said.

Destiny opened Bamena's pussy lips, making her clit slide out. Destiny had to concentrate because of the mask she had on. She licked Bamena's pussy the way Dick licked hers.

Bamena began to cry.

About two minutes later, Bamena stopped crying and became silent. Bamena had never touched herself down there unless she was washing. She dug her nails in the floor and her legs began to shake.

"Baby, I think she like that shit!" Dick said, smiling.

Bamena burst into tears because what Dick said was true, but she didn't want to like it.

Destiny tried to put her finger in Bamena's pussy, but it wouldn't go.

"Hey Gormez, at least she's still a virgin." Destiny said, taking the tape off Gormez' mouth. "Are you ready to talk now?" she asked.

"You black slave, you will die for this!" Gormez yelled.

"I don't take threats lightly. Now it has gotten personal again!" Destiny said and placed the tape back over Gormez' mouth.

Bamena lay balled up on the floor crying. Destiny went to her Gucci bag and pulled out an eight-inch strap on dildo with the small vibrator attached. She slid it on and it vibrated against her clit.

Gormez' eyes grew big as saucers and he tried to talk through the tape.

Bamena looked up at her father, followed his panicked eyes, and saw Destiny walking toward her wearing the strap on. Bamena tried to get up and run, but Destiny pushed her back to the floor.

"Where in the fuck did you get that shit from?" Dick asked.

"I'll explain later," Destiny said as the vibrator made her tingle all over.

Destiny turned Bamena on her stomach. She tried to crawl away, but Destiny put her weight on her back with her knee. Rubbing Anal Ease on the dildo with one hand, Destiny used her other hand to spread Bamena's ass cheeks.

Bamena was begging, crying, and pleading, but it was no use. Destiny aimed the head of the dildo at Bamena's asshole and pushed. She felt a break through as the dildo pushed back on Destiny's clit, making her close her eyes. Bamena let out a loud scream, which caused Lambo to run in the room.

"What the fuck!" Lambo yelled, looking at Destiny trying to go inside Bamena with the strap on.

Destiny pushed harder, splitting Bamena's asshole. Little spots of blood dripped on the wooden floor. Destiny moved in and out of Bamena at a medium pace.

"Let's step out for a minute. I don't want to see any more of this shit," Dick told Lambo as they exited the room.

Destiny fucked Bamena hard until she came. There was shit and blood all over the dildo.

Gormez closed his eyes. He couldn't believe that his baby was being violated like that.

Destiny, weak from her nut, stepped in the bathroom to clean up.

"Her pussy is next, if you don't talk!" Destiny said, snatching the tape off Gormez' mouth, after coming out of the bathroom.

"All right … All right, I'll tell you on one condition. I know you're going to kill me. Let her go, and don't touch her any more. She doesn't know any of you, and hasn't seen your faces." Gormez said in broken English.

"I give you my word, she will live if you talk," Destiny, promised.

"He's ready to talk, guys." Destiny yelled, calling Lambo and Dick back into the room.

Dick noticed the wet spot in front of Destiny's boy shorts, and knew that she had got off on that shit.

"All right, Gormez, if you hold anything back, I'll take her through more pain, and then kill her in front of you," Destiny said in a threatening tone, and then she told Dick and Lambo what she promised Gormez.

"Let me call Dee about all that," Lambo said, dialing Dayself's number.

"Hello." Dayself answered with an attitude.

"He's ready to talk, but he'll only talk if we give our word that we will let the girl live," Lambo said.

"Did she see anybody face or how to get to the house?"

"No."

"Let her live then. Please hurry up."

"We got you in five minutes tops," Lambo said and hung up. "All right, start talking."

"I have seventy five thousand in the safe behind Destiny's mother and my picture, on the wall. There's one hundred thousand in the safe at the club, and there's one point five million in the ground. I own a junk yard in Rocky Mount called Nachos, on 301," Gormez said.

"There's one more thing," Lambo said, handing Gormez the phone. "Make the call." He dialed Dayself's number at the same time.

"Hello," Dayself answered.

"Take your positions."

"What's the problem boss?" Martinez answered, seeing Gormez number.

"Step around the back of the house, there's a package that needs to be taken to the basement," Gormez said.

"Why they didn't bring it to the front door?" Martinez asked.

"Don't question me, just do as I say!" Gormez yelled.

"Sure boss, I'm on it right now."

Martinez turned the porn flick off, zipped up his pants, put his gun his holster, and headed out the door. He pushed the door open fast, and saw Dirty move out the corner of his eye. Martinez, reached for his gun, and tried to turn back inside. Dirty hit Martinez in the back of the head with his gun, and he stumbled toward the floor. Martinez caught his balance, still trying to get his gun out. He turned with the gun pointed, but before he could squeeze the trigger, Trent shot him in the shoulder with his .44 Bulldog. Martinez' shoulder bone shattered, making him drop the gun. He tried to grab the gun with the other hand, but Dirty stepped on his hand.

"Turn your bitch ass around!" Dirty yelled, making Martinez lay flat on his stomach.

"I'm going to check the rest of the house," Dayself said. "We gotta get out of here. The people next door may call the police."

"I've already checked it out. The people who own that house just moved," Dirty said.

"Did any of you find a key? It's two locks in here," Dayself asked, after finding the door to the basement. They looked around and found the keys lying beside the Spanish porn DVD case. "I may need some help down here."

Dirty got on Martinez' back, wrapped the drop cord around his neck, and choked the life out of him. Trent went back to the van, and Dayself went to see what they had. There were forty keys of cocaine stacked in one corner, ten bricks of black tar heroin, and a small barrel of ecstasy pills.

"My niggas, we are rich!" Dayself yelled when Trent and Dirty showed up at the door.

They loaded the stuff on the van fast, and dropped it off at the stash spot, then took the van to Boybaby's paint shop to have it painted.

Dayself wasn't ready to bring Boybaby out with them like that. He had taken care of Boybaby from the time he was six until he went to prison. Dayself wanted Boybaby to be better than he was, at whatever he did.

Dayself, Dirty, and Trent made it back to the hiding spot, where Destiny, Dick, and Lambo were holding Gormez and Bamena hostage. Destiny told them about the different money spots that Gormez had.

"Hold up!" Trent said, stopping everyone from talking. "Gormez has some type of money in the bank. He has a legit business," Trent said, putting on his mask and going into the basement with the others behind him. "Where's the rest of the money, Gormez?" Trent asked, putting his gun to Bamena's head.

"Papi, please tell them!" Bamena said, afraid to die. "Tell them about the accounts in Mexico."

"Okay … okay … just don't hurt her!" Gormez begged. "I have three point five million in an account in Mexico. The account numbers are in the safe at the house," Gormez said, exhausted.

"Damn, you had a good run," Lambo said, thinking about how he could get more money.

"I want one million placed in Dirty and Trent's accounts, and one point five in mine. We already have offshore accounts," Dayself said.

"When did y'all do that?" Dick asked.

"When we made our first fifty thousand," Dirty said.

"Shit, I just bury mine." Dick said, rubbing Destiny's ass.

The next morning, Bamena sat in the corner with her knees pulled up to her chest. Hearing her father make a grunting sound, Bamena tore a piece of her shirt off and went to her father.

"Mena, there's no need for that," Gormez said as Bamena tried to stop his wounds from bleeding. "I want you to listen to me. Move the toy box you had as a little girl. Lift the rug. There is a safe there. Open it with the key on Nana's key ring. Two hundred and fifty thousand dollars, along with the deeds to three houses I own, and the club are in there. It's all I have left here in America. There's other money, but you won't be able to touch it. It's in a fake name. You'll have the insurance money too. I want you to take that money and enjoy your life. The family will avenge my death. Just tell Nana I was robbed and killed at the club. Never mention to anyone that you are my daughter. They may try to hurt you for money that you don't have," Gormez said sadly.

"Please, Papi, don't leave me. You're all that I have left!" Bamena cried.

"There's no need to cry, we both know that they're going to kill me," Gormez said weakly.

"I swear revenge in your name!" Bamena said, angrily.

"Let it go. The family will find out who did this. Promise me you won't get involved."

"Don't make me promise," Bamena cried.

"Promise me, Bamena!" Gormez yelled.

"Okay, I promise, Papi!"

"Don't talk to the police or the family. They still don't know who you are."

Destiny and Dick were eating breakfast when Destiny's phone rang.

"Hello," Destiny answered, with a mouth full of food.

"Baby, Gormez didn't come home last night. That's not like him. Did he call you?" Destiny's mother asked.

"No, he's probably out humping somebody's little girl."

"I'm on my way to church. I don't have time for a bunch of sinful lies," Destiny's mother said and disconnected the call.

Destiny looked at the phone. "Some things never change," she said.

After breakfast, Destiny headed out the door to her mother's house to get the money and papers.

Dick left at the same time, to get the money from the club. Dirty, Trent, and Dayself went to the junk yard, removed the old Toyotas, and pulled a refrigerator up, where the one point five million sat. Everyone made it back almost at the same time. Dirty, Trent, and Dayself took one hundred and fifty thousand, and left the rest for Destiny, Lambo, and Dick to split up.

Dayself went down to the basement, with the cell phone and numbers to the accounts. Destiny took Bamena out of the room, so she wouldn't hear Gormez say Dayself, Dirty, and Trent's names. Gormez called the bank and explained what he wanted in Spanish. An hour later, Trent called to make sure the money was transferred. After checking, Trent looked at Dayself and smiled.

Dick and Destiny took Bamena to see her father for the last time.

"Papi, Papi, I love you!" Bamena cried, dropping down in front of her father.

"I love you too. Don't forget what I told you!" Gormez weakly yelled, watching Dick and Destiny pull her away.

Destiny placed a blindfold on Bamena and taped her hands behind her back.

Bamena walked to the truck with a limp from the previous night's penetration. On the ride home, two things kept going through her head. Her father's face flashed before her eyes. He was all she had left, except her Nana. Nana was an old Mexican lady who had been paid by Gormez to keep Bamena since she was five months old. Gormez never introduced her to friends and family. He always said they lived too much of a violent life. Bamena didn't even have her father's last name. Her thoughts stopped when she felt the truck stop and pull over.

"You're at the park down from your house," Destiny said, helping Bamena out of the truck. She sat her on a bench. "Sit here until somebody comes along. Don't try to walk, you may get hit." Destiny said, walking back to the truck.

One hour later, Bamena was still tied up. An old lady that knew her walked by.

"Child, what happened?" the old lady asked. "Hold on, let me cut that stuff off of you." *How can someone do such a thing?* She thought. "Wait right here, I'm going to call the police."

Bamena jumped up and ran all the way home. She burst through the door, screaming for Nana.

"Where have you been, young lady?" Nana asked with attitude.

"He's gone, my papi is gone. He's dead!" Bamena yelled, falling to the floor crying.

"What happened, baby? Tell Nana what happened," Nana said as Bamena cried on her shoulder.

"He was robbed at the club!"

Nana noticed that Bamena couldn't sit down straight on her butt. She went to make Bamena a hot tub of water, with her favorite body wash.

Bamena ran in her father's office, opened his drawer and

pulled out his gold plated .45. She sat behind the desk, rocking back and forth, with the gun in her hand. She didn't even know where to start looking for the people responsible.

Nana walked through the house calling Bamena's name. She found her on the floor with the gun in her hand. Squatting down beside Bamena, Nana took the gun out of her hand. "Come on, baby," Nana said.

Bamena wrapped her arms around Nana's neck and cried. Nana lifted her off the floor and walked her to the bathroom. She undressed Bamena and helped her get into the tub. Bamena sat dazed in the tub until the water turned cold, and Nana made her get out. She helped Bamena into her gown, tucked her into bed, without either of them saying a word. Nana sat and watched Bamena until she thought she was asleep, and then she left to go clean the bathroom.

Bamena lay in bed, still smelling the burnt skin on her father's feet, and seeing the holes in his kneecaps, and then Destiny walking up to her with the dildo on. Bamena balled up in a knot and cried.

Nana picked Bamena's clothes up and saw the blood in the back of her pants and thong. She grabbed her cross around her neck, got down on her knees and prayed.

"I wish we could've met on better terms. We could've got plenty of money together, but that's life," Dayself said.

"One request? If you're going to kill me, do it somewhere I love. Kill me in my club," Gormez said.

"We were going to kill you in front of the club, but yeah, we can do that," Dayself said, walking over and handing Gormez some papers. "Sign this paper so the junk yard will be in my name."

Eight o'clock came fast for Lambo. He carried Gormez into the club and tied him down to a chair.

"You know, Gormez, you are a true soldier. You are willing to accept death when it knocks at your door," Lambo said.

Dayself and Trent heard two gunshots, and then they watched Lambo walk out of the club and disappear into the night.

Dirty started the car and drove off.

CHAPTER 12

The next morning, Dayself was on his way to stash his money when his phone rang.

"Hello."

"Come by the house," Piepie said.

"Nope, girl, you just kicked me out the other day, after you got some dick."

"Just stop by for a minute, it won't take long."

"I'll be there. Give me about twenty minutes."

"All right, but make sure you come."

Dayself dropped the money off at the stash spot and headed to Piepie's house.

"I'm pregnant!" Piepie said, soon as he opened the door. "You don't seem happy about that," she added, noticing the look on Dayself's face.

"Going through this over and over has put a strain on our relationship and marriage. Then, by you losing kids, it's stressing you to the point that you don't keep yourself up like you used to. I hate to keep seeing you hurt like that. I'm in the streets, and you can't handle that. I don't know what to say or do anymore," Dayself said.

"Just get the fuck out!" Piepie yelled, watching Dayself walk past her and slam the door. "I will never give up on us and our baby!"

～

Destiny stood up and stretched, her fingers were sore from counting money.

"You still haven't told me where you got that strap on from," Dick said, grabbing Destiny's arm, stopping her from walking to the shower.

"I got it from Tape City in Rocky Mount the other day. I was going to get a stripper to help me give you a threesome for your birthday," Destiny said.

"I noticed your panties were wet after you fucked that girl up her ass."

"I like that shit baby, I nutted hard as hell!" Destiny said, rubbing Dick's package and stepping out of her clothes at the same time.

Destiny squatted down, pulled Dick's dick out, and licked around the head. She stuck her tongue in Dick's pee hole and moved it around. Destiny licked up and down, and then deep throated about seven inches of dick. She sucked and jacked until he was nice and hard, and then climbed in his lap, letting half of him slide in her pussy. Destiny worked half until she became wetter, then slid down further, until it felt like his dick was coming out her mouth. She went all the way up to the hood, and let his dick open her pussy back up, and then slid back down, squeezing her pussy muscles. Destiny sped up, moaning loud, as Dick pulled on her nipples.

"Damn, baby, you're in my stomach … oh shit, oh shit … ah … so … big … I'm cumming!" Destiny moaned while cumming on Dick.

Dick grabbed Destiny's waist and bounced her up and down. The more she went up and down, the more her cum coated his dick. Dick felt himself about to cum, so he bounced Destiny faster and harder. Destiny felt herself cumming again. She screamed louder as her pussy muscles squeezed his dick. They came together. Dick exploded deep in her stomach. Destiny got up slowly off of Dick, letting their cum mix together, and run down his balls. She turned around, and went down to the crack of Dick's ass where the cum had run, and licked it from there to the tip of his dick, licking around it like a push up.

Destiny stood up, turned around and made her asshole open and close.

"Look how wet it is, Dick," Destiny yelled, making Dick instantly hard again. He walked toward Destiny with his dick in his hands.

Destiny snatched her clothes up, ran to the bathroom, and locked the door.

"Open the door, girl!" Dick said, knocking on the door.

"I'm not opening this door, 'til that baby arm go down." Destiny said, laughing, and then opened the door so they could take a shower and go shopping.

Dayself was unsettled when he left Piepie's house. He took one of Boybabys' CDs out of the car stereo, and Usher's "Confessions" was playing on the radio. Dayself dropped his head on the steering wheel. His phone rang, and Dirty's number flashed across the screen.

"What's good?" Dayself answered.

"Nothing, just dropped Trent off to his bad ass kids. Soon as he walked in the house, April swung on him for staying out all night.

"How's Laquanda doing?"

"She's good, just feeding and treating a nigga good."

"Tell her I said what's up," Dayself said.

"I'll be sure to do that."

"Yo, call your uncle Yellow to see if he will take this boy off our hands," Dayself said.

I'll do that, but what's really bothering you?"

"It's nothing, just arguing with Piepie."

"That girl love you, nigga, you just can't keep your dick in your pants."

"I know, dog. I just gotta get my money up, then I'll be there for her like I should," Dayself said.

"Your money is up now, there's no excuse."

"After we get rid of this shit, and three more runs, we are through. Then I'll settle down, move away, and enjoy. Be sure to call Yellow. I'm on the way to see old man Curt. I want him to check the boy out for us. I'll get up with you later, peace."

Dayself drove the speed limit to Curt's house. He turned the radio off so he could let his mind travel, hoping badly that the heroin was good money, so he could retire and spoil his kids.

Before he knew it, Dayself was pulling into Curt's yard. He sat in the car and looked at the house. The house was supposed to have been white. The paint was chipped so bad that the house had begun to look mixed with green, the original color. There was plastic covering a broken window, the front door was there, but the doorknob was gone, with a chain running through it. Curt was brown skinned and rail thin. Only 45 years old, but he looked much older, due to his hard living. He put you in mind of Ezel from Friday, but he still had much swag from his status in the game in the early 80's.

Dayself knocked on the door. He was shocked to see Shawn open the door with no fingers.

"Why the fuck you staring at me? Where Curt at?" Dayself asked.

"Let that man in the house, damn!" Curt said, coming out of the back room. "Dayself, I haven't seen you in about three months. What brought you on this side of town?" Curt asked.

"I need to speak with you in private."

"Come on back here," Curt said, leading Dayself to the back room.

"Yo, Curt, I know you're not letting Shawn fuck with her?" Dayself asked, looking at the young white girl sitting on Curt's bed.

"With what?" Curt said, referring to Shawn not having a dick. "Step out, let me holla at my people," Curt told the white girl.

"What you know about this?" Dayself asked Curt, throwing him a gram of heroin.

"I haven't had this shit in years. I know good shit when I see it though," Curt said, examining the boy. "That cut off motherfucker up front do everything in the world. I still know how to cut my ass off, though. We'll, let Shawn test it to see what we got," Curt said, opening the bag and smelling it. "Got damn, what you trying to do, kill somebody? This shit don't have any cut on it!"

Curt yelled for Shawn to go to his friend's house four houses down to get the stuff to mix the heroin. Shawn must have known what Curt was getting ready to do, because he shot out the door. About four minutes later, Dayself stood on Curt's porch, catching a breath from the different smells in the house, and saw Shawn running on his back heels to the house. Shawn came in the house behind Dayself breathing hard, with a strong odor of piss on him. His piss bag had come loose. Still, all he could do was stare at Curt mixing the boy.

"Where your needle at, Shawn?" Curt asked, after putting a three cut on the boy.

Shawn tried to put his hands with no fingers in his pocket. Curt reached in his pockets and pulled the needle out. He heated the boy, and then shot a little into Shawn's veins. The drug entered Shawn's body and he instantly went into a nod, and then fell over on the white girl.

"Get this pissy motherfucker off me!" the white girl yelled.

"How much do a key sell for?" Dayself asked.

"Between seventy five to one hundred thousand dollars," Curt said.

"Damn, I'm in the wrong game!" Dayself said, eyes almost popping out of his head. "I got a job for you," Dayself said to Curt. "Let me call my people first."

"Hello," Castro answered, with two girls laughing in the background.

"I need you to go to the stash house and bring that boy to the hiding spot," Dayself said.

"I'll be there when you get there. I know how slow you are."

"All right, peace," Dayself said and hung up.

Curt and Dayself rode and talked about heroin until they got to the hiding spot.

"Man, you got me riding around with all that shit!" Castro said, looking at the two bags on the table.

"I would've gotten Dirty and Trent to bring it, but I wanted to pay you for the move we made the other night," Dayself said, going to the safe in the back room. "Here's your cut. It's one hundred and fifty thousand." Dayself handed Castro a Footlocker bag.

"Damn, I'm glad you're home, boy!" Castro said, dropping the bag and giving Dayself a hug. "You change lives for real. I gotta run, but I'll get at you later."

"All right, be safe, bruh." Dayself answered, watching Castro walk out of the door.

"Can you put a five cut on that?" Dayself asked Curt, throwing him a key of heroin.

"Is Marvin Gaye dead?" Curt said, looking at the key.

Curt got to work, while Dayself watched him with the mask on. When it was all done, Dayself had fifty keys of heroin for sixty thousand a piece.

"Young blood, be careful. This is life changing money here. A motherfucker will kill his own mama for this shit," Curt said, taking the mask and gloves off and putting his toothpick back in his mouth.

"I'm out the game pretty soon, anyway. Let me call Dirty to see what's good."

"Radio." Dirty answered.

"What's good, did you…"

"I'm trying to program these minutes in this throw away phone, hold on a minute." Dirty said, cutting Dayself off. "I'm back. Did you get a number in a text right then?" Dirty asked.

"Yeah, I got it," Dayself said, after checking his phone.

"Go to the nearest pay phone and call me."

After leaving the stash house, Dayself stopped at the store in front of Double L and called Dirty.

"Radio." Dirty answered.

"What the business is?"

"I just spoke to Uncle Yellow. He said he could use a couple of those thangs if the price is right. He gave me a phone booth number for you to call him ASAP. He said ask for old man."

"I'm on it right now, peace," Dayself said, hanging up and dialing the phone booth in New York.

"Yo." Someone answered.

"Old man." Dayself said.

"What's the business, country boy?" Yellow asked, after taking the phone from his worker.

"I got fifty of them thangs for six five. If you take all of them off my hand, sixty for you," Dayself said, knowing that he wanted sixty anyway.

"Damn, country boy, I didn't know you were going to come that big!" Yellow said, shocked. "You know the old man just got out. I tell you what, I'll cop twenty five for fifty five, and you front me the other twenty five for sixty five."

"I'll do it on one condition. That I get my money off the top, from the front, not the rear."

"How about half at the top and half at the rear?"

"Okay, old man, come check me out."

"I'll send one of my junkies with the runner down there. Soon as he test the work, I'll have my young chick and her sister close by with the money."

"That's what's up."

"All right, country boy, I'll holla at you tomorrow." Yellow said.

"Mrs. Gormez, I'm Sheriff Knight. I'm sorry to tell you this, but your husband was found dead this morning," the Sheriff said.

"Oh God, no ... No!" Mrs. Gormez sobbed.

Mrs. Gormez walked from the door, wobbly. The Sheriff helped her to the dining room table, opened the refrigerator, and handed her a bottle of water.

"Do you know anyone who would've wanted your husband dead?" the Sheriff asked.

"He was murdered?"

"I'm afraid so."

"Oh God, no, I don't. He didn't have any enemies that I know of."

"We need you to come down to the morgue to identify the body."

On the way to the morgue, Mrs. Gormez sat in deep thought. "What have you done, Gormez?" She asked herself over and over.

They entered the room that held Gormez' body. The coroner pulled the sheet back. His face was smashed in beyond recognition. Mrs. Gormez wasn't able to identify her husband by viewing his body. The detective gave her a plastic bag with Gormez' belongings and she spotted his wedding band. Mrs. Gormez took the ring out and looked inside the ring for her initials.

"That's my husband right there!" Mrs. Gormez said, covering her mouth, shaking uncontrollably. She turned and walked out to keep from breaking down.

On her way back home, Mrs. Gormez thought to herself, "That cheating bastard probably got caught fucking somebody's wife. Well, at least I got the million dollar insurance policy and joint bank account. I'm going to find me a young Mandingo."

The Sheriff opening the door took Mrs. Gormez out of her thoughts. She thanked him, walked straight in the house and closed the door behind her.

Destiny's phone rang as she walked through the mall.

"Hello."

"They found your father dead this morning!" Mrs. Gormez said, her voice cracking.

"He's not my father, but I'm sorry to hear that, Ma."

"That's all you have to say, after all he did for you?" Mrs. Gormez yelled.

"What do you want me to say? This is the same man that has kept his filthy hands on me since I was twelve! You never even believed me!" Destiny yelled and hung up.

"Are you all right?" Dick asked Destiny, seeing the look of hurt on her face.

"That was my moms, calling to tell me that they found Gormez' body," Destiny said.

"Let's get back to the house. There's a surprise there waiting for you," Dick said, grabbing Destiny's hand and leading her out of the mall.

Dick and Destiny pulled up at Destiny's house. Dick hit the button, opening the garage to reveal a red 2014 convertible BMW with white leather interior, and a white bow tied around it.

Destiny jumped out of the truck, ran to the car, and opened the door. An all-white pit bull puppy barked at her.

"Baby, I love you more for this!" Destiny said, jumping into Dick's arms and kissing him.

"I love you too, baby. I hope that puppy didn't shit in there." Dick said, checking the floor and seat for shit.

"Can we go for a ride?"

"Take the puppy and go ahead, I need to check on my brothers." Dick said, pulling out his phone and dialing Dayself's number.

"Hello," Dayself answered in a sleepy voice.

"Where you at?" Dick asked.

"I'm at the chill spot, and you woke me up!"

"Call Dirty and Trent so we can come over there and chill."

"You call them. I'm going get in the shower."

Dayself checked his messages. There were four from Piepie,

telling him to come home, one from Muffin, telling him she was coming down for the weekend, and three from Shay-Shay telling him to come get his shit out of her house before she throw it away. He knew that she wasn't going to do it, she just wanted to see him.

Dayself decided to call Piepie to make sure her and the baby were okay.

"Hello!" Piepie's mother answered.

"Mrs. Soloman is Pie—"

"Oh my God, Dayself!" Ms. Soloman yelled. "We're at the hospital. My baby is in surgery. When I got to her house she was laying in the floor."

"I'm on the way!" Dayself grabbed the first piece of clothing that he could get his hands on. He ran out of the house, leaving the door cracked, jumped in the car, doing everything on the dash to get to the hospital.

Dayself pulled up to the hospital, jumped out of the car and ran inside.

"I'm here to see Melissa Burton!" Dayself said out of breath to the nurse at the nurse's station.

"Are you immediate family?" she asked.

"Yes, her husband!" Dayself yelled.

"She's on the fourth floor."

Dayself took off running.

"She's still in surgery," Mrs. Soloman said, soon as Dayself stepped off the elevator. "The doctor said she had a brain aneurysm. I found a purple mark around her neck. The doctor claims it was from her fall, but it didn't look that way to me."

Dayself and Mrs. Soloman sat for another hour before the doctor came out. He walked into the waiting area, slowly pulling his mask down.

"I'm sorry, we did all we could."

Mrs. Soloman fainted. Her family rushed to her aid as Dayself flopped down in his seat and stared in a daze. He couldn't believe his Piepie was gone. He kept saying, "Why didn't I go to her when she called me?"

Dayself stood, walked out of the hospital, and drove to Piepie's house in a daze. He walked into the house, smelling her scent. There were so many memories there. Dayself laid down, put Piepie's pillow over his face and cried. He got up, went to the refrigerator, took out a pint of Hennessey, and tried to drink his pain away. Dayself finally got tired of his phone ringing and answered.

"Hello," Dayself answered in a drunken tone.

"You tell us to come to the chill spot, and you're not even here. And you left the door open," Dirty said in a joking manner.

"She's gone, my Piepie is gone!"

"What the fuck you mean she's gone?" Dirty yelled.

"She's dead, Dirty!" Dayself cried.

"Where you at?"

"I'm at the crib!"

"We're on our way!" Dirty said, running out of the house with Trent and Dick behind him.

By the time they got there, Dayself was drunk, lying on the couch, looking at pictures of his wedding.

"If I would've been home with her, she never would've died!" Dayself said in a drunken tone.

"Don't do this to yourself; you have to be stronger than that," Dirty said.

"It's my entire fault. I killed her." Dayself began to cry.

"Come on, dog!" Dick said with tears in his eyes.

"She loves you. She wouldn't want you to be hard on yourself like that," Trent said.

"She was pregnant, y'all!" Dayself yelled, still turning the bottle up.

"I'm sorry you gotta go through this, bruh, but remember from the earth we shall come, to the earth we shall go," Dick said.

Trent and Dick went outside to smoke a cigarette. Piepie never let them smoke in the house.

"Come on, Radio, be strong. You have to," Dirty said as Dayself broke down crying.

"Let's get out of here," Dayself said, wiping his eyes. "All I can think about is her in here."

Dirty and Dick drove Dayself to the chill spot, with Trent trailing behind in Dayself's car. Dayself called Muffin once they made it to the chill spot to tell her what happened.

"Hello." she answered after about three rings.

"Piepie had a brain aneurysm and died at the hospital this morning," Dayself said sadly, still drunk.

"I'm so … so sorry to hear that! How are you holding up?"

"I'm holding, is all I can say."

"When you want to talk, call me at any time." Muffin said, not knowing what else to say.

"All right, I'll do that." Dayself said.

"Always remember, true love always waits. Bye, Dayself."

"Bye."

Dayself hung up and dialed Yellow's number.

"Hello." Yellow answered.

"What's good, old man?"

"Damn, country boy, I just got off the phone with Dirty. I'm sorry to hear about your loss," Yellow said. "Always remember in life, there will always be losses. You got to hold your head up, and keep living, 'til your turn come."

"I'll keep that in mind, peace."

"Peace." Yellow said, hanging up.

"Give me your phone. I'll handle everything until the funeral is over," Dirty said.

"If I don't stay busy, I'll go crazy."

"All right, we're about to head out. Call us if you need anything. Stay here and sleep some of that drunkenness off," Dirty said.

Dayself nodded, and proceeded to drink himself to sleep.

It was 12:25 the next day, when Dayself woke up. After throwing up two times, he took a shower and headed to Mrs. Soloman's house. Dayself sat in the car in Mrs. Solomans' yard, and looked at all of Prokoshia's toys. He didn't know what to do, or what to tell Prokoshia. She looked like a light-skinned version of her mother. Her father had come to him like a man at the hospital, crying for his daughter. He had asked for custody of his child, and Dayself couldn't deny him that.

Dayself sat there and let his mind roam back to him and Piepie's first phone call. Mrs. Soloman peeped out the window, and Dayself got out of the car wiping his tears away. He walked to the steps where Mrs. Soloman was. She stood at the top step and rubbed his head. Mrs. Soloman was the prototype of her daughter; she and Piepie had the same big eyes, skin tone, and long hair.

"God called my baby home because her work here was done." Mrs. Soloman said, looking Dayself in his eyes, "Don't never hold any guilt. She was with who she loved, regardless of the outcome of things. Come on in," Mrs. Soloman said, walking into the house.

Dayself walked in the house behind her. There were pictures of Piepie as a little girl on the table. Dayself picked the picture up and rubbed her face.

"She and Prokoshia looked like twins." Mrs. Soloman said.

"Yeah, they do." Dayself said, putting down that picture, and picking up the picture of him and Piepie. "Look at my baby."

"She really did love you," Mrs. Soloman said, rubbing Dayself's back.

"I know. I loved her too. I wish so bad that I could bring her back."

"She's not gone. She will always be in here." She touched the center of Dayself's forehead. "Come on and eat, I cooked your favorite. Chicken."

Dayself ate with Mrs. Soloman, and they talked for over an hour.

"I have to go to the funeral home to check on things." Dayself said, wiping his mouth and standing up.

"All right, baby. You take care, okay." Mrs. Soloman gave Dayself a hug.

"Yes, ma'am." Dayself said, walking out of the door.

At the funeral home, Dayself picked out Piepie's casket. She wanted them to renew their vows, and had always talked about a certain wedding dress she wanted. Dayself picked that dress to bury her in.

"Boy, where have you been?" Mabee asked. "I called you ten different times." Mabee had her hands on her hips, watching Dayself get out of his car.

"I went to see Piepie's mother, and then I went to the funeral home."

"I'm sorry to hear about your wife. Sometimes, God takes to give. Baby, I have been having these bad dreams about you. Whatever it is that you're into, it's time to let it go. You have enough money here alone to go straight. You have already lost your wife, if you don't get out, there will be a lot more lives lost. I love you, baby, that's why I tell you this. Grandma see things a lot of people don't."

"I'll be through soon, and then I'll buy you that big house that you've always wanted." Dayself said.

"Baby, I'm good where I'm at, just straighten your life out."

Two days had gone by fast. It was the day of Piepie's funeral. The family arrived at the church in the family car. People walked by the family giving condolences. The preacher preached for an hour about giving your life to God, the choir sang three songs, then the preacher called the family to view the body.

"Baby, you look good in that dress," Dayself said, walking up to Piepie's casket with tears running down his face. "I'm so sorry

I wasn't there when you needed me. I know that you forgive me, because that's the type of person you were. I did a lot of things that I wish I could take back. At the same time, I just wanted the best life for us. I love you, Piepie, even if death have done us part." Dayself leaned over and kissed Piepie's lips, and then laid his head on her chest and let the tears flow until Dirty and Trent came to get him.

Dayself stood up straight, smiled at Piepie, and walked out of the church.

Piepie's mother never made it to the casket; she fainted before she got there. It seemed like the more people cried, the louder the choir got. Piepie's niece stood in front of Piepie's casket and sang, "Walk Around Heaven." After the burial, everyone went to Mrs. Soloman's house to eat.

Dayself gave Mrs. Soloman all of Piepie's things, and a one hundred and fifty thousand dollar cashier's check for Prokoshia when she turned eighteen, if she went to college.

CHAPTER 13

*D*ayself had to visit Shay-Shay; he had not spoken to her in almost a week. He got out of his car in his usual, a white tee and blue jeans. Dayself knew that even clothes bring jealousy in the type of game he was in, so he decided to dress like everyone else. Dayself knocked about twelve times. Shay-Shay came to the door in some pregnant grandma bloomers, a tank top, with her stomach sticking from underneath, and some Tweety Bird slippers. Dayself burst out laughing.

"What are you laughing at?" Shay-Shay asked, putting her hands on her hips, making her stomach come out further.

"At your ghetto ass, you don't answer the door like that." Dayself said,

"I knew it was you. You're the only one that comes to people house this early in the morning," Shay-Shay said, walking to the kitchen. "Are you hungry?"

"What did you cook?"

"I cooked turkey bacon, cheese eggs, blueberry pancakes, and grilled ham and cheese," Shay-Shay said. "What are you doing, boy?" she asked, watching Dayself walk through the house, with his gun out searching rooms.

"I'm checking to see who's here!" Dayself said, going from room to room.

"Come sit down and eat, nobody is here or coming here,"

Shay-Shay said, laughing.

"Fuck that, don't nobody cook that much food to eat by their self."

The phone rang and Shay-Shay ran to get it.

"Hello … not right now … yeah … yeah … yeah," Shay-Shay answered.

"Give me this damn phone!" Dayself said and snatched the phone out of Shay-Shay's hand.

"Why are you at my baby momma house?" a deep voice asked.

"Who the fuck is this?" Dayself asked, with the intent to kill in his voice

"Sike, boy!" Shay-Shay's friend, Cee-Cee, laughed. "Dayself?"

"What girl!" Dayself asked.

"You stupid!" Cee-Cee said and hung up, still laughing.

Dayself turned around with a guilty look on his face.

Shay-Shay laughed until she had to pee.

Dayself finished his food and went to watch the TV in Shay-Shay's room.

Shay-Shay walked in her room naked. "Since I've been pregnant, I have to wear panty liners. My pussy gets so wet, that it soak through my panties, and run down my leg," Shay-Shay said, sticking her hand between her legs, and running her fingers across Dayself lips.

Dayself licked Shay-Shay's juices off her fingers and then pulled her down on the bed.

"Damn, stop being so rough!" she yelled

"Lay on the bed, hold your pussy open, while I eat all the wetness out." Dayself said, undressing as he watched Shay-Shay lay on the bed and open her pussy lips.

Dayself looked at Shay-Shay's bald pussy lips and her manicured hands with juice all over them. He lay between her legs, and rubbed his whole face in her pussy. Dayself went up to Shay-Shay's face. She stuck her tongue out and licked her juices off his face. Dayself went down to Shay-Shay's pussy flicked his tongue softly on her clit.

"Eat this … pussy … eat it … boy … eat!" Shay-Shay moaned.

Dayself slid two fingers in her pussy. He could feel her juices between them. Dayself sucked Shay-Shay's clit as he went in and out with his fingers, moving his tongue fast.

"Shit … I'm cumming … shit … here it … ah …!" Shay-Shay screamed, flooding Dayself's fingers with cum. "I bet you can't make me cum like that again," she said, opening her pussy lips.

Dayself went to work on her pussy again. While licking her clit very fast, he slid the tip of his finger in her ass. Shay-Shay rotated her hips on his finger, trying to push it in further, at the same time trying to push it out as Dayself sucked on her clit. She grabbed the sheets and tried to slide away. He held her tightly, and sucked harder. Shay-Shay's body jerked back as she came all over Dayself's tongue and finger. It seemed like she would never stop cumming. After she finished, Shay-Shay laid there for a minute, and burst out laughing.

"What's so funny, girl?" Dayself asked.

"Boy, your ass eats pussy like a porn star!"

"That shit ain't funny."

Shay-Shay laughed harder.

Dayself lay on the bed with his dick sticking straight up in the air.

"So, you're going to leave me like this?" Dayself asked.

"You can't get on top, you might hurt my baby," Shay-Shay said, getting in the doggy style position. "Pick a hole, baby."

Little drops of cum dripped from Shay-Shay's pussy onto the bed.

"This ain't the price is right, talking about pick a hole." Dayself said, while entering her.

Dayself pushed his dick all the way in, and pulled it out, making Shay-Shay's pussy fart. He moved in and out as she threw it back to him hard. Dayself held on to her waist, and fucked her just like she wanted it.

"Who pussy is this?" Dayself asked, hitting it hard.

"It's yours … baby … it's yours!"

"Who pussy is it?"

"Yours … yours … yours!"

"What's my name? Say it. What's my name?"

"Ahh … Day … Ahh … selfff! I'm … a … cumming … get it … oh shit …get it!" Shay-Shay screamed.

Dayself looked down and saw all the cum Shay-Shay had let out, and exploded deep in her pussy.

Afterwards, they lay in bed thinking of baby names, until Dayself's phone started to ring.

"Hello." Dayself answered, with Shay-Shay lying on his chest.

"Those people arrived," Dirty said, referring to Yellow's runner.

"Tell them to meet me at the chill spot."

"We're already there. We'll be here, peace." Dirty said, hanging up.

"When will I see you again?" Shay-Shay asked.

"Soon, bae. I got some business to take care of. I'm going to use your car." Dayself said, putting his pants on. "Look in the safe and take them ten ounces to Trent for me."

"All right, baby, I got you."

"Here's some money, go shopping for yourself and the baby."

"We don't know what we're having."

"Go and find out, then."

"I want it to be a surprise when it comes out."

"Girl, we are not the Trumps or the Gates."

Dirty, the runner, and the junkie were sitting on the couch when Dayself walked in. The junkie had nodded out. He came back about three minutes later.

"Peewee, how is it?" The runner asked the junkie.

"It wasn't the best I had, but it's some damn good shit," Peewee said.

"That's that Gator!" Dirty said, laughing.

The runner called Yellow and told him everything was a go. Yellow asked to speak to Dayself.

"What's good, old man?" Dayself asked.

"Good looking out. The girls will call you shortly," Yellow said.

"So who's your chick's sister?"

"She's not my chick. I just said that 'cause she was standing beside me. I'm getting too old to be chasing young pussy. Her stepfather was my partner back in the day. She's real trustworthy though. Her sister won't come off the pussy for shit. Some of my buddies have offered her cars and all type of shit. She still won't give it up. Country boy, ain't no pussy even worth that," Yellow said.

"When do you expect them back?"

"They said they were coming back Monday or Tuesday night."

"Let's bet that old caddie you have in the garage I can hit the pussy before she leave."

"All right, what if you lose?"

"I'll knock five gees off each one."

"Country boy, you got yourself a deal."

"I gotta bounce, somebody is beeping in now."

"It's probably them, peace."

"Hello." Dayself answered.

"Is this Dayself?" A girl with a heavy New York accent asked.

"Where y'all at?"

"We're at the McDonald's down from Comfort Inn."

"I'll be there in five minutes. Who will I be looking for?"

"Look for an Asian and an Asian mixed chick."

"All right, peace." Dayself said and hung up.

Dayself went into McDonald's, looking around until his eyes

landed on two of the most beautiful women that he had seen in a long time. One was full Chinese; she looked to be about 26 years old, 5'2", and 135 pounds. She had on white tights, a tank top with Biggie on the front, and some white open toe heels. The other woman was mixed; she was about 5'6", 125 pounds, skin of bronze, with Chinese features. She had on some tight blue jeans, black open toe heels, and a tank top.

"You must be Dayself. I'm Asia, and this is my sister, Amaka," the Chinese woman said.

"I'm good, just can't take my eyes off of two beautiful queens." Dayself said, making them laugh.

"What's so funny?"

"The way you talk, say that again," Asia said, teasing Dayself.

"Nope, Amaka, can I get two of them fries."

"If you're hungry, we can wait until you order," Amaka said, and handed him the fries.

"Naw, I'm good, I just wanted to taste. I don't have anyone at home to cook for me, so I eat out most of the time."

"Poor baby," Asia said. "Are you ready?"

Asia and Amaka followed Dayself to the chill spot. He unloaded the two boxes of money into Shay-Shay's car.

"This place is nice," Asia said, entering the chill spot. There were black leather chairs, trimmed in yellow stitching, black glass tables with yellow circles going around the table holders, a 53 - inch plasma TV trimmed in yellow, pictures of black Jesus, Bob Marley, Malcom X, Noble Drew Ali, and Clarence 13X, on the walls. The smell of different colognes lingered in the air, mixed with the smell of pine oil. Dayself kept the floors mopped, and walls wiped down. Beres Hammond played through the speakers.

"Y'all make yourself at home," Dayself said, going to the back room to change. "Amaka, you don't know nothing about that," Dayself said, referring to her singing "They Gonna Talk" along with the stereo.

"Why not? I'm part Jamaican," Amaka said, watching Dayself put lotion on.

"You trying to take us out tonight?" Asia asked.

"I got y'all. If y'all like, y'all can stay here until y'all go back," Dayself said.

"Your girl won't trip?" Asia asked.

"No, my wife just passed away."

Amaka looked at him and turned her head.

"I apologize for that, Dayself," Asia said.

"It's not your fault. We stayed in another house anyway."

Amaka kept staring at Dayself. He had a wife beater on, showing off his prison muscles and tattoos.

"So, what type of clubs do y'all like?"

Asia said hood, and Amaka said casual.

"I'll tell y'all what. Asia, I'll call my man, Castro, up and let him take you to the hood shit, and I'll take Amaka to the casual."

"I'll just go with y'all, I don't know him." Asia said.

"Shit, you don't know me," Dayself responded.

"If Yellow say you good, then you good."

"I'll let y'all meet him, that's my nigga."

Castro got there in about twenty minutes.

"I love y'all!" Castro said as soon as he saw them, making them laugh.

"Castro, this is Asia and Amaka."

"What it do, y'all?" Castro said, going straight to the refrigerator and coming back with some pizza.

"I got some business to handle. Castro gonna hold y'all down," Dayself said.

"Y'all trying to go with me to the mall?" Castro asked Asia and Amaka.

"Yeah, we need something to wear tonight." Asia said.

"I'll let y'all go if I can pick out the outfits."

"If you're buying, you got yourself a deal," Amaka said.

"Let's get up out of here," Castro said, getting up and heading for the door. "Hold up, if I buy the clothes, y'all gotta buy the food. I want some hot buffalo wings and some cheese fries."

The girls laughed.

Dayself went to meet Dirty and Trent at the stash spot to split the money up from Yellow.

"What's good, partners?" Dayself asked, walking into the stash spot. "Where Dick at?"

"He's riding around, collecting and dropping off," Dirty said.

"What are we going to do about the ecstasy pills?" Dayself asked, setting the money on the table.

"I called my people in Greenville, North Carolina. They took one thousand for five dollars a pill, Shameka in Raleigh took two thousand, and your man, Tray, in Newbern said he's on the way to get two thousand," Trent said.

"That still leaves so many, that I refuse to count," Dayself said, splitting the hundreds and twenties up.

"Let's sit on them, they'll sell themselves. I told my people to spread the word, but we will only deal with them. The spots have been bringing in dough also. The police are kind of hot, we can handle it though. Since you've been down lately, we've sold ten keys of coke in weight. Three to your cousin in Virginia, two to the Crips in Rocky Mount, three to the Bloods in Greenville, and two to your man, Sadiq, in Rocky Mount. With all of them people calling, how do you have time to sleep?" Trent asked.

"I hardly do, that's why we're where we are now," Dayself said.

"The connect been asking what's up," Dirty said, helping count the money.

"I'll get at him later, after we finish the shit that we have. If he don't drop the price, we'll go somewhere else. Three more re-ups, and we should be ready to retire. I'm looking for some business investments, y'all should do the same," Dayself said, getting up to leave and dialing Muffin's number on his way out the door.

"Hey, baby daddy, how are you?" Muffin answered.

"I'm good, just missing you."

"I was offered a job down there. It's a little less than I make now, but I can handle it. I wanted to see what you thought about it, before I took it."

"Doing what?" Dayself asked, getting into Shay-Shay's car.

"I'll be a real estate agent."

"Why would you take a job for less pay?" Dayself asked, driving down the street.

"To be close to you."

"What did you go to college for?"

"I majored in Business Management with a concentration in International business. I've just finished my real estate license, now I'm trying to get my masters in Marketing."

"I'll tell you what. If you make me a silent partner, I'll give you the money to start your own real estate company. I'll also buy five foreclosed homes to start us up. Give me two months. Go ahead and look for office space and the houses."

"That's another reason why I love you. You try to make life better for all the people around you," Muffin said, starting to cry.

"I'll call you later, all right, bae?" Dayself said, not wanting to hear Muffin cry. He was a sucker for tears.

Dayself thought to himself, *It's time to clean up some of this dirty money.*

He called his uncle, Pap. Everyone thought he was Dayself's father, because Dayself looked like a younger version of him. Pap had retired from the fire department, and owned his own fire extinguisher business.

"Hello," Pap answered.

"Unc, you home?"

"Yeah, I'm taking the day off."

"I'm on my way over there. I need to talk with you about something." Dayself said, waiting for the light to turn green.

"I'll be here. You're not in any trouble are you?" his uncle asked. "Last time, my mason brothers bent over backwards to get you them five years. You supposed to be doing twenty."

"Naw, Unc, I'm not in trouble." Dayself said, pulling up in his uncle's yard and ending the call.

"Why haven't you come by before now?" Pap asked, soon as he stepped outside. "I told you I would give you a job."

"You know I make my own way. I want to build a club with a studio hooked to it."

"Boy, you got the money to do all that?"

"You already know what I'm into."

"So what do you want me to do?"

"I want you to get it financed through your company. Put me down as the owner, but let it show on paper that you got it financed through the bank. I'll give you the cost to have it done, plus ten thousand dollars for doing it," Dayself explained.

"I'll do this for you because I want you out of them streets. You go back to prison, it'll kill your grandmother, and I want my mother around a little longer. Meet me at the bank Tuesday at one."

"Thanks, Unc, you won't regret this!" Dayself said, excitedly.

"Where will you build all of this?"

"I own a junk yard. I'll sell the cars to another junk yard for two dollars a car. They'll do all the work moving the stuff."

"Where the hell did you get a junk yard?" Pap asked, and then thought about the way Dayself moved. "Never mind, just have the paperwork with you."

CHAPTER 14

*A*sia and Amaka were shocked at what Castro picked out for them. They knew that they were going to be the shit at the club.

"All right, my queens, it's time to feed the king." Castro said, coming out of the bathroom.

"Boy, you're crazy!" Asia answered, following Castro to the food court. "Girl, you see that dick print? I'm giving him the pussy tonight!" Asia said, squeezing her legs together.

"You are a freak," Amaka said and shook her head.

"Shit, you need to get your cob webs dusted off. Justice has been gone for six years now."

"Can we talk about something else?"

"They are paying." Castro said, pointing at Asia and Amaka.

"No, we are not. He's trying to eat for free." Amaka said, making the cashier reach for the phone to call security.

"We got it," Asia cut in, and she and Amaka burst out laughing.

It was close to seven thirty when Asia and Amaka made it

back to the chill spot. Dayself still wasn't home, so Amaka decided to call him

"Hello," Dayself answered, in a stressed tone.

"What's up?" Amaka asked, in her New York accent.

"Who is this?" Dayself asked, not able to catch Amaka's voice.

"Amaka, we got back at seven thirty. It's nine o'clock now, are we still going out?"

"Yeah, I've been handling some legal decisions today."

"Kind of stressful, right?" Amaka said.

"Yeah, baby girl."

"Who are you talking to?" Asia asked.

"Dayself." Amaka said, in her strong New York accent.

"I'll be back later. I'm going to Castro's crib. I'll probably change clothes over there."

"Whore!" Amaka said, covering the phone.

"Hello … Hello …" Dayself said.

"I'm sorry, Dayself, I usually don't ask this, but how long will it be before you get home?"

"About thirty minutes."

Thirty minutes later, Dayself pulled his keys out to open the door. Before he could get the key in the lock, the door Amaka opened it, wearing a Marc Jacob bodycon dress, wrap around MJ heels, and a tiny diamond necklace and bracelet to match. Dayself's mouth dropped open. She had her hair pinned up with Chinese sticks.

"You like?" Amaka asked, backing up into the house and turning around.

"Hell yeah, I love it!" Dayself said, making Amaka laugh.

"Your food is in the oven."

"What food?"

"Go and see."

Dayself let the smell lead him to the oven. He opened it, and there was BBQ chicken, macaroni and cheese, sweet corn, and biscuits.

"Who taught you how to cook like this?" Dayself asked, licking his fingers.

"My grandmother on my father's side is full Jamaican."

"I bet your man loves for you to cook for him."

"I don't have a man, my boyfriend died six years ago. He was mistaken for his twin brother."

"Damn, baby girl, I'm sorry to hear that."

"It's all right, I guess we kind of went through the same thing."

"Is that why you looked at me that way, when I said my wife died?"

"Yes, but tonight I want my mind to be free. I just want to laugh and enjoy," Amaka said, standing up. "Go ahead and finish eating, I'll turn the shower on for you. How do you like it?"

"Warm."

Dayself got into the shower, thinking how Amaka would look in front of him, with him washing her long black hair. He went ahead washed off, and went old school, with some Gravity cologne.

By the time Dayself came out of the bathroom, Asia, Amaka, and Castro were sitting on the couch waiting for him. Amaka stared him down. He was wearing a silk black, brown, and cream Coogie button up, cream Coogie slacks, and black and brown Tom Fords.

"Fuck this, I'm going home to change!" Castro said after seeing Dayself. He was still dipped in his white dress pants by Kenneth Cole, all brown suede KC dress shoes, a white KC button up, stitched in pink.

Asia had on a semi tight white dress by Vera Wang, open toe white heels by Christian Louboutin.

Castro drove his 2014 money green 500 Benz, customized pecan brown interior, with money green 6 inch lip and Phantom 22s, when they went out of town. All eyes were on the Benz when it pulled up, and after the four of them got out. The eyes followed them even after they took their seats and Dayself went to the bar and brought back two bottles of Cristal.

"I know you're not drinking?" Asia asked Amaka after seeing

Dayself pour the fourth cup. "Dayself, what did you do to my sister?"

"Shit, all I did was kiss at her." Dayself said, making everybody laugh.

They drank, joked, and laughed until the DJ played Sean Paul.

"Let's dance," Amaka said, grabbing Dayself's arm and pulling him to the dance floor.

"I can't dance, girl!" he yelled over the music.

"Well, just stand there. I'll show you how my Jamaican blood do it!"

Amaka did a dance where only the bottom part of her body moved. She pulled Dayself's leg out, squatted like she was riding it, while rotating her hips. Niggas' mouths dropped open, and chicks peeped her moves.

"Sis, it's been a long time since I've seen you dance. I almost forgot you know how," Asia said when Dayself and Amaka returned to their seats.

They danced a couple more times, and then went to the chill spot. Asia wanted Castro to stay longer, but he wasn't with sleeping on the couch, when he had a bed at home. Amaka and Dayself stayed up and watched the Biggie movie. After the movie went off, they both went to bed, staring at the ceiling, waiting for the other to come in their room.

The next morning, Dayself woke up to the smell of French toast. It was strange, because it had been a long time since he'd woken up to the smell of food. Amaka was in the kitchen cooking French toast, eggs, ham, cheese, and green pepper omelets, and hash browns. Dayself went to brush his teeth. As he came out of the bathroom, Asia was coming out of the bedroom in a see through nightgown. Her brown nipples and triangle cut black hairs were the center of his attention.

"Good morning … stop looking at me like that, my sister feeling you too," Asia said.

"Hey Asia … bye Asia," Dayself said, running past Asia into the kitchen.

Asia burst out laughing.

"Go put some clothes on!" Amaka screamed when Asia came in the kitchen with the gown on.

Asia popped her mouth, and went to change. She came back in pajama shorts with the string tank top to match. Asia, Amaka, and Dayself ate everything, and then Asia and Dayself fired up some sour diesel.

"Where are we going tonight?" Amaka asked.

"Don't too much be going down on Sundays, we can go to the bar and chill." Dayself said, watching Dick and Castro come through the door.

"I smell food." Castro announced.

"All that shit is gone," Asia said.

"You should've stayed with me last night so you could've cooked for me," Castro said.

"Boy, you better go to Burger King, somewhere," Asia said.

"I was going to buy you a ring out of the bubble gum machine. You ain't getting shit now," Castro said, making everybody laugh.

"Asia and Amaka, this is our brother, Dick." Dayself said.

"Did you say Dick?" Amaka asked.

"Yeah, I did. Show 'em why, Dick," Dayself said.

"Please don't." Amaka said, looking away.

Asia didn't say anything, she just stared at his dick print.

The door came open, and Trent and Dirty walked in.

"These are my other brothers, Trent and Dirty." Dayself said.

"Y'all are real brothers?" Asia asked.

"You can say that, but not blood brothers. This is our main crew right here. There is one more, but I try to keep him away, his name is Boybaby," Dayself explained.

"We're taking our girls out to eat, and then to the skate center. Y'all trying to go?" Trent asked.

"We already ate. We'll meet y'all at the skate center." Dayself said.

"Damn if I ate!" Castro said, making everybody laugh.

"Did you say skate center? Asia asked.

"Yeah, we country boys make dough, and still live in our childish ways." Trent said.

At the skate center, Amaka stayed her distance from Dayself until Dirty clipped him. He rolled over about three times, and lay out on the floor. Amaka skated around him laughing. Dayself got up and chased her around the circle, until he caught her. She tried to scream, but he had already made her fall. Amaka got up laughing.

"What's on your mind, karate girl?" Dayself asked, stopping near Asia.

"Thank you, I haven't seen my sister laugh so much in years." Asia said, in tears.

"No sweat, you my nigga right?" Dayself said, sticking his hand out to give Asia dap, then clipped her, and took off around the circle.

Everybody just started clipping each other, and they ended up being kicked out.

Later on that night, Dayself, Asia, Amaka, and Castro went to the bar. Asia and Castro were drunk, and arguing about whose fuck game was the best, until the host screamed, "Karaoke time!" Over the mic.

"Sing something, Amaka, please!" Asia begged.

"One more drink, and I'll build my nerve up to do it." Amaka said. "Look, Asia, its blue," Amaka said, referring to the drink Dayself had just bought her.

Amaka drank half, and went to the stage. She came from behind the curtain as "Baby," by Ashanti came through the speakers.

"Damn!" Dayself said, listening to how good Amaka sounded, and looked. She had on some black leather pants, a black semi-transparent string top, and black heels. When she finished, everyone stood and clapped.

"That was for you," Amaka said, kissing Dayself on his cheek.

Asia decided to go home with Castro, and Amaka and Dayself made it back to the chill spot, and took their showers. Dayself was watching *Blow*, when Amaka came out of the bathroom in a long shirt, and sat beside him.

"I know I'll probably never see you again. I see that you have a camcorder in your room, already setup. I want you to fuck me and record it, so I can take it back with me. I haven't had sex in six years. I usually don't come on to men like this," Amaka said, blushing.

"Why me then?" Dayself asked.

"You just make me happy, without really trying. I haven't felt this way in a long time. It's the only way I'll have you with me."

"Why not make love then?"

"Because I don't want to love you then leave. If you fuck me hard and good, something I never had done, and then I can leave with you in my mind, not my heart."

Dayself grabbed Amaka's hand and led her to the bedroom. He turned the lights to high beam, and then turned the camcorder on. Amaka took her shirt off in front of the camcorder, letting her black wavy hair fall to her back. Her nipples were light brown, and stuck out from her small breasts. Her stomach was flat, her pussy hairs were cut in a line, and she had skin of bronze. Amaka turned around to show her body off to Dayself. She had a nice ass to be a small size.

Dayself's dick got hard instantly. By the time Amaka turned back around, Dayself had stepped out of his shorts, and stood there naked, rubbing his dick. He lay on the bed, and Amaka crawled between his legs, with the camcorder on them.

"Tell me how to do it," Amaka said, grabbing Dayself's dick and licking it.

"Lick it like a blow pop," Dayself said, watching her.

"These too?" she asked, cupping his balls.

Dayself shook his head up and down. Amaka came up, and

placed his dick in her mouth, scraping her teeth against him.

"Don't use your teeth, baby, use your lips." Dayself said, in teacher mode.

Amaka finally got the hang of it, and Dayself had to make her stop before he came too quickly.

"Lay on your back and open your legs."

"Put it in, Dayself."

"Not yet, baby," Dayself said, as he went straight to Amaka's nipples.

Dayself sucked and nibbled on them until they were extra hard. Amaka's breathing had become heavy. He went to her lips, sucked and kissed them until they swelled. Dayself ran his tongue over Amaka's lips, then down the middle of her body. Being careful not to touch her pussy, he went down to her toes, sucking them one by one. Amaka's breathing got heavier. Dayself flipped her over. He grabbed her hair, lifted it up, licked and sucked the back of her neck. Dayself ran his tongue down the middle of Amaka's back, causing her toes to curl. Tracing his tongue past her butt, licking her calf muscles. Dayself ran his tongue back up to Amaka's butt cheeks, sucking on them until he saw red hicky marks. Amaka moaned like she was singing. Dayself flipped her back over, spread her pussy lips open, and blew on her clit softly, making her flinch with every lick.

"Damn, Day, that feels so good! I never thought it felt this good. Damn … damn!" She cursed.

Dayself inserted his finger in Amaka's pussy; she jumped. She then grabbed his finger and pushed it back into her pussy. Dayself went in and out of Amaka's pussy, sucking her clit at the same time. He felt her pussy tighten around his finger.

"I feel dizzy … o shit … ooo shit!" Amaka moaned as her pussy squirted cum all over Dayself's face and chest.

"Damn, your pussy just did some porno shit!"

"Is that what cumming feels like? Damn!" Amaka said, opening her eyes, seeing her cum dripping off Dayself's face. "Did I do that? I'm … ooo shit!"

Dayself had pushed half of his dick in her pussy. Amaka

wrapped her arms around Dayself and held him tight, while saying, "shit," over and over. Dayself lay there until she was ready. Amaka pushed up, sliding the rest of his dick in. Her pussy was squeezing his dick.

"Are you ready?" Dayself asked, with most of his dick in.

"What am I supposed to do?"

"Move like you're dancing on the floor," Dayself said, moving in and out of her very slow. The more he sped up, the more Amaka danced on his dick.

"Ah ... Day ... ah ... ah ... feel dizzy ... again ... shit!" Amaka moaned, cumming all over Dayself's dick and stomach. Dayself pushed her legs back and fucked her like she asked.

"O...o...stop...Day...stop!" She moaned, causing Dayself to stop. "Please don't stop ... please don't stop!"

Dayself felt himself about to cum. He pulled out of Amaka's pussy and slid his tongue inside her, moving it around in circles.

"Boy ... Boy ... what ... are ... ooh ... you ... doing ... down ... oh ... oh ... down there!" Amaka screamed, sliding back.

Dayself stopped, flipped Amaka over, and showed her how to put the arch in her back. He slid in her pussy real slow. After he got it all in, he sped up.

"Ah ... o ... ah ... it ... hurt ... so good!" she moaned loudly.

Dayself had to slow down to keep from cumming. He pulled out and lay on his back.

"Ride it like you did my knee," Dayself said, watching Amaka climb over him and slide down on his dick. "Ride baby, ride this dick," Dayself moaned, causing Amaka to go wild on his dick.

"You ... oh ... oh in ... my stomach ... ooo ... dizzy ... shittt!" Amaka moaned.

Dayself felt himself cumming, but his words wouldn't come out. He tried to lift Amaka up, but she sat down flat and moved around in circles, causing him to cum all up in her.

"I can't move," she said, falling over.

Dayself rolled Amaka over with his dick still in her. Amaka's pussy was throbbing so hard, his dick instantly came back to life. They fucked two more times before going to sleep.

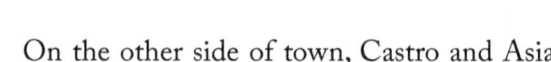

On the other side of town, Castro and Asia walked into the house. Castro flopped down on his leather couch, opened the candy dish on the table, and popped an ecstasy pill.

"This is the first time I've gone to someone's house, and they had a candy dish full of ecstasy pills."

"That's because you never came across a Double L nigga."

Asia reached in the dish, popped a pill, then went to the refrigerator and came back with two bottles of water. Castro went to his room, pulled out his supply of Viagra, popped a little piece, then jumped in the shower. He was getting out as Asia stepped out of her clothes. She had her hair in a bob type cut. Her nipples were light brown, it looked like she had just shaved; her pussy was bald.

Castro reached for Asia's pussy as she took the towel out of his hands.

"Let me take care of you, you'll have all night to get this," Asia said, moving his hand from her pussy, and wiping him down with the towel. After wiping him down, she threw the towel in the hamper. "I'll be out in a few," Asia said, kissing Castro on the cheek, then getting into the shower.

"About five minutes later, Asia walked into Castro's room. He was watching a cartoon porno flick and laughing.

"Damn, that pill got you tripping, and my pussy wet," Asia said, standing in front of Castro naked. "So what's up with all that tough talk?" Asia said, getting between his legs and sucking just the tip of Castro's dick, then taking all eight and a half inches down her throat slowly.

Castro gritted his teeth. Asia came up, wrapped her hand around his dick, and jacked it fast, sucking the head at the same time.

"You like that shit, right?" Asia asked, watching Castro with his eyes closed, still jacking his dick. Asia leaned down to sucked him some more.

"I let my tongue and dick do the talking," Castro said, pulling

Asia up. "Lay on your stomach."

"Oh, you ain't said shit," Asia said, laying on the bed, then flipping on her stomach.

Castro spread Asia's ass cheeks, first licking around the rim of her ass. He rammed his tongue in her ass and tongue fucked her. Asia started speaking Chinese. He reached behind them and grabbed the little vibrator, called a bullet, and stuck it to Asia's clit, while still tongue fucking her ass. Asia almost jumped off the bed when the bullet touched her clit. The feeling in both holes started connecting like two positive wires. Asia came all over the little toy, while yelling in Chinese. Castro flipped her over, and went to sucking her clit.

"Put your finger in my ass," Asia yelled.

Castro reached under Asia and slid his finger in her ass. She moved back and forth on his finger and tongue. Asia gripped the sheets and moved her body up and down, until she screamed in Chinese, cumming all over Castro's tongue and finger. Castro slid his finger out, and Asia grabbed her legs and pulled them all the way back to her head. Her pussy was sitting up like a muffin. Castro slid into Asia's wet pussy, all the way to the balls. He pounded away on her pussy for five minutes, then she put her legs on his shoulders, and he pounded away five more minutes. Asia held her nipples tight, throwing it back to Castro, the whole time still speaking in Chinese. They went ten more minutes in that position. Asia had cum two more times. Castro flipped Asia over; he still had not cum.

"Damn, give the pussy a break, you're killing me ... take the other hole."

"Not yet, I told you I was going to show you what time it is with these country boys!" Castro said, slamming his dick into her pussy, fucking her with force.

"Okay ... okay ... I'm ... sorry ... y'all win!" Asia screamed.

"Hell naw, come here!" Castro yelled, pulling Asia by the waist, fucking her hard.

"Ahh ... ahh you ... kill ... ah ... ah!" Moaning loud dropping flat on her stomach, Asia was incoherent.

Castro kept pounding her out. Asia's body started to tremble.

She came and just lay there. Castro pulled out and came all over Asia's back.

Castro went to get a washcloth to wipe them off, and when he came back, Asia had dozed off. He dropped the washcloth on the bed, stuck his hand in the drawer, and pulled out some K-Y jelly. Castro rubbed some on his dick, and spread her ass.

"Please tell me you're not ready again!" Asia said, waking up quickly.

"Ah … ah … fuck … me in … my … ass!" Asia moaned as Castro slid in.

Castro fucked Asia so long, she begged him to cum. Asia tried to slide away, but it was no use. He grabbed her hips and pulled her back. Castro still couldn't cum. He slid out of her ass, wiped himself off, and went back in her pussy.

"O … help … o … help me!" Asia screamed.

Castro fucked both holes, for ten more minutes before he came. Asia was out of it.

I got to tell my girls about these country niggas. She thought to herself.

When Asia and Castro woke up the next morning, Asia couldn't even walk. Castro had to carry her to the tub.

"How am I going to drive back like this?" Asia asked.

"Do you want a pain pill?" Castro asked.

"Hell no, I'm not fucking with you and those pills! Boy you like to gave me a hysterectomy and shit bag!" Asia yelled, rubbing her ass and pussy in the bubbled water.

"I thought I could get a little more this morning," Castro pulled out his dick, showing her he was hard. Asia became quiet. "I thought that would shut you up."

Castro walked out of the bathroom laughing.

Amaka and Dayself were eating breakfast when Asia and Castro walked in. Asia was walking like she had been riding horses for two days straight. Dayself started laughing. He knew Castro had given her the EV dick, Ecstasy and Viagra.

"What are you laughing at?" Asia asked.

"Nothing," Dayself answered with a big smile.

"Girl, what's wrong with you? Why are you walking like that?" Amaka asked.

"Let's just say I tripped down last night," Asia said.

"On a dick." Dayself mumbled, making everybody laugh.

"Fuck y'all, I'm going to the bathroom." Asia said, walking to the back of the house.

"Do you need any help?" Castro asked, watching her ass.

"No … hell no … I'm good!" Asia said.

"What you keep smiling for?" Asia asked Amaka on her way to the bathroom, making her smile harder.

Asia sat on the toilet to pee. It took her so long, Castro went to check on her.

"Excuse you!" Asia said.

"What are you doing, shitting?" Castro asked, walking in the bathroom.

"Do you smell shit?"

Castro pulled out his dick, and Asia went to work.

At the breakfast table, Amaka asked Dayself, "If you come to New York, you'll stop by and check me out, right?"

"I promise to stop by, if you ride me like you did last night. Shit, I'll make a special trip for that," Dayself said.

"That's a promise I'll hold you to. You can get it however, whenever, and wherever you want it. This is yours," Amaka said, putting Dayself's hand on her pussy print.

When Asia and Castro finally came out of the bathroom, Amaka had already packed their things.

"Go change clothes," Asia said after kissing Castro and getting into the truck.

Castro looked down at his pants and smiled when he saw a red lipstick kiss print. He laughed as Amaka and Asia drove away.

Asia and Amaka stopped to get gas halfway to New York. Amaka had watched her portable DVD player for almost the whole ride. She had turned it so Asia couldn't see what she was watching. After Asia returned from paying for the gas, Amaka went into the rest stop to use the bathroom. Asia was curious to know what had held Amaka's attention for the last few hours, so she pressed play on the DVD player.

The image of Amaka riding Dayself's dick popped on the screen.

"Damn, sis, you handling the dick," Asia said, laughing at Amaka as she got back into the truck.

"What?" Amaka asked.

"I didn't know that you could ride dick like that! Shit, I can't even do that."

Shocked, Amaka looked at Asia and burst out laughing.

CHAPTER 15

Two months had gone by, and most of the work was gone. Dayself arrived at the chill spot, and the Cadillac Yellow owed him was sitting in the driveway. Dayself smiled, then dialed Yellow's number.

"Country boy, what's up?" Yellow answered. "I see you've noticed your winnings."

"How did you know?"

"Amaka was getting thick. I asked Asia was she on depo or something. Asia told me that she was pregnant."

"I know like hell you didn't say pregnant!" Dayself said, almost dropping the phone. "By who?"

"You're the only one that got that pussy in six years, that I know of."

"Yo, where she at now?"

"She decided to go to Jamaica until she have the baby. Man, shit, call Asia. Fuck it, tell her I told you."

"All right, bet."

"That's the first half, in the trunk. I'll have the other half in thirty or forty days."

"All right, old man, I'll speak with you later," Dayself said, hanging up the phone, then dialing Asia's number.

"Hello." Asia answered.

"Asia."

"This is her, who's calling?"

"Dayself."

"Hey brother, I knew Yellow would tell you. It's not that you're a bad person or anything like that. Amaka is still smiling, talking about you. It's just that her father was this king pin, and some Colombians wanted in on his money flow. He disrespected them, so they say, and they killed him and our mother. Amaka still thinks the world of you, she just don't want her baby around the activities that you got going on. Shit, every time the bitch gets hot, she looks at the DVD y'all made. She thinks I don't be hearing her in there moaning, playing in herself. The next morning, she got the biggest smile on her face, like you are there. Just give her a little time, she'll come around. She knows you're doing you, but she got a special place in her mind and stomach for you."

"All right, be sure to tell her I called."

"I'll do that." Asia said, about to hang up. "Oh, Day, it's not your money she wants. Her father left her enough money that'll last her grandkids the rest of their lives."

"Well shit, she need to take care of me. I'll clean the house, wash the dishes too."

"You're a trip, but I know you're the type of man that make your own way."

"Well, karate girl, let me go."

"Before you do, tell Castro I told my girls about the fuck game he put down. They're trying to get some."

"Y'all some wild cats, I'll do that though." Dayself said and hung up.

Dayself got into the caddie and smiled. Thinking about the night with Amaka, he drove the Caddie to the stash house so he could split the money with Dirty and Trent.

Bamena looked at the calendar and placed a check mark on the date of her father's death. It had been two months. She had since graduated from high school at the top of her class. East Carolina University offered her a scholarship, but she had turned it down to run her father's club. Bamena's life had started doing a full circle in her mind. She had a fake ID, which said that she was twenty-one. No one knew Gormez was her father, except the kidnappers and Nana. Bamena had just received three million dollars from an insurance policy. She made many changes to the club, then she remodeled the two houses that were willed to her. The last house was the whorehouse Gormez got caught slipping at.

Bamena knocked on the door and a Spanish girl answered. They spoke in Spanish, then the girl let Bamena in.

"I'm the new owner of this house. You owe me two months' rent, and two months' pay for prostitution. I'll forgive the debt if you agree to my terms," Bamena said.

"What are your terms?" one of the Spanish girls asked.

"I'm opening the club back up. I want some Mexican strippers in there. Three of you will stay here, while the other three work at the club. Y'all will rotate every two days."

"Why can't we all strip at the same time?" one of the Spanish girls asked. "I hear it's a lot of money in that."

"I own the house right beside the club. All of you will move there. You will rotate on night and day shifts. I have a friend who will teach you all the ropes," Bamena said.

"You have a deal, boss," the same Spanish girl said.

"Are you the only one that speaks English?" Bamena asked.

"They can speak it a little, but not like me. Everyone call me Spanish."

"All right, y'all move today," Bamena said, walking out the door.

Bamena went to different clubs and recruited three black strippers. One was named Kia; she was about thirty years old, light brown skin, 5'6", 150 pounds, a short haircut and a fat ass. The guys at the club called her Superhead number two. The other girl was named Crystal; she was about twenty-four years old, 5'9",

145 pounds, long hair. The burn mark on her arm stopped her from being a dime, but she had the body like Beyoncé. Brandy, the third girl, was about twenty-three years old, 5'7, 145 pounds, jet-black skin tone, dread locks, and she could shoot marbles out of her pussy. Spanish was twenty-two years old, 5'5, 123 pounds long black hair, a model face, and a body shaped like Kim Kardashian.

"At my club, anything goes, except fucking, fingering, and a little sucking. If they want to fuck, y'all can use the four bedroom house beside the club," Bamena explained. "Y'all will charge them one hundred dollars a fuck. If y'all want to do anal sex, you can keep the extra money for that. We will split the hundred dollars down the middle. I don't know how ecstasy pills feel, but I do know that we need them. Do any of you know where we can get a connect on the pills?" Bamena asked.

"Hell yeah, we need them!" Kia said. "I know who got them for cheap."

A month went by, and the club was in full effect. So much money was coming in that Bamena had to get a money machine. The pussy, alcohol, and ecstasy pills were selling like water. Bamena never came out of her office. She always used a secret door that her father had installed, connected to the office. She watched the people on the monitors, almost the whole time. Bamena recorded all of the freaky scenes and sold them on the internet. The girls didn't care, as long as they got paid.

There was a knock at the door. Bamena looked at the monitor and saw that it was one of her Mexican bouncers.

"Boss, there's a gentleman out there who wishes to speak with you. He says to tell you that he comes in peace," Bamena's bodyguard, Angelo said.

"What does he have on?"

"The Mexican, in the black cowboy hat."

Bamena zoomed in on the man's face. Her eyes widened.

He looked just like a young version of her father. She could not swallow.

"All right, tell him to come back." Bamena cleared her throat. "Wait outside the door after you escort him back."

The Mexican entered and took off his hat. He was about thirty years old, 5'5", thick mustache, 140 pounds. He had on a black cowboy hat, blue jeans, white button up shirt, and brown cowboy boots.

"I'm Bonito Gormez, you look like my uncle Gormez," Bonito said. "Are you sure, y'all are not related?"

"No, we're not."

"He always said he had a kid, but no one has ever met him or her."

"Well, I'm not his daughter. He sold me the club before he died," Bamena said with her finger on the trigger of her father's gold .45.

"I like what you've done with the place. I tried to tell your father, I mean, Uncle Gormez, to do it like this. He always chose to go the old route."

"Thank you. What are your intentions in speaking with me?" Bamena asked, gripping the gun and trembling.

"I know you're selling ecstasy pills. I heard the blacks in Tarboro are selling them five dollars a pill to weight buyers. If you buy from me and my family, I'll sell them to you for two dollars a pill. As for the coke, I'll front you whatever you buy for seventy five hundred a key, if you buy twenty or more," Bonito said.

"I'll take fifty thousand pills," Bamena said.

"All right, they'll be here tomorrow night."

"No, not here. I own a house on 115 Morgan St., deliver them there."

"That's one of Uncle Gormez's old houses," Bonito said, smiling.

Bamena quickly turned her head away and looked at the monitor, knowing she had revealed too much.

"They will be to you soon," Bonito said, turning the knob to leave. "Bye cousin," he added and looked back, causing Bamena to smile at him. "Oh yeah, one more thing, we're on to the people who killed Uncle Gormez."

"What do you mean, on to them?" Bamena's smile turned into a frown.

"We have an idea who it was; we just can't prove it yet. When we do, there will be hell to pay," Bonito said. "Three body-guards straight from Mexico will be here to look after you. We brought their wives and kids down here, and put them in homes. They think that you're responsible for bringing their families to America, so they will die for you. Bye cousin, it was nice meeting you," Bonito said, closing the door behind him.

"Damn, I knew they would figure it out." Bamena said, staring at the wall.

Instead of selling her father's houses, she moved the black strippers into one. They sold pills to most of the black customers. Bamena fronted a white guy she went to school with to bring in the white customers, and she sold weight in pills for four dollars a pill. The other house was used for the stash house. In two weeks, the pills were gone. Bamena called Bonito.

"Hello." Bonito answered.

"I need one hundred thousand roller blades," Bamena said.

"Little cousin, you're moving the roller blades mighty fast. Are you ready for the other thing we talked about?"

"Yeah, bring me ten of them on front."

"I'll have to charge you ten a piece for them."

"That's cool. When they get to the spot, tell them to knock three times, pause, then two more."

"All right, cousin, be safe."

"I will not slip like my father," Bamena said.

Bamena never told Bonito what really happened. She felt it was a personal revenge, which she would someday get. So much money was coming in that Bamena rented out the house that she and Nana stayed in, and bought them a fenced in baby mansion.

CHAPTER 16

*M*uffin had the real estate business up and running. She had sold two of the houses for a hundred and fifty thousand dollars each. After paying seventy thousand for each house, and putting fifteen thousand dollars' worth of remodeling in, Dayself and Muffin made one hundred and thirty thousand dollars in profits. Muffin moved in one of the houses, and they still had two more to sell.

"Come get your gun off of this floor, boy!" Muffin yelled.

"Damn, why when you're around them white folk at work, you talk all proper. When you get home, you turn to Remy Martin?" Dayself asked.

"Oh, nigga, I'm hood. I just play my role to get on top."

"I gotta get ready to go. Has the baby kicked yet?"

"No, bring me back some ice cream and pickles."

"Girl, you go get them. I don't know when I'm coming back. Your ass need to eat some nutritional foods, so he'll be healthy."

"He good, trust me," Muffin said, rubbing her stomach.

"I'm out."

"Don't be letting Shay-Shay trick you out of no dick either! I can see right through her sneaky ass."

"You tripping, I'll see you later."

"You better come kiss my stomach."

"I forgot to tell you, my man called, he want to look at one of the houses."

"Why did you wait so late to tell me?"

"I smoke, I forgot."

"How's the club and studio coming along?"

"The walls are up now. They have to put the soundproof booth in next week. Yo Gotti and 2 Chainz will be at the grand opening."

"I'll be there shaking my pregnant ass!" Muffin said, snapping her fingers.

"Your ass will be here looking fine and thick, with your legs propped up."

"Get out of my house then." She poked out her lips.

"You need to go look at some more houses."

"That's what I hired the two agents for. One more thing before you go, bae. Starbucks corporate offered me a regional manager position, responsible for all the locations in eastern North Carolina.

"Tell them no, but we are interested in buying into the franchise. We'll open three up to start off."

"We don't know anything about that shit. Why in the hell would you open one up in these little ass towns?"

"First, we can put in the contract that they have to fully train three of our employees for each shop. The reason why I say the small towns, is because we can have the buildings small, and just make a two lane drive thru."

"I'll make the call tomorrow. You and your ideas."

"I'm gone, let me give mommy tummy a kiss." Dayself lifted Muffin's shirt and kissed her stomach, causing her to laugh.

Dayself got into the car and checked his messages. Amaka said she will call back later, Shay-Shay said, "Dayself answer this damn phone, if this baby kick me like that one more time, I'm cutting her ass out! You better come calm her ass down! Yeah, I said her." Then she hung up. Dirty called and said, "We got one puppy left. She looking real low."

Dayself called Dirty back first.

"Radio." Dirty answered.

"What's good, where you at?" Dayself asked.

"Over Castro's crib, playing dominos."

"Have you seen Trent and Dick?"

"Trent home with his bad ass kids, and you already know Dick is home with Destiny."

"Who's running the spot?"

"Boybaby."

"You think he can handle it?"

"Pretty boy is you in the making. He got it."

"I'm pulling up right now."

"What are we going to do about the re-up?" Dirty asked Dayself as soon as he walked in.

"The connect won't go down on the prices. I told him that we wanted thirty joints, he still saying eighteen. I told him to go kill hisself, and then hung up. The other connect wants us to come get it, and only knock five hundred off each key. I'm not fucking with that. Yo, Castro, give Boybaby a break. He been at the trap house for two days," Dayself said.

"Fuck that, he won fifteen stacks from us playing In The Line of Duty," Castro said. "I'm making his ass suffer."

"Let him enjoy his winnings. You know soon it's going to be you and him," Dayself said.

"That's what's up, I got you." Castro said.

"Don't worry, something will fall in our lap," Dayself said, watching Dirty sit down with a stressed look.

"It's not that. We're not on point like we used to be. We usually keep coke and three or four people in the trap house."

"We're good now, bruh. We got legal businesses jumping off. Stop sweating the small shit. We're in the big league now," Dayself said.

"That's what's up, you know I'm with you one hundred percent. We just made money so fast, it slips my mind that we have millions now."

Boybaby left the barbershop and headed to the mall. He got out of his 2014 Jazzy-blue 300 Chrysler, with 22-inch Jazzy-blue deep lip rims to match. A white trimmed in pink Porsche truck, with white 24-inch Porsche rims to match, and a pink Porsche symbol on the center of the rim, pulled up two parks away from him. Bamena got out of the truck.

Boybaby stared at her body, shaking his head, then he yelled, "Damn!"

Bamena looked back at Boybaby and smiled with her Prada shades on. She had on a Prada black bubble jacket with fur around the hood, a pair of tight Prada jeans, a black and silver sweater with precious on the front, and black and silver Prada heels. Boybaby had on an all-white Lacoste sweater, Lacoste blue jeans, and some brown Timberlands with the white sole. Boybaby walked fast to catch up with Bamena. He didn't see the Jet Black Yukon parked beside her.

Bamena shook her head at the bodyguards, and they closed their doors. She thought Boybaby was cute. Bamena has always been attracted to black guys. Her father had always told her to never mix the blood. She said to herself, *who the hell having babies? I'm still a virgin, as* Boybaby walked with her into the mall.

"What's your name?" Boybaby asked, checking out Bamena's beauty.

"Salita, and yours?" Bamena asked.

"Boybaby."

"That's not what your mama named you," she said, lifting her shades onto her head and looking into his eyes.

"It's Taeshawn, but everyone calls me Boybaby. So what brings you to the mall?" he asked, breaking the stare.

"I came to do a little shopping."

"Can I shop with you?"

"I don't know you like that."

"That's why I want to shop with you, so I can get to know you.

Can I buy you one of them big ass pizzas then?"

"How do you know I even like pizza?"

"You ain't shaped like that eating salads, that's in a good way. You're trying to get rid of me."

"Now why would a girl like me do that?" Bamena said, looking at him smiling.

Boybaby and Bamena went in several stores together, laughing and talking. Bamena wanted to go in Victoria Secrets to pick the girls out some new outfits, but she didn't want Boybaby to see what she was doing.

"Let's go in there," Boybaby said, pointing to Victoria Secrets.

"For what? You won't see me in anything in there."

"At least let me pick you something out, it's on me."

"If you say so, but I got my own money."

They walked around, looking at different G-strings and bras. Bamena had never worn G-strings, she had a couple of thongs, and mostly boy shorts. Boybaby picked her out a hot pink pair, with the bra to match. Then he grabbed some apple body lotion to go with it.

"Are you trying to tell me something, do I stink to you?" Bamena asked when Boybaby put the lotion on the counter.

"No, if you're going to put these on, you gotta smell extra good." Boybaby said, holding the G-strings up, then placing them on the counter to be bagged up. "Here you go." He handed Bamena the bag.

"Thank you, you're so sweet," Bamena said, blushing.

Bamena and Boybaby walked to their vehicles with their hands full of bags. He helped her load her bags in her truck. Bamena got in, turned the heat up, put her lip-gloss and shades on, and started backing out.

"Boybaby, here is my number. I usually don't give it out, but I'm feeling your swag."

"I'm feeling yours to baby girl." He said, reaching for her number.

Bamena backed out of the parking space with the Yukon right

behind her. Her phone rang.

"Hello," Bamena answered, with J-Lo playing in the background.

"You forgot to eat pizza with me," Boybaby said.

"Why don't you come by my house around seven thirty? My Nana cooks the best steak and cheese tacos."

"I'll be there. You stay pretty 'til then."

"My address is 212 Master St."

"Peace, my queen," Boybaby said, hanging up.

Boybaby didn't have anything to do, so he hung around Wilson for a while. It's a place of it's own, full of different sections of houses, wood houses, all you hear is reggae, all day long. Seventy percent of the people there have dreads. You can get any weed in the world from that area. Then over past the mall, is the white people section, or people with money. Big houses, gated communities, you can tell the money is on that side for sure. It's like night and day.

Boybaby got out of the car, and rang the doorbell at ten after seven. Bamena already knew that he was there by the motion sensors going off, and the camera zooming in on him.

"Who is it?" Nana said.

"Taeshawn"

"Who are you here to see?"

"Salita."

"I'm sorry, she's not expecting you."

"Well, Ms. ..."

"Just called me Nana," she said, opening the door.

"My name is Taeshawn, but everybody calls me Boybaby."

"Oh, I'm sorry, you're the one Salita said was coming over for dinner."

Bamena came down the stairs in black tights, white tank top and white air ones, wiping her face with a towel.

"What's up, Boybaby?" Bamena said smiling.

"Nothing. Nice crib y'all got here."

After a quick tour, they went straight to the kitchen to eat, then the sun room to talk. They watched *Friday After Next*, and laughed together until Boybaby's phone went off.

"Hello, hold on a minute Stro. Salita I need to step outside to take this call."

"Sure, you can go out there on the patio."

Bamena had trust issues, so she pressed the intercom to listen in on Boybaby's conversation.

"He still haven't found a connect yet ... what are we supposed to do til then ... I hope so, cause I'm trying to stack some dough fast and get out of the game."

Bamena knew then that Boybaby was hustling something. She had gotten rid of her last key, to a guy in Wilson. Bamena never touched it herself; she always used the bodyguards.

Boybaby walked back into the house, with a stressed look on his face.

"What's bothering you, you're not acting yourself?" Bamena asked.

"It's nothing."

"Where do you work?"

"Um ... I own a paint shop."

"But you hustle, right?"

"Something like that, you're not the Feds are you?"

"No, I hate to tell you this."

"What's good, my queen?"

Boybaby looked into Bamena's eyes, as she smiled at him.

"I was listening to your conversation when you were on the phone. So tell me what's going on?" she crossed her legs Indian style in the chair.

"You won't understand."

"Try me. I may be able to help."

"I have some brothers, and their people sold jewelry. They went out of business."

Boybaby looked at her to see if she caught on to what he was saying. She stared at him in the quiet house for a minute.

"I have an uncle who has pull with the Mexican cartel. I'm sure he can help out, but he will want to do a background check on you."

"A background check for what?"

"To see if you're a snitch."

"You know a lot to be a spoiled rich girl."

"Who said I was spoiled or rich."

"My name is Taeshawn Harper, Jr."

"I'll let you know what he says."

"I'm about to bounce, I'll call you tomorrow."

"Since you brought me such a nice gift today, here you go." Bamena said, handing him a bag with a Castleberry button up inside.

"You didn't have to do that."

"It goes with the Jordans you just bought. I had to go back and get you something real quick."

"You have a good heart. Don't ever let anyone destroy that," Boybaby said, walking out the door.

Boybaby pulled his phone out and called Castro soon as he drove off.

"Hello." Castro answered.

"I need to see you ASAP."

"I'm at the spot. Come through."

Boybaby arrived at the spot less than twenty minutes later.

"You're not going to believe what happened to me today," Boybaby said. He ran the story down to Castro, from the mall until he left Bamena's house.

"Nigga, are you crazy? She could be a fed!" Castro yelled.

"She's not the feds."

"How in the fuck do you know?"

"Feds don't sell coke, and if you keep yelling at me, we gonna have to shoot it!"

"The Feds do what the fuck they want to do!"

"If she's Fed, I'll take full responsibility, because her people will only deal with me."

"Let me call Dayself and see what he says," Castro said, dialing Dayself's number.

"Hello." Dayself answered.

"Your protégé wants to speak with you. Are you on a good line?"

"Yeah, if he codes it out."

"Hello."

"What's good sun?" Dayself asked.

"I found us a stripper."

"Is the pussy any good?"

"She's Mexican, they keep that good pussy."

"Sun, I'm going to put my trust in your hands. Don't let me down."

"I won't, that's my word. What will we ask for?"

"Thirty dollars to get in, under seventeen not allowed."

"All right, peace." Boybaby said, rushing Dayself off the phone, to answer the beep.

"Peace." Dayself said, hanging up.

"Hello." Boybaby answered.

"This is Salita."

"Girl, I know your voice."

"My people just called back, it's a go."

"Your phone good?"

"Yeah."

"How much for thirty of that white?"

"He said for twenty or more fifteen a key."

"We'll take thirty."

"You're only getting them for fifteen because I told him you're a good friend of mine."

"I owe you. Let me take you out to dinner on Friday."

"We can do that, handle your business first."

"All right, I'll talk to you later. Peace, my queen."

"Peace." Bamena laughed and hung up.

Bamena called Bonito with a smile on her face. Every time she looked in Boybaby's eyes, she wanted to kiss him.

"Hello." Bonito answered.

"I need fifty squares."

"Around three or four in the morning, they should be there. Cousin, why don't you come up here to visit the family?" Bonito asked.

"I'll try to get up there soon, let me stack just a little more money first."

"Be safe and take care."

"Thanks Bonito," Bamena said, hanging up. Bamena called Boybaby back.

"Hello." Boybaby answered.

"The meet will be at the old S&J store in Princeville, tomorrow morning at seven."

"Not a problem, let me call my people," Boybaby said, hanging up and calling Dayself.

"Hello." Dayself answered.

"One five at S&J, at seven a.m.," Boybaby said.

"That's peace, we'll be there, but not seen. Take the tester, and test our lucky 7. Fifteen sounds too good to be true.

"The price might drop after I get the pussy."

"Don't mix business and pleasure, haven't I taught you anything? Learn from my mistakes."

"That's peace."

"That's not peace. You're like me, got to have the pussy."

"Peace, Day," Boybaby said, laughing

"Peace G."

Dayself drove up and saw Shay-Shay sitting on the porch tapping away on her laptop.

"Nigga, where have you been? You know I'm pregnant, and you won't answer your phone!"

"I'm here now, what's wrong with daddy's girls?" Dayself

asked, smiling.

"I'm going back to work with this big stomach."

"For two and a half months? Shit, you act like you're making twenty five dollars an hour."

"So, shut up, at least I have a job, and don't ask you for shit. The money you give, that I don't ask for, I just put it in the bank."

"Well, I need to borrow that back."

"Sure, it's yours anyway."

"I'm just playing. What are you doing, on the sex chat line?" Dayself asked, laughing.

"Real funny. I'm ordering little girl clothes that they don't have down here."

"It's dark, turn the porch light out and come inside."

"You're not getting any pussy."

"Did I ask for any?"

"Do you ever?" Shay-Shay said, getting up.

Shay-Shay sat on the couch with her legs open. Her grandma bloomers were soaked under her skirt. Dayself stuck his hand under her skirt to feel her wetness. Shay-Shay stared Dayself in the eyes, not saying a word. He got on his knees and bit her pussy softly through the bloomers, causing more juices to sink through. Shay-Shay lay down on the couch while Dayself slid her bloomers off. He spread Shay-Shay's pussy lips, letting his tongue run from her pussy hole, to her clit. Then Dayself slid two fingers into Shay-Shay, as her juices ran down his fingers and dripped onto the couch. Dayself fingered in and out of her pussy, causing it to make a smacking noise, while sucking her clit at the same time. Shay-Shay gripped Dayself's close cut head, screaming. She came all over the couch, and then lay there, breathing hard.

Dayself went to the kitchen, and walked back past Shay-Shay to the door, with two chicken drumsticks in his hand.

"Where are you going? Come back and finish what you started!" Shay-Shay said, lying there with her skirt up.

"You told me I wasn't getting any pussy."

Shay-Shay stood up and wobbled to the door.

"You big nose motherfucker! Don't come back," Shay-Shay yelled, slamming the door.

～

Dayself stopped to the stash spot, and then headed to the chill spot. He counted out four hundred and fifty thousand dollars with the money machine. He was taping the boxes, when his phone went off.

"Hello," Dayself answered.

"Boy, you not know who you play wit!" Amaka said in a Jamaican accent.

"Who the fuck?" Dayself said, looking at his phone like he could see the person.

Amaka burst out laughing.

"What's good, baby mama?" Dayself asked.

Amaka stopped laughing. "It's not like that. I was going to tell you, but we won't be a part of your life until you go straight. I lost my mother and father behind the drug game. I love my life and my baby's life too much to feel that pain again. I just can't get attached, and then lose you too," Amaka said in her strong New York accent.

"That's understandable. Things will change for the better soon."

"Everybody say that, and end up dead or in prison."

"You'll see, just stay in contact with me. That's all I ask for right now."

"I can do that, Day."

"Try to call me tomorrow."

"All right, bye."

"Bye." Dayself said, hanging up and going in deep thought about leaving the game.

Dayself took the money to Castro, so Boybaby could pick it up. Then he went to Muffin's house. She was in the kitchen going over taxes. Dayself walked straight to the DVD player, put in *Paid in Full*, and lay on the couch.

"Boy, your ass can't speak?" Muffin asked.

"What's good, baby mama?" Dayself said, rolling up a blunt of bubble gum dro.

"What's wrong with you? Let me leave you alone. I see that you're in one of your moods, Mr. Bipolar," Muffin said, walking upstairs eating a pickle.

Dayself smoked the dro, took two drinks of Hennessey, and passed out on the couch.

"Bae, get up and go to bed," Muffin said, waking him up with a kiss two hours later.

"You're right, I have a long day tomorrow, wake me up at five."

CHAPTER 17

$\mathcal{D}$ estiny had been begging Dick to take her to the strip club for months. Finally, he agreed and they decided to go to club Megos in Wilson. It was the new strip club that everybody talked about. The place was jammed packed with all races of people. The strippers were in full money mode. The good thing about it was that all of them were fine. They determined who they gave pussy to, and plenty of ballers of all races, were after them.

Bamena always watched the cameras. She spotted Destiny and Dick's new faces as soon as they walked in. Bamena was doing illegal activities, so she kept a look out for the cops. Dick and Destiny went straight to the bar and ordered a bottle of Cristal and two cups of Hennessey. A stripper was already at their table waiting for them. Spanish could spot money a mile away. Dick wore an all-white Marco Polo jogging suit with the zip up hooded sweater, brown suede Timberlands 2.0 Boat Moctoe Chukkas, a platinum chain with a charm made of a circle of diamonds and Double L wrote in diamonds in the middle, with a platinum L on each side. Destiny had on a cream Vera Wang fitted dress, with her hair done up Chinese style, and white open toe Liz Claiborne's. She wore a tiny platinum chain, with a tiny charm, that read, Them L's.

"I'm Spanish, would y'all like a lap dance?"

"Yeah, right here," Dick said, pointing to his dick.

Spanish grinded on his dick, while Destiny put money in her G-string. After two dances, Spanish went to another table.

Dick and Destiny had drank most of their drinks and loosened up. Dick called Spanish back to give Destiny a lap dance. As Spanish grinded on Destiny's lap, she pulled Spanish's bright orange G-string from between her cheeks, and stuck her finger in Spanish's ass. Spanish hopped up and gave Destiny a shocked look. Destiny handed her a ten dollar bill.

"I've never seen y'all in here before," Spanish said, taking the money out of Destiny's hand.

"I'm Destiny, and this is Dick."

"Why do they call you Dick?" Spanish asked, looking down at his print.

"Do you want to find out?" Destiny asked, grabbing Dick's dick.

"That can be arranged, it'll be one hundred for one, and two fifty for the both of you," Spanish said, lying about the extra fifty.

"The boss wishes to speak with you," the security guard said, tapping Spanish's shoulder.

Spanish looked at the security guard, rolled her eyes, and walked to Bamena's office.

"Come in and close the door behind you," Bamena said through the intercom.

Spanish walked in staring at Bamena, scared to ask why was she fucking with her money.

"What's the problem, Boss?" Spanish asked.

"I saw the look on your face when you hopped out of the young lady's lap. What happened?" Bamena asked.

"She stuck her finger in my ass!"

"Did they say what their names were?"

"Yes, she said their names were Destiny and Dick."

The two names that Bamena remembered shot straight to her brain. Her heart started beating fast, her hands shook, and sweat popped on her forehead.

"I don't care what you do, I want you to stay close to them!"

Bamena said with shaky hands. "Find out everything about them! If you have to go home with them, then go! Don't fail me, Spanish, or you will be on the first flight back to Mexico, understood?"

"Yes, Boss."

"All right, handle yours."

Bamena broke down in tears after Spanish left the office. She tried her best to hold it, but a loud whine, like a newborn baby escaped. Bamena lifted her head slowly and stared at the monitors.

"You will die for what you did to my father!" Bamena said with trembling lips.

Bamena picked up the phone and dialed her manager, Pedro's number.

"Hello."

"I'm leaving, be sure to lock up when you leave."

"Not a problem, Boss, take care."

Spanish walked back over to Destiny and Dick's table.

"Are y'all down with the price?" Spanish asked, licking her lips. "We can use the house beside the club."

"We're trying to go back to our crib. We'll give you five hundred for the whole night." Destiny said, pulling out five one hundred dollar bills.

"Let me go change, I'll be ready in a minute. Pull in front of the club and wait for me." Spanish said, walking away, making her ass jiggle with each step.

Spanish quickly put on a skirt, tee shirt, brown shearling coat and Indian Timberland boots with wool around the top, then left out of the front door. Dick and Destiny were parked in front of the club waiting for her. They went straight to their house. Spanish made sure she remembered the address.

Dick poured them a cup of Hennessey, and then went to shower.

"Do you be getting checked for STD's?" Destiny asked.

"Every two weeks. I just got tested this week," Spanish said, pulling her results out of her pocketbook.

Destiny pulled Spanish's shirt over her head, and pulled her orange G-string and skirt down at the same time. Destiny then pulled her dress over her head. She was braless and pantyless.

"How about we go get this sweat off of us?" Destiny said, making her breasts touch Spanish's breasts.

Dick walked in the front room with no shirt on and gym shorts.

"Before we do, let's get in the game," Spanish said, going to her skirt pocket and pulling out three ecstasy pills.

Dick and Spanish took theirs with a chase of Hennessey.

"I don't know. I never fucked with them shits," Destiny said.

"Go ahead, baby, it won't kill you. If you don't like it, you don't have to do it again," Dick said, holding a pill out to her.

"Fuck it, give me the shit!" Destiny said, taking the pill and swallowing it. "Come on, Spanish, let's get this sweat off of us." Destiny said, guiding Spanish to the bathroom.

While Destiny and Spanish were in the shower, Dick went in the bedroom and popped another ecstasy pill to put him where he needed to be. He went to the door of the bathroom; Destiny was staring at Spanish's breasts. She grabbed a breast with one hand, and rubbed Spanish's clit with the other hand.

"Y'all coming out or what?" Dick said, rubbing the head of his dick through his shorts.

They dried off and went into the room. Dick moved the camcorder on them every step they took.

"All right, ladies, bend over and spread them."

Destiny and Spanish turned around and opened their ass cheeks, letting Dick zoom in on their ass and pussy holes. The ladies got on the bed so Dick could get the focus right. Destiny climbed on top of Spanish's face, with her pussy inches from her lips. Spanish jiggled her tongue on Destiny's clit. Destiny grabbed her breast, as a chill shot through her body. A hot sensation came right behind that, causing Destiny to move her pussy back and forth, with Spanish's licks. Dick slid his fingers in Spanish, then smelled his hand. He closed his eyes, slowly, got on his knees, spread Spanish's pussy lips open and watched her fat clit slide out. Dick slid two fingers back in and sucked on her clit.

Spanish jumped, sliding her tongue deeper inside of Destiny. The more Spanish moaned, the more she ate Destiny's pussy. Dick felt the other pill kicking in. He stood up, and stepped out of his shorts. Since Spanish was already to the edge of the bed, he slid half of his dick into her pussy. She moved on the half like she was salsa dancing. Dick pushed about four more inches in.

Spanish pushed Destiny off of her, and slid away from Dick.

"Hell no … what the fuck is that!" Spanish yelled, looking at Dick's dick.

"You wanted to know why they call me Dick. Now you know," Dick said, standing with his dick in his hand.

Spanish thought about what Bamena said about sending her back to Mexico, and slid back to the edge of the bed. Destiny got back on her face, and Dick went back up in her pussy. He fucked Spanish at a medium pace, with about ten of his twelve inches. All of them were feeling the ecstasy and moaning loud. Destiny felt herself cumming, she squeezed the headboard and moved her body faster. Spanish stuck her tongue in Destiny's pussy. She rode Spanish's tongue like a dick, letting her cum run down Spanish throat. Destiny slid down, rubbing her pussy all over Spanish breast. She slid off of Spanish, and licked her own wetness. That turned Dick on more, he slid the rest of his dick in Spanish and started giving her the dick.

"O … o … hurt … oh … oh it hurt!" Spanish moaned.

"Ride it!" Dick said, pulling out of Spanish.

"I can't, you're too big!" Spanish said, looking at his dick sticking straight up and curving to the left a little.

"Baby, show Spanish how to do it." Dick said, reaching for Destiny.

Destiny got on top of Dick, grabbed his dick, and slid down inch by inch, until about eleven inches was in. Spanish's eyes were bucked open, watching as Destiny took most of the dick. The pill had taken full effect; Spanish became turned on watching Dick and Destiny.

"Spa … nish … ah … lick … ah … and … tongue … my … ass … o … o!" Destiny said, riding Dick's dick.

Spanish had never licked, tasted, or tongue fucked any one's ass before, and never had it done to her. The pill had her wanting to try all kinds of shit. She got behind Destiny as she rode Dick's dick, she licked Destiny's ass every time she came down on his dick. When Destiny went up, she would lick Dick's balls. Destiny went up and down as Spanish shoved her tongue in Destiny's ass.

"Oo … shit … oooo … ooo!" Destiny moaned, cumming all over Dick's dick and balls.

Destiny lifted up, got between Dick's legs with Spanish and helped her lick her cum off of Dick.

Spanish climbed on Dick, grabbed his dick tightly with her manicured hand, put it at her pussy entrance, and slid down half way. "It won't work!" she screamed, feeling Dick stretch her pussy.

Dick grabbed Spanish's waist and went up in her real slow. Spanish screamed and cursed in Spanish. When almost eleven inches was in, Spanish grabbed her stomach and let out a scream. She leaned over on Dick's chest, letting Dick move in and out of her. Spanish felt her ass cheeks spread and Destiny start licking her ass.

"Oh shit!" Spanish screamed, feeling Destiny lick her ass, and then insert her tongue in it. "Damn … it … it's … good!" Spanish moaned. She started to grind on Dick's dick. Her eyes rolled back and she came all over Dick, speaking in Spanish.

"Keep working that dick!" Destiny said.

Spanish's stomach was killing her. She could barely move. She felt her ass cheeks being spread again. She thought Destiny was going to tongue her ass again until she felt a strange slippery object.

"Please, Destiny, no. I've … never … had … it back … there before," Spanish said, as Destiny pushed the head of the strap on into her ass. "Oh shit!" Spanish screamed.

Once Destiny got most of it in, she penetrated her softly. About two minutes of doing that, and Spanish reached back and spread her ass cheeks so Destiny could go deeper. Dick moved half of his dick in and out of her. Spanish rocked back and forth until she came out of both holes. Destiny came right behind Spanish, pulling on Spanish's hair. Dick still had not cum. He lifted Spanish off his dick and she flopped down on the bed. Destiny lay beside her with the strap on sticking straight up.

"Come ride it, baby," Destiny said.

It turned Spanish on to see a chick who favored Tatiana Ali, and had a bad body, with a strap on. She slid one leg over Destiny, lifted up, and slowly went all the way down on the rubber dick. As she went down, Destiny felt the dildo vibrating her pussy, causing her to meet Spanish as she rode the fake dick. Spanish bent over and slid her tongue in Destiny's mouth as Dick spread Spanish's cheeks open.

"Noo ... Dick ... nooo!" Spanish begged and moaned at the same time.

Dick slid the head into Spanish's asshole. Spanish dropped her mouth to Destiny's mouth, and sucked hard on her bottom lip. Dick pushed about three more inches in Spanish's ass; she dropped her face beside Destiny's ear, and moaned with a whine. Dick moved in and out of Spanish's ass, until he felt himself about to explode. Destiny moved in and out of Spanish's pussy fast, feeling herself about to cum again. Dick tried to pull out, but Spanish wanted him to cum, maybe it would be over. She squeezed her ass muscles tight, not letting him out. Dick and Destiny moaned, and yelled at the same time. Dick let his load off deep in Spanish's ass. They fell over beside each other, staring at the ceiling.

CHAPTER 18

*B*amena lay on her bed staring at the wall; it was time to get serious about her payback plans. She had over four and a half million in the bank, four hundred thousand in the basement, and three hundred thousand in her safe at the club. Bamena decided right then, that she was ready for war. The phone ringing took her out of her thoughts.

"Hello," Bamena answered.

"The pianos have arrived," one of the bodyguards said in Spanish.

"Twenty to S&J, be there at seven a.m."

"Ok, Boss."

"Make sure all three of y'all go."

"You got it, Boss."

Dayself woke up with Muffin's leg wrapped around him. He wondered why Piepie couldn't have wanted more out of life.

"Stop staring at me," Muffin said, turning over.

Dayself smacked Muffin on the ass. She turned back around and put him in the headlock.

"Stop, Day, I got to pee!" Muffin laughed as Dayself tickled her.

Dayself tried to put his dick in her, with them laying on their side. Muffin got up and ran to the bathroom.

"Boy, you need to come in here and brush your teeth. Breath smelling like liquor and shit," Muffin said, brushing her teeth.

"I know you ain't talking, Ms. Pickle Shit Breath," Dayself said, going into the bathroom to brush his teeth.

Dayself was checking his teeth out in the mirror when Muffin grabbed his hand and put it on her stomach. Dayself felt his little man kick.

"That's my boy. Show 'em what it do!" he said, smiling.

Dayself went downstairs to fix them some cereal.

"I want some fried chicken and an apple pie," Muffin announced, walking into the kitchen.

"It's five o'clock in the morning, and you're talking about chicken and pie? Fuck around, our baby gonna come out weighing seventy pounds."

"No he's not, because I drink Slim Fast every day, and I eat a lot of fruit."

"Then you eat five pickles, a quart of ice cream, and two whole chickens."

"Be quiet. I forgot, could you bring me my briefcase? We got the deal with Starbucks."

"That's what's up, now we have to find the buildings."

"It's already been taken care of. We only have to pay fifty percent when the store opens, and fifty percent at the end of the year, so we can see what our profits may be. We also own five more houses. Our agent sold the last one Tuesday to Lambo. Your money has been transferred to your account."

"Get it, big girl!" Dayself said, doing the two-step.

"Watch your mouth before I swing on you."

"I'm gone … I'm gone! Are you going to the office today?"

"Yes, I need to cover some things."

"Like what?"

"I'm opening up a clothing store in Raleigh that will be run by my cousin. I'm selling name brand women and baby clothes in the same store."

"Just as long as they're not knock offs. If they are, you and your cousin going to jail," Dayself said, laughing.

"Oh, honey, I have a contract with a major New York fashion buyer. Her partners are some of the world's top designers of women and children's clothing. My store will be exclusive because we will have the latest fashions before anyone else in Raleigh, hell, actually anyone else in North Carolina."

"Marry me!" Dayself yelled, falling to his knees.

"Don't play, boy!" Muffin said in a serious tone, laughed, then headed upstairs.

Dayself grabbed the keys to Muffin's Galant. While getting into the car, he said, "She got all that money in the bank, and she driving this shit." His phone rang as he started the car.

"Hello."

"Boy, bring my car!" Muffin screamed.

"Drive the Lexus, the keys are on the table."

"Don't have no bitches in my car. I'd hate to bust your shit!"

"Bye, gangsta big draws."

Dayself checked his messages. A couple of cats had called for weight. There was a message from Asia, telling him to call her. He dialed her number.

"Hello," Asia answered, sounding like she had been sleeping

"What's good?"

"Damn, you get up early."

"A hustler with ambition don't sleep much."

"I'm at the Comfort Inn, I need to see you."

"All right, meet me at the chill spot. You could've stayed at my crib last night."

"With these two bitches, I don't think so!"

"Who are you with?"

"Not Amaka!" Asia said quickly. "She would've blanked if I'd done that."

"Is she still in Jamaica?"

"Yeah, she's showing now. She done gained weight, I'll send you some pictures to your phone."

"I'll see you at the chill spot."

Dayself's phone beeped three times and a picture of Amaka appeared on the screen. She had her shirt lifted, with a fake tattoo on her stomach that said, "Lil Dayself," the next picture was of Amaka in an emerald green maxi dress looking down at her belly, and the third picture was from the back of Amaka walking through a field of purple ground orchids.

Asia and her friends were asleep in the truck when Dayself pulled up. He blew the horn, scaring them, and they got out of the truck. Asia opened the back of the truck and pulled out two tote bags.

Dayself felt the girls eyes on him. He had on his usual white tee, blue jeans, Timbs, and a yellow and black Pittsburgh pirate's jacket. Monique was dark skinned, about 26 years old, 5'9", 152 pounds, with long dreads. She had on some tight blue Seven jeans, a white leather coat with buckles, and white Louboutin heels. Keara was light skinned, about 24 years old, 5'8", 130 pounds. She had her hair cut on the side like Rhianna; she looked like a slimmer Faith Evans in her pink jean coat, tight Levi's, and pink and white Air Ones. Asia had on a black leather coat, blue Baby Phat jeans, and black heels.

"He got to be broke. This nigga got on all that cheap ass shit, and pull up in a damn Galant," Keara said, laughing.

"If I was broke, would you not want to come in my crib? Oh, I get it, you're one of them chicks, your nigga hold you down, he get knocked, go to prison, and you shit on him. I smell it on you," Dayself said, sniffing towards her.

Asia gave Keara a funny look to shut up.

"Damn, Keara, he seen right through your ass." Monique laughed as they walked in the chill spot.

Asia handed Dayself two bags. He went straight to the safe to lock them up.

"Day, Yellow said call him soon as your hand touch the bags." Asia yelled.

Dayself walked in the front room, dialing Yellow's number.

"Hello."

"What's good, old man?"

"Tell me something good, country boy."

"I got some new people. Give me a couple of days. It'll be worth the wait."

"I'll do that, are the girls still there?"

"Yeah."

"The dark skin one with dreads, that hardly talk …"

"Yeah?"

"When she's drunk, she's the total opposite. I seen her on tape smoking a cigar with her pussy, no hands attached."

"You're lying!"

"You can't do shit anyway, Asia will tell it on your ass."

"I gotta go, old man. Everybody is in my mouth."

"All right, peace."

"Peace."

"Call Castro over here," Asia said.

"You do it. He supposed to be on his way."

Five minutes later, Castro arrived. The girls stared at his dick print.

"This is Monique and Keara. Y'all, this is Dayself, and our baby, Castro," Asia said.

Asia started slapping her pussy, and then fanned it with her hand.

"What it do, y'all? What's wrong with you, chin chung?" Castro asked.

"My pussy got hot and started running and jumping when you walked in here!" Asia said, holding her pussy. "You put a root on my shit, boy!"

Everybody laughed at Asia. Keara bit her bottom lip and

looked at Castro, then at Dayself's dick print.

"I gave that to Boybaby," Castro said.

"All right, I'll call him later." Dayself said.

"After we smoke this, y'all taking me to IHOP in Rocky Mount, and take turns feeding me." Castro said, pulling out two bags of blue berry haze.

"The way Asia said you put it down, oh nigga you can get fed," Keara said.

"I gotta couple runs to make, I'll be back later." Dayself said.

"All right," Asia said, pulling Castro in front of her.

Dayself went and picked up Trent and Dirty. They parked at the club that used to be a grocery store, and walked the railroad tracks until they were in front of S&J. It was only six forty five. They knew it was best to arrive early so they could peep the scenery. Dayself called Boybaby.

"Hello," Boybaby answered with his CD playing in the background.

"Where you at?" Dayself asked, looking down the street. "Nevermind, I see you pulling up now. Don't look around, nigga, you won't see us. Soon as you get the other business straight, ask them can they get that boy, and how much."

"I'll do that, peace."

"Peace."

Boybaby pulled up at S&J, then a white van with a cross, and Jesus saves written on the side, pulled up beside him. Three men got out of the van in suits, with guitar cases in their hands. Dayself watched Boybaby get into the hooptie, and back it in. He got out and went into the building. One Mexican unloaded the money out of Boybaby's car, one counted the money, and the other one unloaded the keys of coke. They all looked the same, except one was a little taller than the other two.

Boybaby pulled out the tester, looking around for water. One Mexican stacked the coke in stacks of ten. Boybaby spotted the sink in the corner. He went to put water in the little test tube. The Mexicans stopped and watched him every step of the way there, reaching for their weapons.

After filling the tube, Boybaby walked back to the coke. Instead of checking every seventh one, he checked every third and seventh one. Each time, the water turned blue. Boybaby knew that they had some official shit. He and the Mexican counting the money looked at each other and smiled at the same time. Knowing that everything was good.

"How much for a key of heroin?" Boybaby asked after loading the last bag into the hooptie.

The Mexican stared at him, and then dialed a number, spoke in Spanish, and hung up. Two minutes later, his phone rang back. The Mexican kept saying, "Si … Si … Si …" Then hung up the phone. "Seventy thousand if you buy ten or more. Eighty-five if you buy anything under that. They can take a five step." The Mexican said, in broken English.

"All right, I'll get back with y'all on that," Boybaby said, getting into his car and sliding the small .25 from the sleeve of his Four Square snow jacket. He looked in the mirror to see if he was safe. The Mexicans had walked off, and left him at the site alone. Boybaby thought to himself, *Damn, Salita got pull, I gotta hit that.*

Boybaby headed to the stash spot. Trent, Dirty and Dayself pulled in the back of the cleaners, beside Boybaby's car. The family members of one of Dirty's white friends, who was down on their luck, ran the cleaners. They had been living on the streets in New York for two and a half years when Dirty gave them the cleaners, for a fifty/fifty split in profits. There was another building attached to the cleaners that the crew used as a stash house. The cleaners sat in front of the police station.

"The Mexican said seventy thousand if you buy ten or more. Eighty-five for anything under that. They can take a five step." Boybaby said after unloading the coke.

"Hold on, let me call Yellow," Dayself said, pulling his phone out and dialing Yellow's number.

"Hello," Yellow answered.

"I told you I had you. There's one thing, I need the money upfront. Three hundred and fifty thousand, they're going for seventy thousand a piece," Dayself said.

"Shit, I thought you were going to look out. I can go to the

Columbians; I'm just beginning not to trust them. Something doesn't seem right."

"Let me finish, you can step on them three to four times."

"No bullshit country boy?"

"I'll also front you five more that you can step on three to four times."

"You got a deal, country boy. The money will be there tomorrow, peace."

"By fronting Yellow the five and selling him five for what you paid for them, you won't be making anything," Boybaby said.

"Why won't we? I'll step on the ten one time, which will give us twenty keys of heroin. He's buying five for three hundred and fifty thousand, then I'm fronting him five. That's the three hundred fifty thousand we spent back, and we'll have ten keys left. That'll give us a seven hundred thousand dollar profit."

"So you're eating, while you let somebody else eat too," Boybaby said and smiled.

"So you remember?" Dayself asked, looking at Boybaby with pride. He recalled what he had told Boybaby one day when he wouldn't let any of his friends get weed money with him. "If they don't eat, you won't eat long. Let somebody eat with you." Dayself came out of his daydream. "Call your people and tell them we want ten of them thangs," Dayself said.

"I tried calling on the way here. Her phone is off."

Dayself went to check out the club and studio. The construction workers were putting the last wall to the booth up. Double L had announced the club's opening through flyers, the radio, Facebook, Mocospace, and Twitter that weekend. The security and bar had been taken care of.

After leaving the club, Dayself went to visit his grandmother. He pulled up in Mabee's yard, and got out of the car.

"Why are you doing that?" Dayself asked, watching his

grandmother rake the yard. "I could've paid somebody to do all that for you."

"I want to do it," Mabee said, raking up blunt guts.

"So what's going on with my favorite girl?" Dayself asked and kissed Mabee's cheek.

"Nothing, baby, I'm still having these bad dreams. You need to be careful out there. You still have money in this house that I haven't touched."

"I know. I'll leave it there for hard times."

"You need to stop spoiling your son so much. He has gotten to the point where he won't wear his clothes or shoes more than three times. He definitely don't have any business with a cell phone.

"I'll talk to him. You know I'm trying to make up for being gone out of his life for five years."

"He understands. All he needs is you here with him."

"I'll call you later. I love you," Dayself said, giving Mabee another kiss on the cheek.

"I love you too, baby."

After several tries, Boybaby was finally able to reach Bamena.

"Hello." Bamena answered in a stressed tone.

"What's wrong, bae?"

"Nothing, and you haven't earned the privilege to call me bae."

"You mad today?"

"No, just got something on my mind."

"Wanna talk about it? Thinking of talk, you turned your phone off on me last night."

"My phone went dead, I didn't know until I checked it," Bamena lied as she leaned back in her office chair.

"Word. Tell your people we want ten of that boy, ASAP."

"I'll hit you right back," Bamena said, hanging up in Boybaby's ear. She dialed Bonito's number.

"Hello." Bonito answered. He was in the tub being washed by two beautiful Mexican women.

"Cousin, I need ten of that boy on face. You'll get your money two or three days, tops," Bamena said.

"I'm not worried about the money. It could be yours, if you come up here. Until you do, I gotta charge you forty thousand a piece for them, and that's because you're family."

"Thank you so much, Bonito."

"That's what family is for. It'll arrive tomorrow night."

Bamena called Boybaby back.

"They said Wednesday morning, same spot, at eight o'clock."

"That will work … I …"

"I'll call you later."

Boybaby looked at his phone, shook his head, and laid it down on the table.

Bamena continued to count the club money until the sensors at her door beeped and the camera zoomed in on Spanish standing at the door wiping tears from her eyes. Bamena buzzed her in. Spanish limped in. Bamena already knew what had happened; she'd had the same limp before.

"Have a seat," Bamena said.

"No thanks, I'll stand." Spanish said, handing Bamena Dick and Destiny's information.

"Thank you, Spanish, you don't know how much this means to me," Bamena said, with tears in her eyes, "Take two days off to get yourself together." Bamena said and handed Spanish two thousand dollars.

"Thanks, Boss, I'm forever loyal to you for giving me a job and keeping me here in America," Spanish said, with tears in her eyes and limped out of the office.

Bamena watched Spanish walk out of the club through the monitors. Soon as Spanish was out of sight, she called the bodyguards.

"Y'all meet me at the stash house, now!"

Bamena drove up to the stash house in her black 2001 Dodge Shadow, almost hitting the house. She jumped out of the car, and ran in.

"I want y'all to go to this address tonight and bring me the two people that live there!" Bamena said, handing her guards the address.

"Here, Boss?"

"Yes, here. That way, nobody will hear them scream."

"All right, you're the boss," one of the bodyguards said.

The Mexican bodyguards left immediately and headed to Destiny's house. They sat across the street for half an hour, trying to figure out how to get in. Finally, the two of them came up with a plan.

Spanish called Destiny's phone.

"Hello," Destiny answered.

"This is Spanish. Could you go and see if I left my keys in the truck?"

"Damn, baby, you coming back tonight?" Destiny asked, walking to the truck.

"Yes, come and get me. Y'all be gentle this time, okay?"

"Baby, you know you …"

One of the bodyguards hit Destiny in the back of the head with his gun, knocking her out cold. He picked her up and carried her to the van. The other two guards went through the cracked door. Dick was asleep on the couch. One of the Mexicans tapped him on the shoulder. Thinking it was Destiny, Dick sleepily pushed the hand away. The Mexican guard slapped him in his forehead. Dick sat up to the sight of two Mexicans pointing Glock .40's at him. He tried to jump up, and was knocked back down by a bullet to his shoulder. The guards turned Dick over and handcuffed him. He tried to kick, but one of the Mexican guards tasered both of his thighs, then carried him to the van.

Boybaby picked Bamena up at seven thirty and took her to IHOP to eat. Bamena was quiet and picked through her food.

"Are you all right?" Boybaby asked.

"No, I don't feel too good."

"What's the matter?" Boybaby asked, chewing on his hot wings.

"My stomach is killing me."

"Let's leave then!"

Boybaby paid for the food and they walked out of the restaurant.

The ride back to Bamena's house was silent. When they pulled in front of Bamena's house, she reached over and tongue kissed Boybaby until she felt a tingle between her legs.

"I'll see you tomorrow," Bamena said, removing her arms from around Boybaby.

"Okay, can I have another kiss?" Boybaby asked and poked out his lips.

"Bye, Boybaby," Bamena said, stepping out of the car smiling.

Boybaby watched her go in the house, and then drove off. Once he was out of sight, Bamena opened the door back up, ran, and jumped into her car, headed for the stash house. She walked in and Destiny sat there naked, handcuffed and taped to a chair. Dick had on jeans, no shirt or shoes, bleeding out his shoulder, chained and taped to another chair.

"Hey, Dick and Destiny," Bamena said.

"Bitch, I knew I should've killed you!" Dick yelled.

"Do you have anything to say, Destiny?" Bamena asked, laughing at Dick.

"Don't do this, I let you live!" Destiny said.

"Bitch, after you violated me! I got a little surprise for you this time, though!" Bamena yelled, squeezing Destiny's chin. Bamena walked out of the room to call Spanish.

"Hello." Spanish answered. She was in the tub, soaking for the third time that day.

"Come to the old whorehouse ASAP. I have two people I want you to meet."

"Them motherfuckers! I'm on my way!"

Ten minutes later, Spanish arrived limping, with a tape city bag in her hand.

"Y'all really damaged me last night," Spanish said, walking in the room, seeing Dick and Destiny tied up. "The doctor said it'll be hard for me to have kids!"

"I can't believe I let a fucking hooker set me up!" Dick said.

"Yeah, I did. Y'all didn't have to do me like that!" Spanish said.

"Bitch, you liked it!" Destiny yelled.

"Give me the names of the people that were involved in killing my father!" Bamena yelled over everyone.

Dick and Destiny became quiet. Spanish walked up to Dick, unbuttoned his pants, and pulled his dick out. Bamena and her bodyguard's eyes grew big. They looked at Spanish's ass, and then started speaking in Spanish.

"Destiny, you're going to miss this dick!" Spanish said, holding Dick's dick.

Bamena called Spanish over to her and whispered in her ear. They walked out of the room together. About five minutes later, Bamena walked back in the room, staring Destiny in her eyes. Dick sat there weak from the gunshot wound.

"Put her on the floor," Bamena said.

"No … no!" Destiny yelled, trying to crawl away.

The bodyguard kicked her back to the floor. Dick was hurt; there was nothing he could do to help.

"Does this scenery look familiar, guys?" Bamena asked. "Spanish, come on in."

"Dick, you've got a big dick, but I got a bigger one," Spanish said, holding on to a thirteen-inch strap on dildo.

"Please don't do this!" Destiny cried, looking up at the dildo.

Dick tried to get free, but he was growing weaker from the

gunshot wound. The strap on was big and round like a baby bottle.

"You can handle it, big girl," Spanish said, rubbing baby oil on the dildo.

"Who else was involved?" Bamena asked again.

"Fuck you, bitch!" Dick yelled. "Destiny, don't tell them shit. They're still going to kill us!"

"Shut the fuck up, if you're not going to talk." Bamena yelled and pointed at Dick.

"Bitch, I breathe this shit!" Dick yelled with spit flying. "You ain't getting shit out of me! It's Double L 'til my casket drop!"

Bamena nodded at one of the bodyguards. The tallest one took a machete out of the corner, drew back, and swung with all his power, cutting Dick's whole head off. His head rolled by Destiny's face and stopped, standing up on its neck, pouring blood. Dick's eyes were wide open, staring into Destiny's eyes. She screamed and cried out of control. The guards untied Dick's body and sat him in the corner. One of the guard's picked Dick's head up and put it in a bag.

"Who were they?" Bamena asked.

Destiny lay there in shock, not hearing anything Bamena was saying. Her eyes were stuck on Dick.

"I gotta piss!" Spanish said, limping towards Dick's headless body.

"Leave him alone!" Destiny yelled. "Get up Dick, she's coming over there!"

Spanish turned around, pulled the string hooked to the strap on to the side, sat on Dick's neck, and pissed down his throat. She got up with blood and piss smeared on her pussy lips and butt cheeks. Spanish squatted over Destiny and rubbed it all over her face.

Bamena wanted to throw up. She held it in with all the energy she had.

Spanish lifted up, laughing. Growing up in Mexico, she was used to people dying, and headless bodies.

"Who were the others?" Bamena asked again.

Destiny laid on the floor, staring at Dick's body, in shock.

"Spanish, she's all yours," Bamena said.

Spanish opened Destiny's legs without a fight. Destiny knew she was going to die. She was ready to join Dick. Spanish pushed a little of the dildo into Destiny's pussy. Destiny gritted her teeth hard, with tears running down her face. Spanish slammed most of the dildo into Destiny, splitting her pussy half way to her asshole. She let out a loud scream. Spanish fucked her hard, as blood ran out of her womb. Destiny fainted, and Spanish kept right on fucking her.

"All right, Spanish, stop!" Bamena yelled. "Can't you see she's out?"

Spanish got up, looking like she was just about to cum. The bodyguard poured ice cold water on Destiny, bringing her back to consciousness. She lay still, with her eyes closed, breathing hard, hoping that when she opened them this would all be a bad dream. Destiny opened her eyes to see Dick's headless body still sitting in the corner.

"Dick ... Dick, baby ... get up baby ... get ... up!" Destiny screamed.

"Who were they?" Bamena yelled.

Destiny still lay on the floor, staring at Dick's body in shock.

"Flip her over!" Bamena said to the bodyguards.

Bamena looked at Spanish and nodded. Spanish got behind Destiny with blood and clumps of meat still on the dildo. Spanish forced the head of the dildo into Destiny's ass. Destiny yelled and beat her head on the floor. Spanish pushed the dildo half way in, and felt something pop. Destiny's asshole split to meet the other split from her pussy. She bled badly out of both holes. The strap on had shit and blood all over it.

"Who were they?" Bamena yelled.

Destiny still wouldn't answer. Spanish slammed the dildo back into Destiny.

"Day ..." Destiny said, passing out.

"They what ... They what!" Bamena yelled. Seeing Destiny out cold, she pulled Spanish off her.

The Mexican guards, poured water on Destiny, but she never

regained consciousness. Spanish stood there with sweat, blood, and shit all over her.

"If I don't find out who was behind the death of my father, you will die the same way." Bamena said angrily to Spanish.

Bamena placed the latex gloves on, walked over to Dick's body, and cut his dick off. She took his head out of the plastic bag, pushed his dick in his mouth, and pushed the other end in Destiny's pussy.

"That's how I want them found!" Bamena said, walking out of the stash house.

CHAPTER 19

*Y*ellow had the runner to drop the money off at the chill spot. Dayself counted the money up along with his, to be boxed up for Boybaby.

Boybaby knocked on the chill spot door at 6:30 a.m. Dayself opened the door and smiled at his protégé.

"Early bird gets the worm." Boybaby repeated what Dayself had taught him.

"I see you still hungry," Dayself said as he let him in. "I wanna thank you for the plug. You really came through for the team. The spot over east has slowed down. Lil man is not handling his business like he's supposed to. I'm going to put his ass in the studio to make beats, since he's good at that. I'm giving you the spot as a gift for keeping the crew eating. All I want you to do is cop from me. I know you're like why would you cop from me, when you can just fuck with the connect. By me backing you, it'll make you bulletproof over there. I'll charge you the price I get them for. Another month, I plan to be out of the game. The spot is yours, and the one over Southern Terrance."

"What about Dirty and Trent?"

"They'll be out of the game too. I'm giving Castro the other spots."

"That's what's up. No homo, I love you for being you."

"Y'all can put y'all money together and buy anything y'all want. Y'all young niggas straight. I have taught you since you were eight. I didn't come around you when I got out, because I wanted to see how your mind had grown, with me trying to enlighten you from behind the walls. You're ready now. I see the fire in you."

"I won't let you down."

"I know, that's why I'm giving them to you," Dayself said as his stomach growled. "Let's make this move, I'm hungry."

Dayself met Trent and Dirty on the tracks in front of S&J again.

"I hope this don't take long. I'm sleepy, and it's cold out here," Trent said, rubbing his hands together and pulling his NorthFace tight.

"Damn, sun, we all are, but we gotta get this shit so we can retire at a young age. In another month, you can sleep all you want," Dayself said.

"The van is pulling up now," Dirty said, staring at S&J.

Boybaby backed in about two minutes later, and everyone was gone in thirty-five minutes.

Dayself stopped by Curt's house to pick him up.

Shawn stuck his head out the door and snatched his head back in fast when he saw Dayself. Curt pushed Shawn out the way, and pimped to the car.

"What's good, young blood?"

"Can you ride with me for a minute?"

"Let's ride," Curt said, getting into the car. "I'm not doing shit anyway."

Dayself noticed that Curt had stepped his appearance up. He had on a brown coat by Andrew Marc, green sweater by Calvin Klein, brown Kenneth Cole dress pants, and brown dress shoes by Kenneth Cole. They rode and talked all the way to the hiding spot.

"You be careful out here, young blood." Curt said, wrapping the last key of heroin. "Sometimes you gotta accept what you have and live with it. I have seen plenty of babies don't know when they're full, and throw everything back up," Curt said, chewing on his toothpick.

"A month tops, and it's over for me. Then we're going to pimp straight dime piece white girls."

Curt laughed like his chest hurt.

"Young blood, drop me off over Tabia's crib, I know she need a hit this morning."

"Bet. Let's go."

Fifteen minutes later, Dayself pulled up in front of the crack house.

"Remember what I told you, young blood," Curt said, getting out of the car.

Dayself's phone started to ring.

"Have you seen my sister?" Amaka asked.

"Not since yesterday, I think they're over Castro's house."

"Where did those girls stay the other night?"

"Not at my crib. Where you at?"

"I was going home to New York, but when I called Asia she was down there, so I caught a plane to Raleigh airport."

"I thought you were staying in Jamaica until you have the baby."

"I was, but grandma is into the voodoo shit too bad. It was scaring the shit out of me."

"You didn't bring any of that shit back home with you, did you?"

"No, but she did say if you don't do right by her first and only great grandbaby, she was going to get you."

"Word up!"

"I'm just playing," Amaka said laughing.

"I'll be there in an hour."

Dayself did everything in the dash of his Lexus, the whole way to Raleigh. He got to the airport in thirty-five minutes. Dayself walked in the airport and started laughing. Amaka was sitting down eating a Reese's cup on top of a honey bun, licking her fingers. She saw Dayself and hopped up. Amaka ran to Dayself and gave him a big kiss, letting him taste the sweets on her tongue.

"Let's go. That's how I ended up like this," Amaka said, walking off rubbing her stomach.

On the way back, Dayself dialed Dirty's number.

"Radio."

"Have you heard from Dick and Destiny?"

"Nope."

"They haven't been answering their phone. I'm going to swing by there to check on them."

"Ain't no telling what those two freaks are up to."

"Call the runner and meet him at the spot with my son."

"All right, peace, partner."

"Peace."

"You want to ride with me to check on my people?" Dayself asked.

"Do I have a choice?" Amaka responded. "Don't you get to Rocky Mount before you get to Tarboro?"

"Yeah."

"I'm riding with you then."

"You got a smart mouth today."

Dayself reached over and rubbed Amaka's pussy through her jeans. She closed her eyes, and bit her bottom lip.

"I gotta do something about that heat down there," Dayself said.

"You sure do. I'm ready this time," Amaka said. "Let me call my sister and tell her you picked me up. I should let her ass drive all the way there, for being late."

The garage was up, with Dick's truck door open when Dayself and Amaka pulled up in Destiny's driveway. Dayself got out of the car and saw a blood trail leading to the house. The front door was slightly ajar. He went back to the car, went in his secret compartment and pulled out his Glock .40.

"Turn the car facing the street, and keep the car running. Don't get out of the car," Dayself said, cocking his gun back.

"What's going on?"

"I'm about to find out. I'll be back."

Dayself pushed the door open slowly, calling Dick and Destiny's name. Dayself followed the blood trail all the way to Destiny's bedroom. He pushed the door open and couldn't believe his eyes. Dick's body lay beside Destiny. His head was cut off, with his dick in his mouth, and the other end was in her pussy. Dayself called Dirty immediately.

"Radio."

"This is some crazy shit, come to Destiny's crib now."

"The runner just leaving, we're on our way."

Dayself heard a noise behind him. He swung around with the gun pointed. Amaka stood there with her hand to her chest.

"Didn't I tell you to stay in the damn car?" Dayself yelled, walking toward Amaka as she tried to look around him.

"I thought you were —" She screamed, ran out the house, jumped in the car, and locked the doors.

Dayself called her name over and over before she unlocked the door.

"Didn't I tell you to stay in the car?" Dayself said, sitting in the driver seat.

"It took you too long. I thought something happened to you," Amaka cried, opening the door and throwing up on the pavement.

"Stay here, I gotta wait on Dirty and Trent." He patted her back and put the gun in her lap as Dirty and Trent pulled up.

"What's going on?" Dirty asked, jumping out the car with his gun out.

"Y'all follow me." Dayself said, walking into Destiny's house.

They walked into the house, looking down at the blood trail that led them to Destiny's room.

"Got damn!" Trent said.

"I stopped by to check on them. This is what I found."

"Somebody gotta answer to this shit!" Trent said, angrily.

"They will, believe that!" Dirty said, looking at Dick and

Destiny. "Here, put these latex gloves on. We gotta find the money and guns."

Trent noticed the camcorder was set up. He pressed play, and moaning and screaming came through the surround sound speakers. Dirty and Dayself stopped and looked at the screen. Dick and Destiny were having a threesome with a Spanish chick. Trent forwarded it the video to the end. There was nothing up there.

"Look at the date, this was the other night," Dirty said.

"Take the camera. If we find her, she might be able to tell us something." Dayself said.

Dayself checked the closet in their room. He felt around, until he found the slant installed in the same place his was at the chill spot. Dayself pushed the slant, and it opened to reveal two shopping bags with money in them, and a bag of guns.

"I got the money, let's get the fuck out of here!" Dayself said, stuffing the guns in one of the bags with the money. "Look at this shit. I tell them to invest; instead, they got all this money in one spot. Y'all meet me at the stash spot. I gotta drop Amaka off at the chill spot first," Dayself said, handing Dirty and Trent the bags.

"Take me to my sister at Castro's house," Amaka cried when Dayself got into the car. "I should've listened to Grandma. She told me not to come, that there was trouble in the air. I had tried to tell you so many times, that I don't want that to be you!"

"It won't happen to me." Dayself said, driving off.

"How do you know?"

Dayself became quiet.

"I can't take this! When I saw them, all I could think about was seeing my mother and father lying in a puddle of blood!" Amaka cried, answering her phone.

"Sis, I'll be at the chill spot."

"Okay."

When Asia saw Dayself's car, she jumped out of her truck and ran to the car.

"What happened?" Asia asked.

Dayself gave them the house key, and drove off to the stash spot.

Dirty and Trent were passing a bottle of gin around, smoking some O.G. Kush, when Dayself walked into the stash house.

"Who could have done that shit to them?" Dirty asked.

"They couldn't have been trying to rob them; there were about eight gees on the kitchen table. It had to be somebody that got money. Something will come up, and then we'll punish their ass the same way."

Dayself, Dirty, and Trent counted the money with the money machine. It was six hundred and thirty five thousand dollars.

Dayself knew Dick had another stash spot. He always talked about burying his money. Dayself took two hundred thousand out for Dick's sister. She was in her last year at Tarboro high school. They took thirty five thousand out for both funerals.

"I just remembered, Dick said he want to be cremated." Trent said.

"We'll just place his ashes in an urn, and put it in Destiny's casket," Dirty said.

Dayself, Dirty, and Trent split the rest of the money.

"Let's go home, Asia!" Amaka begged. "I can't stay down here around this shit!"

"Dayself won't let anything happen to you!" Asia said.

"Daddy said that too, and look what happened." Amaka yelled. "Just take me to the airport. I'll catch a plane back! If you don't, I'll call a cab!"

"All right, Amaka! I really do think that you're overreacting!"

"Overreacting!" Amaka yelled. "I saw a man with his head cut off, his dick in his mouth, and the other end stuffed inside a dead woman's pussy! How the hell am I supposed to act? Come on, Asia, think!"

"Let's go. Y'all are lucky that I love y'all," Asia said and rubbed Amaka's stomach.

"We love you too, sis, but I have to protect me and my baby."

Boybaby put two young guys, Antrail and Skip, from the Double L in charge of his spot in East Tarboro. Since he had the spot, he had free time to chill and open up other businesses, but he was a rapper at heart. He turned the CD up and rapped along with his demo. "I'ma get this cake 'til Betty Crocker resurrect/stay strap with the sound proof teck/just in case a nigga run up on me/ so I can send you back where you belong homie."

Boybaby's phone vibrated in his lap.

"Hello."

"Boy, turn that down!" Bamena yelled.

"My bad, what's good, Salita?"

"I have something for you, can you come by today?"

"I'm around your way now."

"Why are you out and about so early?"

"I'm riding around looking for old cars."

"Why?"

"I restore them with rims and all, then sell them for twice as much as I put into them. I already have a paint shop, and I just bought a mechanic shop, now I'll make three times as much."

"That's a nice hustle. Can you come through?"

"Yeah, I'm on my way."

Boybaby rang Bamena's doorbell five times, and got no answer. Bamena finally came to the door.

"I'm sorry, I just got out of the shower, and Nana went to the grocery store. Come in, I didn't know that you were so close," Bamena said.

It's cool." Boybaby said, staring at her red Victoria Secret nightgown that came to her thighs and her wet hair. Boybaby gave her a hug, and smelled the apple body lotion he had given her. "You can come up to my room."

Boybaby followed Bamena, watching her ass every step they took. Bamena's bed was shaped like a heart, with hot pink and white bed sheets, a trimmed in pink 43" Plasma TV on the wall, white dresser, with a big heart shaped mirror, and a hot pink and white leather chair sitting in the corner.

Boybaby sat on the bed, watching Bamena bend over in the closet. She came out with a Footlocker bag and handed it to him

"What's this?" Boybaby asked.

"It's fifty thousand dollars. My uncle sends it to you as a thank you, for bringing him business. He knew that you wasn't buying for yourself. He said that he looks forward to doing business with you in the future."

"Thank you, Salita, I wanna give you half."

"Don't worry, he already straightened me out."

"Girl, you sound like the mob." They laughed.

Boybaby dropped the bag and kissed her. Bamena felt her panties become damp. He pulled her straps off her shoulders; the gown fell to the floor. Bamena stood there in a red thong. Boybaby took a step back, looking at her body as Bamena dropped her head shyly.

Boybaby walked up to Bamena, pulling his shirt over his head. He let his lips softly tough hers. Boybaby gently rubbed Bamena's nipples, causing her to flinch. It was a feeling she had never felt. Her breasts were small, with large nipples. Boybaby leaned down and sucked on Bamena's right nipple, while backing her on to the bed. Bamena closed her eyes to the good feeling. Boybaby ran his hand under Bamena's thong, and tried to push his finger in her pussy, but only the tip would go inside. He pushed harder and Bamena jumped and slid away.

"Why didn't you tell me?" Boybaby asked, staring into her eyes.

"Just finish what you started, please!" Bamena said, staring back into his eyes.

Boybaby slid down, pulling Bamena's thong off. She had a panty line cut, and her hairs were slicked down like they had been greased. Boybaby lay on top of Bamena and kissed her softly. He kissed down to her pussy. Boybaby rubbed the hairs on her pussy, and then opened her pussy lips. The feeling of Bamena's clit coming out made her bite on her bottom lip. Boybaby licked Bamena's clit like a snake. He went in circles around her clit with his tongue.

Wrapping his lips around her clit, Boybaby sucked on it like candy. Bamena's whole body trembled. He could hear her teeth hitting together, as she moaned and came all over the sheets.

Boybaby came up and kissed Bamena. She could taste her pussy juice on his tongue and lips. He lifted up, and removed his shoes, pants, then his boxers. Bamena let out a sigh of relief that he wasn't like the one she had cut off the other night. Bamena had a scared look, thinking about the eight inches that had to go in her. Boybaby got between Bamena's legs, and slowly tried to push his dick in her pussy, but it wouldn't go in. He rubbed his dick up and down her slit, coating it with her juices. Finally, Boybaby pushed into her, gritting his teeth as the head popped in.

"Boy … it … hurt … it … hurt!" Bamena moaned and screamed.

"You want me to stop?" Boybaby asked, sliding the head out.

"No … finish!" Bamena moaned, wrapping her arms around Boybaby, holding him there.

Boybaby pushed about two inches in, and Bamena's wall came down.

"It's in … oh … oh … it's in!" Bamena screamed, squeezing him tight.

Boybaby went in inch by inch, until it all was in. They lay there staring into each other's eyes. Boybaby moved in and out of Bamena slowly. He could feel her pussy molding just for his dick. He sped up just a little. Bamena squeezed him tighter, and he sexed her like that for ten minutes. Bamena's pussy muscles tightened around Boybaby's dick. Boybaby felt himself cumming, and he tried not to fuck Bamena hard, but he just couldn't help it. Bamena's tight, wet, and warm pussy was driving him crazy. He moved in and out of her with speed. She looked up at him with her mouth wide open.

"Boy … ba … ba … ba …!" Bamena screamed, cumming all over Boybaby's dick and the sheets.

"I'm cumming too, bae … o … shit!" Boybaby moaned as he came.

Breathing hard, they lay on the bed holding each other, not wanting to break the mood.

"Where's the bathroom?" Boybaby asked.

"As soon as you go out the room, to your left."

Bamena got up feeling like something was still sticking in her pussy. She looked at the sheets, and saw the spots of blood and cum. Bamena grabbed the sheets, wrapped them up, and threw them in her closet. Bamena went to the bathroom, and found Boybaby cleaning up with baby wipes. She turned the shower on.

"Can I join you?" Boybaby asked, taking off his socks.

"I don't care," Bamena said in an innocent voice.

Bamena winced as she raised her leg to step into the shower. Boybaby sat her down on the toilet lid, turned the shower off, and ran her some bubbles in the tub.

"You don't have to do that for me," Bamena said.

"Let your King take care of his Queen."

Boybaby lifted Bamena up, and put her in the tub. Bamena closed her eyes and enjoyed the warmth of the water, as Boybaby grabbed the sponge and washed her body in circles.

CHAPTER 20

The grand opening of Club IMPRINT had finally arrived. All ladies wearing anything sheer, without a bra or thong got in free. The club was jammed packed. Ballers from all across North Carolina were in the VIP section popping bottles. There were two floors; upstairs played reggae all night, and downstairs played hip-hop and R&B music. The seating area was comfortable, with booth seating and tables. Waitresses lingered in the area, ready to serve the patrons.

The dance floor was packed. Yo Gotti, and 2 Chainz hit the stage and the crowd went crazy. They sold all six hundred Dirty Water mix CDs for ten dollars a CD, from the Double L label. The club jumped so hard, after the last song played, people still stood in the club talking. Security had to tell them to leave. After the club cleared out, Trent and Dirty went to Dayself's office.

"You did it, boy!" Trent said excited. "This is the hottest club in eastern North Carolina. I know y'all ain't ready to turn in yet. Let's go to Megos in Wilson. I heard that shit is bananas."

"We can go check it out," Dayself said.

Trent, Dirty, and Dayself walked into Club Megos and everyone showed them love. They ordered three double shots of Hennessy. Strippers were everywhere. Three came to their table and gave them lap dances. Spanish sat on Dayself's lap. She had on a silver bra and G-string, long silver eyelashes, and her long black hair hung down her back. She danced and rubbed on Dayself's dick, and then switched positions, facing him. Spanish looked very familiar to Dayself, he just couldn't place her.

"Don't I know you from somewhere?" Dayself asked.

"No, I don't think so, papi," Spanish said, still grinding on Dayself's dick.

"What's your name?"

"Spanish, and yours?"

"Dayself."

Spanish turned back around the other way, put Dayself's hand on her pussy, and bent over. Dayself saw a tattoo of some pussy lips, with a sombrero hat on top of it, on the side of her ass. He lifted Spanish's G-string and slid his finger in her pussy. Dayself pulled his finger and smelled it. He almost gagged; Spanish's pussy had a strong fish odor that had been covered in perfume.

"Here you go, I'm good," Dayself said, handing her two dollars.

"You can put more than your finger in there for the right price."

"I'm good, baby girl, take better care of yourself."

"What's that supposed to mean?" Spanish asked with attitude, looking at him with her hand on her hips.

"You'll figure it out in due time."

Spanish walked away feeling embarrassed. It was the third time that night she had offered pussy and was turned down.

Dirty, Dayself, and Trent bought two more drinks, then left. Dayself hadn't said a word since his encounter with Spanish.

"What's troubling you, partner?" Dirty asked.

"The Spanish chick looks real familiar,"

"It's probably one of the chicks you done fucked," Dirty said.

"Naw, partner, I would remember her, bad as her pussy stink."

"You're bullshitting!" Trent laughed.

"I'm for real, nigga!" Dayself laughed. "Y'all drop me off at Shay-Shay's crib."

They got back to Princeville and Dayself called Shay-Shay.

"Hello." She answered half asleep.

"Come open the door, I'm staying the night."

"It's four fifty seven in the morning, so I guess you're staying the morning."

"Girl, come open the door!"

"I'm at the door!"

Dayself walked on the porch, Shay-Shay had the door cracked, peeping out.

"Move out of the way, your scary ass."

"I'm not scared. I thought your ass was high, playing again." Shay-Shay said, walking back to her room, in big grandma bloomers, no shirt or bra, and tweety bird slippers.

Dayself slapped Shay-Shay on her ass, as he walked behind her to the room.

"Stop, Dayself, it's too early to be playing!" Shay-Shay screamed.

"You're giving me some ass. I don't care how early it is."

"You gotta eat it first," Shay-Shay said, stepping out of her bloomers. She lay on the bed and opened her legs.

Dayself got between Shay-Shay's legs and opened her pussy lips, licking the wetness up. He sucked on her clit, making her jump as he flicked his tongue back and forth over her clit for three minutes.

"Here it comes … oh … shit!" Shay-Shay moaned. She came in Dayself's mouth, pulling his head to her pussy. After Shay-Shay came, she let his head go and started snoring like she was asleep.

"Yo, stop playing!" Dayself said as Shay-Shay dropped her legs down flat and continued snoring. "That's fucked up!"

"Payback is a bitch!" She laughed.

Shay-Shay finally fell asleep, and Dayself lay next to her, trying to remember where he knew the Spanish chick at Megos from. He closed his eyes, dozed off to sleep, and began to dream.

Dick walked up, in all white fatigues, and said, "Dayself, be careful. She fucks well, but lies better."

"Dayself, get up, get up baby!" Shay-Shay said shaking him.

Dayself woke up, frantically looking around for Dick.

"What time is it?" Dayself asked.

"It's eleven thirty. Why did you keep asking, 'which one, Dick?' were you dreaming about him?"

"Yeah, that shit was crazy."

"Have the police found who killed them?"

"No, we haven't either."

"Do you want some breakfast?"

"Yeah, run me some bath water too."

"You don't have any boxers here, unless you're going to free ball."

"You always got some crazy shit to say. I know our baby is going to be something else."

"Bitch, she might be, bitch she might be!" Shay-Shay danced.

"Don't let Gucci Mane get your ass tore up."

On the way to the chill spot to shower, what Dick said kept playing in Dayself's head. After taking his shower, he took some of the money out of his safe, and spotted the DVD that they took from Destiny's house. Dayself got dressed and put the DVD in. He could hear the chick speaking in Spanish. She faced the camera, and Dayself stood there shocked when he saw Dick eating Spanish's pussy.

"Damn, my nigga, you go hard." Dayself said, thinking about how her pussy smelled.

Dayself forwarded the video to where Spanish was leaning over with Dick's dick in her pussy. Her tattoo was plain as day. Dayself called Dirty.

"I know you ain't still in the bed?"

"Yeah man, what?"

"The chick from Megos, I know where I know her from."

"Where?"

"On the tape with Dick and Destiny."

"How do you know it's her?"
"The face and the tattoo on her ass."
"That's your word."
"I said it, didn't I?"
"We gotta question her ass."
"All right, let me call Trent."
"I'm getting up now, peace."
"Peace."

CHAPTER 21

$\mathcal{B}$amena had been spending most of her time with Boybaby, and hadn't been to the club in a week and a half. She had tried to call and check in at the club late the night before, and got no answer. Bamena picked up the phone to call Pedro's house.

"Hello." Pedro answered.

"Why didn't anyone answer the phone last night?" Bamena asked.

"Boss, we were short. I had to help out behind the bar."

"If anyone asks, or try to go to my office, you're the boss. You got that?"

"Yes, I got it, Boss."

"I'll talk to you later, bye."

"Bye." Pedro said and hung up.

Bamena dialed Bonito's number.

"Hello." Bonito answered.

"Hey family, how are you?" Bamena asked.

"What's happening, little cousin?"

"I need one hundred thousand more roller blades."

"They'll be dropped off tomorrow. I see that you're handling your business."

"I'm trying to. I might as well go ahead and get thirty of the soft (kilos of cocaine) too."

"I can manage that. You know this is a dirty game for a woman. Hurry up, get yours, and get out of the game. Open up a couple of businesses or something."

"I'm handling that today."

"I'll be back down that way to see you next weekend. I want to freak that girl, Spanish."

"You don't want her. I got this black chick named Kia that you'll love."

"How is she?"

"I don't know!" Bamena yelled. "I hear her vagina stays like a virgin, regardless of what goes in her."

"Yeah, hook that up!"

"She's all yours, bye cousin."

"Bye."

Bamena then called this Spanish chick named Sabina that she had gone to school with. Sabina had to drop out of school to support her twin sisters. Their mother and father kept the garden cleaned for a Colombian family, and another Colombian family that wanted to take over their drug line killed them. Bamena tried to get Sabina to work in the clubs, but she would rather work in the fields. In school, she always talked about cooking. Sabina was about twenty-one years old, 5'5", 135 pounds, long black hair, and hazel brown eyes.

"Hello." a female answered.

"May I speak with Sabina?"

"This is she."

"This is Bamena. I promised I would call if something came up. I'm opening a Mexican restaurant in Princeville at the old S&J store. Are you and your family still interested in the job?"

"Yes!" Sabina almost yelled.

"It'll be complete in another week. I'll give y'all a call about when to start."

"Okay, and Bamena, thank you so much!" Sabina said excitedly.

"You're welcome, bye."

"Bye."

Bamena made her last call to an Arab she met at a jewelry auction in Raleigh

"Mr. Muhammad?"

"Yes, speaking."

"This is Bamena, the girl from the auction in Raleigh."

"Oh yes, how are you?"

"I'm fine. I'm calling to see if you're still trying to open up the jewelry store in Golden East Crossing Mall, in Rocky Mount."

"Yes, but I still haven't found a fifty percent investor yet."

"I'll invest. Draw the papers up, give me a call, and we'll sign them. You'll still take the cash to buy the diamonds?"

"Yeah ... yeah, sure!"

"Fine, I'll be waiting on your call."

"Talk to you later, young lady."

"Bye, Mr. Muhammad." Bamena said, hanging up as her other line beeped.

"Hello."

"This is Wilson County Health Department. We are calling for a Kanoni Santiago.

"This is she."

"Your test came back positive for gonorrhea. We need you to come in for treatment as soon as possible."

"I'll be there in the next hour."

Bamena hung up and called the strip club.

"Megos." Spanish answered.

"Bitch, get dressed now!" Bamena yelled. "The health department called. Your ass has gonorrhea! I thought I told you to use a condom!"

"I did, Boss. Someone must have put a hole in it or slipped it off."

"You should check the shit every time he comes out and wants to go back in!" Bamena continued to yell.

"I'm sorry, Bamena."
"Just be ready! Now your ass can't work for a whole week!"
"I'm sorry. I'll make it up to you, I promise."
"Just be ready, Spanish!"

CHAPTER 22

The Double L crew didn't want their faces to be known at Club Megos, so they sent old coons, Boybaby's uncle, Big Buddy, and Eugene. Big Buddy was about sixty years old, 5'8", 179 pounds, brown skin, with waves to the side. He favored the rapper, KRS-One. Eugene was about sixty-two years old, 6'1", 205 pounds, brown skin, and small afro, with a slight limp from the Gulf War. They went to the club three days straight looking for Spanish, and the security kept saying that she was out sick.

Muffin was on her way back from Raleigh, and Dayself wanted to beat her home.

"I'm gone, lock up when you leave," Dayself said.

"I got one more verse to put down, and then I'm out too," Boybaby said, turning the trumpets down on the board. "I can't believe that Dick is gone."

"Me either. I lost him, Destiny, and my wife this year. You know when we do wrong, things come back on us. I'm a strong believer in three hundred and sixty degrees. Sometimes you gotta accept the bitter with the sweet."

"I feel you, but whenever we catch who did this, we gotta punish them severely."

"You already know. I'm on to something now," Dayself said, and walked out of the studio.

Muffin still beat Dayself home. She was sitting on the edge of the chair, looking like her stomach was about hit the floor.

"Hey baby daddy!" Muffin said, smiling.

"Damn, girl, your shit hanging almost to the floor! You better get somewhere and put your feet up."

"Oh, nigga, I'm still that bitch!" Muffin said, standing up trying to do the stanky leg, but she couldn't put her leg out far enough.

"Girl, sit down," Dayself said, sitting down.

Muffin sat down and put her feet in Dayself's lap. "Massage my feet."

Dayself kissed each of Muffin's fat toes, and then massaged her feet.

"Bae, we sold one of the houses today."

"Damn, them shits selling like hot cakes."

"I'm thinking about putting some rims on my car."

"It's 2014, you got all that money in the bank, and you want to put some rims on a 2000 Galant? Stop that shit."

"So, it's mine and paid for!"

"I'll buy you a car next month. I need to push your shit anyway."

"I bet you do. You don't have to buy me a car, shorty got her own."

"Damn, I missed you."

"Come here then, baby."

Dayself stood up and walked over to Muffin.

Muffin unzipped Dayself's pants and pulled his dick out with her manicured tips. She slowly licked around the head of Dayself's dick. While looking up at him, Muffin slid Dayself's dick in and out of her mouth. She wrapped her lips around the head of his dick, and sucked like she was sucking a blow pop, while jacking his dick at the same time. Muffin looked up at Dayself. He had his head leaned back, eyes closed, and mouth wide open. Muffin sped up as Dayself moved in and out, with her hand and mouth.

"Oh … shit … damn bae … damn … here it comes!" Dayself moaned.

Muffin sucked harder on Dayself's head, and jacked faster. Dayself shot his cum to the back of Muffin's throat. It ran out of the sides of Muffin's mouth as she tried to swallow all of it. Dayself flopped down on the couch, weak and satisfied.

"Come on, let momma bathe the baby," Muffin said, stepping out of her bloomers, walking towards the bathroom, with Dayself behind her.

After showering, Dayself sat on the couch and fired up some haze, letting his mind roam. Dick was the first person that popped into his mind. He picked up the phone and called Eugene.

"Y'all need to get back on the job," Dayself said.

"We'll start tomorrow."

"I got a beep, y'all get at me with that information soon."

"Alright, young blood, be safe."

"Hello." Dayself answered his other line.

"What's good, country boy?" Yellow greeted.

"Nothing much."

"Are you still looking for good friends? I met this Jamaican chick. She's only sixteen and a half."

"Naw, old man, I'm good right now."

"Her people and I go way back. I don't deal in that area too much. She wants too much of my time. She's driving though, and doesn't mind coming to your crib."

"I'll keep you posted."

"It's good to have a woman on the side. You never know when your main girl will up and leave you, or her pussy goes dry. All right, chat back, country boy."

"Will do, peace."

"Peace."

Dayself hung up the phone and made a mental note to pass on the information that Yellow had just given him about a new connect to Castro and Boybaby. Although things had been working well with Boybaby's connect, Yellow was right. It never hurt to have another connect on standby, and sixteen and a half thousand for a key was a fair price.

CHAPTER 23

*B*amena stared at the phone, debating whether she should call Boybaby. Every time she turned, she always looked back at the phone. Bamena wanted nothing more than to hear Boybaby's voice, but she didn't want him to think she was worrying him.

"What the hell?" Bamena said, grabbing the phone and dialing his number.

"Hello."

"What's good, Boybaby?"

"Nothing, in the studio finishing up this last verse."

"What do you do, rap or sing?"

"The only R&B in me is running a block."

"You're crazy. You need to let me hear something sometime."

"All right, I'm just about finished with this track about my man's that died."

"I'm sorry to hear about that."

"When are you going to wear the G-string and bra that I bought for you at the mall?"

"Tonight. Nana went on a trip to visit her relatives in Colombia. If you want, you can stay with me for the next two weeks."

"We'll see about that. You know I have a business to run, but I can spend some nights."

"Whatever works for you."

"Give me an hour, I'll be there."

"Hurry up. I learned some new moves too."

"How did you do that?"

"Not with anybody, I've been reading books."

"Damn, my Queen, you getting it right ain't you?"

"You better hurry up before I forget."

Boybaby wrapped the last verse up, and went to Bamena's house. He rang the doorbell, and Bamena pulled the door open, wearing the hot pink G-string and bra Boybaby had bought her. She wore open toe hot pink heels to match, with her hair pinned up, smelling like vanilla.

"Do you like what you see?" Bamena asked, turning around, bending over, and looking back at him, like she saw the girls do in the club.

Boybaby walked toward Bamena, licking his lips.

Bamena turned to Boybaby, pushed him to the wall, unzipped his pants, got on her knees, and pulled his dick out. She put half of Boybaby's dick in her mouth, and sucked in a back and forth motion, like the strippers had taught her. Bamena grabbed the other half of Boybaby's dick and jacked it. Boybaby grabbed Bamena's head, and moved it with her sucking motion.

"Am I doing it right?" Bamena asked, looking up at Boybaby.

Boybaby's throat had dried; all he could do was shake his head up and down. Bamena unbuttoned his pant, and pulled his boxers and pants down at the same time. Boybaby slipped his shoes off. She stood up, and pulled Boybaby's red Akoo sweater and t-shirt over his head. Boybaby was now naked, except for his socks.

"Follow me," Bamena said, walking toward the stairs.

Boybaby followed Bamena with his dick sticking straight out, thinking about bending her over on the stairs. Bamena pulled Boybaby into her room, pushed him on the bed, unhooked her bra, and threw it at him. She turned around, bent over, and pulled her G-string down slowly. Bamena crawled backwards to Boybaby, until her pussy was over his face. She leaned over and placed Boybaby's dick in her mouth, forming the sixty-nine.

Boybaby touched Bamena's pussy with his tongue. She moaned and increased her sucking speed on his dick. Boybaby ate her pussy until he felt her trembling. She bit her bottom lip, and came in his mouth. Bamena laid her head on Boybaby's thigh to catch her breath. She lifted up, turned to face Boybaby, and tongued him down. While doing that she reached back, grabbed his dick, and slipped the head into her pussy. Bamena went down inch by inch. She had her eyes closed, and mouth open in an O shape, but no words came out.

"Damn, so tight!" Boybaby moaned.

Once all of Boybaby's dick was in, Bamena leaned over and tongue kissed him, moving up and down real slow. She felt her pussy getting wetter as she sped up on his dick.

"Ah…Boy…ah…oh…hurt…my…stomach…ah!" Bamena moaned.

"Ride this dick, ride it baby!" Boybaby moaned, holding Bamena's waist, bouncing her up and down as she came.

Cum ran down Boybaby's dick and balls as Bamena dropped down on his chest with his dick still in her.

"We gotta try one more position."

"All right, what position?"

"From the back."

Boybaby got behind Bamena, and showed her how to put the arch in her back. Bamena started having flashbacks of Destiny raping her.

"Boybaby, no anal sex, okay?" Bamena said in a scared tone.

"Trust me, my queen."

Bamena put the arch in her back like Kia had showed her.

Boybaby went in her pussy, thinking, *Damn, who taught her how to put her ass in the air like that?*

"Play with that, while I do me," Boybaby said, grabbing Bamena's hand and putting it on her clit.

Bamena rubbed her clit with her pointer finger. Her pussy got wetter, and Boybaby fucked her harder.

"Boyba … ah … ah … Boy … Ba … by!"

Bamena started to tremble again. Her pussy seemed to grab Boybaby's dick. He exploded deep in Bamena's pussy. She fell flat on the bed, and Boybaby collapsed beside her.

They rested for a little while, and went at it again.

The next morning, Boybaby went down stairs to get his CD out of his back pocket, and then went back upstairs.

"Check this shit out that I did for my man," Boybaby said, placing the CD in the CD player.

When the song came on, Bamena thought she had heard Boybaby wrong. He said, *RIP Dick*. When Boybaby started rapping about how Dick fucks chicks, and makes them pass out. Bamena went into a daze.

"Are you all right?" Boybaby asked, stopping the CD.

"Yeah, who is Dick?"

"Dick was one of the Original Double L niggas. He and his girl, Destiny, got killed. They found them dead in her house, with Dick's head and dick cut off. His dick was stuffed in her pussy, and the other end was in his mouth."

Bamena felt sick to her stomach. She thought to herself, *I may have to kill Boybaby, but I love him so much.*

"I just remembered that I have to go to the grocery store if I'm going to cook for us."

"I'm going to get some rest while you're gone."

"I think I can walk. my pussy is throbbing like a heartbeat."

Bamena put on a skintight J-LO jogging suit and headed out the door, dialing a number at the same time.

"I want y'all to follow my boyfriend. I think he'll lead us right where we need to be," Bamena said.

"No problem, Boss." The bodyguard said in Spanish.

"He's at my house right now, he'll probably leave in the next two or three hours."

"We're on it, Boss, we won't let you down."

Bamena made it back home, and Boybaby was sound asleep. She leaned over and kissed Boybaby on the lips, waking him up.

"Damn!" Boybaby said, looking at the clock.

"What's wrong?" Bamena asked, concerned.

"I was supposed to meet Dayself to handle some business."

Bamena's mind flashed to Destiny saying "Day …" before she died.

"I'll see you later," Boybaby said, giving Bamena a kiss.

"Be sure to call me after you handle your business."

"I will."

Bamena walked with Boybaby to the door. After the door close, she pulled out her cellphone and called the bodyguards.

"He's leaving right now."

"We're right behind him."

"Stay out of sight."

"We got it, Boss."

While waiting for Boybaby at the stash spot, Dayself read all the comments on Facebook about his club. His phone rang.

"Spanish should be back at the club in thirty minutes." Eugene said.

"Make sure that y'all are there."

"What do you want us to do?"

"Even if y'all got to pay her to leave, find out if she knew Dick and Destiny. If she says no, tie her ass up and call me.

"All right, peace."

"Peace."

The Mexican bodyguards followed Boybaby to the studio. They sat across the street at the store, watching his car. Double L never drove their cars to pick work up. They kept three late model cam-up cars behind the club. The Mexican bodyguards watched Boybaby's car on one side, as he drove out of the other side.

Bamena paced the floor with her phone in her hand. She dialed the bodyguard's number.

"Where is he now?" Bamena asked.

"He went into the studio, but he hasn't come out yet."

"Stay on him!"

"We got you, Boss."

Spanish walked over to Big Buddy and Eugene's table, wearing, a yellow G-string and bra. Big Buddy wore a white button up by Calvin Klein, black dress pants by Gucci, black square toe Gucci slip on shoes, gold Rolex, and black brim hat pulled low. Eugene was sporting a white button up by Kenneth Cole, brown dress pants by Kenneth Cole, square toe dress shoes by Stacy Adams, sunglasses, and a brown suede brim hat.

"Would you like a lap dance?" Spanish asked.

"Hell yeah, come get me first. He can wait!" Big Buddy said, chewing his gum.

Spanish sat in Big Buddy's lap and grinded on his dick, while Eugene put dollars in her G-string. She got up, sat in Eugene's lap, and grinded while holding his dick at the same time.

"You can do more for the right price," Spanish said, still holding Eugene's dick.

"How much are you talking?" Eugene asked through gritted teeth.

"One hundred or one fifty for anal sex. I've only tried it with two people," Spanish lied.

"We can do that at my spot, beautiful," Eugene said.

"That'll be two hundred a piece," Spanish responded.

"Let's go," Eugene said, handing Spanish four hundred dollars. "Drive around front in five minutes."

Five minutes later, Big Buddy and Eugene picked Spanish up from in front of the club.

"I'll have to be back in two hours," Spanish said, getting into the car.

They made it to the hiding spot, and Spanish took off her clothes at the door. Big Buddy and Eugene looked at each other, hunched their shoulders, and took their clothes off along with her. They both stood there in only black dress socks.

Spanish got on her knees at the door, and put Big Buddy's dick in her mouth, while Eugene went and sat on the couch. He stroked his dick as he watched them. Spanish got Big Buddy hard then she went to Eugene, bent over, and sucked his dick.

"Get you," Spanish said, looking back at Big Buddy.

Big Buddy rolled a condom on and went up in Spanish's pussy, from the back. He fucked her hard with all eight inches. Spanish seemed not to be bothered by it. Big Buddy banged her pussy harder, and she didn't moan. Big Buddy and Eugene weren't used to such young Spanish pussy and head. Big Buddy quickly felt himself cumming, and he grabbed Spanish's waist and fucked her hard. Spanish sped up sucking Eugene's dick, as he felt himself cumming also.

Big Buddy and Eugene came almost at the same time. Spanish swallowed all of Eugene's cum, and then licked her lips. Eugene and Big Buddy sat down on the couch breathing hard. Spanish walked to her clothes and pretended to look for more condoms. She pulled four ecstasy pills out, and went to the bar to fix them a drink, dropping a pill in their drinks, and taking two of them herself. Spanish walked over with the drinks.

"Girl, you got the best head around!" Eugene said, turning his liquor up and draining the glass.

"Yeah, I heard that before," Spanish said, still horny.

"In the old days, a Spanish woman wouldn't give a black man the time of day," Big Buddy said, finishing his liquor.

"This girl loves black dick!" Spanish said, getting on her knees and grabbing Big Buddy's dick.

Spanish put Big Buddy's whole dick in her mouth, as Eugene rubbed his dick and waited. Spanish saw that Eugene was about an inch or two bigger than Big Buddy, and she stopped sucking Big Buddy's dick, walked over to Eugene, took the condom out of his hand, put it in her mouth, and rolled it down his dick. Spanish squatted over Eugene, grabbed his dick, and put it in her pussy. She went all the way down to the balls.

Spanish got a small feeling, and closed her eyes as she bounced on Eugene's dick. When she felt Big Buddy spreading her ass cheeks, Spanish stopped and leaned over. Big Buddy slid into her ass with ease. Spanish got the feeling she had been looking for. She bit down on her bottom lip and rocked back and forth as she was double penetrated. They fucked in that position for ten minutes until Spanish felt herself cumming.

"Fuck it … Fuck it … o … o Fuck it!" Spanish moaned.

She squeezed her ass and pussy muscles, rocking faster. Big Buddy grabbed Spanish's waist, and gave it to her harder. He came hard, like he did at sixteen. Eugene came right after them. Spanish hopped up, rolled the condom off, and caught some of Eugene's cum still running out of his dick. She kept sucking, trying to get more. Eugene held Spanish's forehead, and pushed her up off his dick. Big Buddy and Eugene flopped down on the couch out of breath. They stood up and started putting on their clothes.

"The two hours isn't up yet!" Spanish screamed with attitude.

Big Buddy and Eugene looked at each other and shook their heads.

"Dick told me that you loved dick," Big Buddy said, staring at her.

"Wha … what did you say?

"Dick told me that you love dick," Big Buddy repeated.

"I don't know anybody name Dick."

"Are you sure about that?" Big Buddy asked.

"Yes, I'm positive!" Spanish said.

"Dick told us that you love threesomes too," Eugene said.

"Is that all whoever this Dick is told you? Because I don't know him," Spanish said, walking to the bar.

"No, Destiny told us you can eat some pussy," Big Buddy said.

"I've never met either of them," Spanish said, with her back turned, at the bar, fixing a drink.

Eugene crept up behind Spanish and hit her in the head with a Hennessey bottle. Spanish fell to the floor, unconscious.

"Call Dayself and tell him to get over here!" Eugene yelled.

Big Buddy dialed Dayself's number.

"Hello." Dayself answered.

"She's denying the shit!" Big Buddy said.

"Soon as your nephew come see me, I'll be there. Tie her up and strip her."

"The bitch is already naked! She wouldn't put her clothes back on!"

"All right, peace!"

CHAPTER 24

*B*amena couldn't wait another second for the Mexican body-guards to call her back, so she called them.

"Hello."

"Where are y'all now?" Bamena asked.

"We're still at the studio."

"Boybaby told me he was going to see Dayself," Bamena said, remembering that Boybaby had left the money she gave him again. "I'll call y'all right back!"

"Hello." Boybaby answered with his song about Dick playing in the background.

"You left your money," Bamena said.

"Damn, I was intending to get that."

"Where are you now?"

"I'm just getting in Tarboro. This old lady is going slow as hell in front of me."

"Just pick it up when you're done."

"I'll be there late tonight or tomorrow."

"All right, bye."

"Bye."

Bamena called the bodyguards back.

"How is it that Boybaby is on the highway, and y'all are still there?" Bamena yelled.

"He can't be. We're sitting here looking at his car."

"I tell y'all what. Kill everybody in the studio, and burn it down!" Bamena said angrily.

"What about the club?"

"Burn that too!"

The guards had watched Trent, Lil Man, and Moot-Moot go inside the studio. They got out of the truck, walked across the street, and peeped through the window. Trent, Lil Man, and Moot-Moot had their backs turned, listening to a beat Lil Man had just made. The Mexican bodyguards opened the door to the studio with AK-47s in their hands.

Trent looked back and saw them raising their guns. He reached for his gun, but it was too late. The Mexican guards opened fire on them. Moot-Moot and Lil Man never knew what hit them.

Shay-Shay had called Dayself's phone and left numerous messages. His son kept calling crying, saying he needed to talk to his daddy. She only knew three places to look for him. Having already checked Double L and the stash house, Shay-Shay pulled up in front of the studio and heard gunshots. She thought they were coming from the beat machine.

Shay-Shay opened the door, and one of the guards turned and fired, hitting her in the shoulder. She spun around from the impact of the bullet, and fell back out of the door.

The bodyguards went through the connecting door and continued throwing gas all over the club.

Shay-Shay got up and staggered to her car. She drove off, weaving in and out of traffic.

One struck a match and laughed as he threw the match to the floor. The three guards ran out of the club as it ignited.

Shay-Shay dialed Dayself number, but still got no answer. She left a message. "Day, help me, I've been shot. Our baby!" she cried weakly.

Shay-Shay dialed 911, trying not to pass out. She felt her eyes getting heavy. Her head dropped, and feet pressed the gas petal.

Shay-Shay swerved to the right, and hit a light pole. The impact threw her through the windshield.

Bamena thought hard about what she had told the guards to do. To take her mind off things, she headed to the club. Pedro was sitting in her office with his leg kicked up when she came through the secret door.

"What's up, Boss?" Pedro asked, jumping up.

"Nothing. Don't you have your own office?" Bamena asked, pulling her ringing phone out of her purse. "Hello," Bamena answered.

"Boss, it's done. We had to lay a pregnant chick. We went to burn the place, but when we ran out, she was gone."

"What!" Bamena yelled. "Are y'all fucking crazy? Meet me at the spot, now!"

"Is there a problem, Boss?" Pedro asked.

"No, how are things coming along at the club?"

"Everything is good, except Spanish left with two guys earlier and hasn't returned."

"Did you check the camera to see who the guys were?"

"I couldn't tell, one had on shades, and a hat, and the other one had his hat pulled low. Spanish wrote in the books, gone for two hours, but she never showed back up." Pedro said as Bamena went back on the camera. "Hold on, Boss, those two guys came here looking for her several times before!"

"Did they ask anything out of the ordinary?"

"No, they just wanted to see Spanish for some fun."

Bamena went in her safe and took out two weeks of the club earnings to be dropped off at the bank on her way to the stash house.

Boybaby finally showed up at the stash house.

"Damn, Sun, how you going to have the connect waiting on you? Dayself asked.

"My bad, I'll try my best to not let it happen again," Boybaby said.

"What are you trying to get, Sun?"

"Two joints."

"I only have three left," Dayself said, holding up two fingers to the tiny camera in the corner.

Dayself walked in the bathroom and opened the mirrored cabinet. He pulled the mirror open, a white hand handed him the keys from the bathroom in the cleaners. Dayself hit the button on the bottom of the counter, closing the inside of the mirror. He flushed the toilet. Only he and Dirty knew that the cleaners belonged to Dirty. They thought he kept the coke in the wall in the bathroom.

"We'll be ready to reup in the next two days," Dayself said, weighing the keys on the triple beam. "Here you go."

"I'll get in touch with my people. Your phone done went off about ten times."

"I'll get it in a minute, you headed to the studio?"

"In about an hour."

"I'll see you then."

Dayself went to get his phone in the back room, where the table and chairs and two hidden safes were. He had missed fifteen calls.

Three were from Muffin, two from his Uncle Pap, five from his son, and five from Shay-Shay. Muffin said, "Your uncle Pap is trying to get in touch with you, he said it's important." Hanging up, Dayself dialed his uncle Pap's number.

"What up, Unc?" Dayself said.

"What the fuck is going on?" Pap yelled.

"What are you talking about?"

"The studio and club were set on fire!" Pap yelled. "They found three bodies in there! I thought it was you, boy!" Pap said, tearing up.

"What? Whose bodies were they?"

"They won't know until the DNA test come back. Your friend's cars were out there."

"Whose?"

"Trent and Boybaby's."

"Unc, I gotta go," Dayself said sadly and hung up.

Dayself called Trent's phone and got no answer. Then he called his girl, April.

"Hello." April answered.

"Have you seen Trent?" Dayself asked.

"No, Dirty just left here looking for him. He's probably somewhere with his bitch, Tonesha! I don't even care! Dayself you know where the fuck he at!" April said and hung up.

Dayself pressed the play button to check his voicemail. Big Buddy was calling.

"Hello." Dayself yelled.

"Young blood, what do you want us to do with her? We gotta go."

"Hog tie the bitch with chains, and leave her there!"

Dayself ran out of the stash spot, down the street to his car. He called Boybaby while getting in.

"Hello." Boybaby answered.

"Somebody burnt up the club and studio. They found three bodies in there. Call Dirty and tell him, and y'all meet me at the chill spot."

"I'm leaving my spot now!"

One of the hoopties, and Dirty's Chrysler was out front when Dayself drove up. Dayself walked through the door checking his voicemail.

"Yo, what ..." Dirty started and then stopped.

He watched Dayself frown. Dayself held the phone tight to his ear, closed his eyes, opened them, and dialed Shay-Shay's number.

"That was Shay-Shay. She said she's been shot!" Dayself said.

"What the fuck, dog!" Dirty yelled, punching his open hand.

"Hold on, Dirty, let me call the hospital," Dayself said, dialing the hospital number.

"Heritage Hospital, Eve speaking." The nurse answered.

"Do y'all have a Shameka Willis there?"

"Hold please."

"Y'all some strange shit is going on," Boybaby said.

"Sir, yes we do," the nurse said.

"How is she?"

"She's in surgery right now."

Dayself ran out of the house with Dirty and Boybaby behind him. The whole way there, Dayself kept saying, *this can't be happening.*

Dayself parked his car and ran into the hospital.

"I'm here to see Shameka Willis!" Dayself said, out of breath.

"She's in surgery on the fourth floor," the receptionist said.

The elevator took so long that Dayself took the stairs, two at a time. He burst through the exit door. Shay-Shay's mother was in the corner with her sisters, aunts, and cousins around her praying. Detective Carrell and Barfield, the same two Detectives that testified against him in the robbery case stood in another corner staring at him. Detective Carrell is white about 40 years old, short and on the chubby side. Detective Barfield is black slightly taller than Carrell with a close cut, and a lazy eye.

"Are you Dayself Burton?" Detective Barfield asked.

"Y'all know who I am. Stop the games," Dayself said.

"You've been gone so long, we almost forgot who you were." Detective Carrell laughed.

"At the car accident, your baby mother gained semi-consciousness," Det. Barfield said.

"What the fuck you talking about a car accident?" Dayself yelled.

"She was shot, and then had a car accident getting away. She said some Spanish guys shot her, and then she passed out again. Shameka's mother said that Shameka called her and said she was looking for you, for your son," Det. Barfield said.

"Are you trying to say that I —" Dayself said before being cut off.

"Not at the moment, but we've been hearing some things about you. Believe me, if we hear, the Feds will hear soon. Have a good day, big time," Det. Barfield said, walking to the elevator.

"My baby mother and baby have been hurt, and y'all come at me with this bullshit?" Dayself said a little too loud.

Det. Carrell looked at Dayself, smiled, and then winked as the elevator door closed.

The doctor came to the waiting room wearing a concerned expression.

"She made it through surgery," the doctor said.

Shay-Shay's family screamed, "Thank you Jesus, praise the Lord!"

"If she makes it through the next three days, she'll pull through," the doctor said.

"What about the baby?" Dayself asked.

"I'm sorry, she didn't make it. Shameka will be in the ICU in about an hour."

Dayself sat by Shay-Shay's side from one day until the next. He sat and rubbed her hand until he dozed off. He was about to fall over, but he caught himself and opened his eyes. Shay-Shay had her eyes open, staring at the pitcher of water on the night-stand. Her whole face was wrapped up, her jaw was broken, and her neck.

Dayself sat up and kissed her scratched up hand, smiling.

"I ... Lo ... yo ... Da." Shay-Shay said, softly.

"I love you too, bae. Get well, so I can take you home." Dayself said, rubbing Shay-Shay's swollen hands.

"Spani ... at ... stu ... o."

"An ... res, Da ... we ... lo ... yo."

The monitors flat lined. Dayself jumped up and pressed the emergency button.

"Help ... help ... somebody help!" Dayself yelled, running out of the room screaming.

The nurses and doctors ran into the room and pushed Dayself out while they worked. "Don't leave me!" Dayself yelled through the window. "Shay-Shay, I need you!"

Only ten minutes had passed, which seemed like an hour to Dayself. The doctor came out shaking his head.

"I'm sorry, Mr. Burton, we did all we could." The doctor said in broken English.

"Can I see her?" Dayself asked, dropping his head.

"Sure … Sure!" The doctor said, walking off.

Dayself walked in, sat in the chair, and rubbed Shay-Shay's hand.

"Baby, I'm sorry." Dayself said, with tears falling. "I blame myself for not answering my phone again. If you would just get up so we can start over! Please, Shay-Shay, get up!" he cried.

Dayself laid his head on Shay-Shay's empty stomach. After the last tear fell, he stood up.

"I will always hold y'all to my heart. I love y'all!" He kissed Shay-Shay's lips and walked out.

CHAPTER 25

*B*amena had been throwing up, since late the night before. After throwing up her breakfast, she remembered she had skipped her menstrual cycle last month. She said aloud, "I can't be pregnant!"

Bamena left the house and came back with a pregnancy test. After peeing on the stick, she sat and stared at it for thirty minutes. It was positive. Bamena dropped her head, grabbed her phone, and called Boybaby. His phone went straight to voicemail.

Boybaby stared at Spanish, wondering where she had come from, and what she had done. She was stretched out, with her arms and legs apart, and mouth taped. Boybaby kept looking at her pussy. It was wet, but looked ragged, and swollen. He pulled out his phone to call Dayself to ask what was up with the chick, and noticed that his phone was dead.

Boybaby went to get his charger out of the car. He returned to the room to see piss flying out of Spanish's pussy onto the floor.

Dayself walked out of the hospital and called Dirty.

"Radio."

"Partner, they gone!" Dayself said with anger.

"Damn, Day, are you all right?"

"Hell no, I'm not all right!" Dayself yelled. "I won't be all right until I kill every person responsible!"

"Yo, don't talk like that over the phone. Where are you headed?" Dirty asked.

"I'm going to Shay-Shay's crib to move some things. Meet me at the hiding spot in ten minutes."

"All right, peace."

"Peace." Dayself said and dialed Muffin's number.

"What's up, baby daddy?" Muffin answered.

"I need you to pack some things and go to your grandfather's house in Rocky Mount."

"Why? You sound strange."

"Just do what the fuck I said."

"What's wrong? You're scaring me!"

"Shay-Shay was shot. Her and the baby are dead."

"Oh my God … oh my God!" I would never wish that on her. Can I go to the funeral?"

"That might not be a good idea, being you're pregnant by me too."

"I'll go pack," Muffin said, getting up. "Dayself."

"Yeah?"

"Be careful. If something happens to you, I don't know what I would do."

"I will Ms. G.P." (Good Pussy)

"We love you, Day."

"I love y'all too."

Dayself stopped at the chill spot and got the DVD of Dick,

Destiny, and Spanish, and then went to Shay-Shay's crib to remove his things out of his safe. Shay-Shay's tweety bird slippers were on the bedroom floor when he walked in. He smiled as tears ran down his face. Dayself stared at the picture that he and Shay-Shay had taken in the club, until he felt weak. He lay down on her bed to smell her scent one more time.

After a few minutes, Dayself jumped up, snatched the tote bag, the picture of them in the club, and headed to the hiding spot.

Dirty noticed the look on Dayself's face when he entered the hiding spot. It was a look he had never seen before.

"You can leave now. I need to speak with Dirty," Dayself said, with a big bag in his hand.

"If you need me, give me a call," Boybaby said, walking out of the house.

"Talk, partner," Dirty said.

"Trent's girl called me. She said that was him they found in the fire. He had been shot seven times. The other two were Lil Man and Moot-Moot. Shay-Shay was shot at the studio too. Before she died, she said it was some Spanish cats."

"I know how it feels to lose someone you love. I haven't been the same since my brother died in my arms. We can't bring them back, bruh, but we can get revenge on the people responsible."

"Let's get started then."

"What's in the bag?" Dirty said.

"Nothing major, a little something for our little Ms. Spanish. I think she knows who the people are that's responsible for all of this."

"You think she really knows?" Dirty whispered at the door.

"We're about to find out," Dayself whispered, walking into the room.

The room was empty, except a slab of metal with four legs bolted to the middle of the floor, with a queen size mattress on top of it. Spanish laid on top of the mattress, with her legs and arms chained, stretched out. She looked at Dayself and tried to remember where she had seen him before. Then it came to her.

"What's good, Spanish?" Dayself asked, removing the tape from her mouth.

"Why am I here?" Spanish cried.

"You know why you're here!" Dayself said.

"No, I swear I don't!" Spanish cried.

"Do you know Dick and Destiny?" Dirty asked.

"No, I've never seen them before!" Spanish said, trying to move her arms and legs.

Dayself pulled a saw knife out of the bag. Spanish watched the shiny steel out of the corner of her eyes. The closer he got to her nipple, the more she believed what was about to happen. Dayself sawed Spanish's nipple until it fell over in the center of her chest. Spanish screamed out in pain.

"I'll ask you again. Do you know Dick and Destiny?"

"No!" Spanish screamed.

Dayself reached over and sawed her other nipple off. This one rolled onto the bed beside her. Blood ran from both nipples to the bed. Spanish started speaking in Spanish. Dayself reached in the bag and pulled out some wire cutters.

"Do you know them?" Dayself yelled.

"Please … please, I told you no!" She screamed, watching Dayself with the wire cutters.

Dayself reached down, spread Spanish's pussy lips, and put the wire cutters around her clit.

"Yes … yes, I know them!" Spanish yelled.

"Now we're getting somewhere. Where do you know them from?" Dirty asked.

"They used to come in the club!" Spanish cried.

"That's it?" Dayself asked.

"Yes, I swear!" Spanish yelled.

"You know, I really do hate liars," Dayself said, pulling the portable DVD player out of the bag. He turned it on and pressed play. Spanish was flabbergasted. "So you're saying that's not you?"

Spanish became quiet. Dayself grabbed the cutters, opened Spanish's pussy lips, put the clippers around her clit, and cut her clit off. She cried and screamed, as blood shot from her clit, like a water gun squirting.

"Bitch, shut the fuck up. Why did you lie to us?" Dayself screamed.

"Fuck you, puta!" Spanish yelled then spit on Dayself's shirt.

"All right, we'll see about all that." Dayself said, wiping the spit off. "I bet Dick fucked you real good, didn't he?" Spanish laid there quiet. "The doctor said my girl Destiny was penetrated in both holes, with a thirteen and a half inch object. Let me show you how it felt," Dayself said, reaching in the bag and pulling out a thirteen and a half inch dildo.

"Where in the fuck did you get that from?" Dirty asked.

"I had bought it years ago as a joke present for Mabee, but Shay-Shay talked me out of doing it. It came in handy though," Dayself said.

"Please … please no!" Spanish yelled.

"Don't say that yet, baby girl," Dayself said, pulling out a plastic tube, with a skeleton head screwed on top. "Usually, warm liquid is put into these, but I've decided to use acid."

Dayself screwed the balls off the dildo, poured the liquid in them, and screwed them back on. "Which hole shall I start with?"

"I'll tell you! Please don't do this!" Spanish yelled. "My boss told me to go home with them, and find out where they live! I set them up to be kidnapped. That's all I done, I swear!"

"What's your boss name?" Dirty asked.

Spanish became quiet. Dayself shoved the dildo in her pussy.

"Pedro!" Spanish yelled.

"That wasn't so hard, was it?"

Dayself pulled his Glock .40 off his waist and shot Spanish between her eyes.

Dirty picked up the liquid acid and burst out laughing.

"What's so funny?"

"Man, that won't no acid, you got that shit from the store. That's some liquid candy!" Dirty laughed.

Dayself had a smile on his face, then he got right back serious.

"Shit, it's your turn to do some work. Here, take this," Dayself said, handing Dirty the axe.

"What do you want me to do, cut off her limbs?"

"Man, hell naw! Just cut her head off, leave the dick in her pussy, and shove the other end in her mouth."

Dayself thought for a minute about who he could get to go to club Megos. He dialed the lawyer, Becky's number.

"Hello." Becky answered.

"I need a favor."

"Sure."

"I need you to drive to the strip club, Megos, in Wilson, and find out who the boss is, and how he looks."

"I'll do it, but don't make this a habit, and don't mention this to anyone."

"There will be a guy in a black and tan coat there. Make eye contact with him, then nod your head at the boss. Wait about ten minutes then leave."

Becky drove straight to the club, thinking to herself, *damn, I haven't done anything like this since college.* Becky had on a black St. John's pantsuit, and black suede pumps by Liz Claiborne. She walked to the bar.

"Can I have a martini please?" Becky asked.

"Coming right up," the bartender said in broken English.

Becky looked around until she found the guy in the black and tan coat.

"Here you go." The bartender said, handing Becky the Martini.

Becky took two sips, turned and spit it on the floor.

"This stuff is watered down!" Becky screamed.

"Ma'am, I just opened the bottle," the bartender said.

"I want to see the owner of this dump!" Becky yelled. "I want my money back!"

The security came over fast, trying to figure out what was going on. Pedro saw the commotion on the security cameras. He put the straw down that he was sniffing his cocaine through, and went to the bar.

"What's the problem?" Pedro asked, wiping his nose.

"This lady says her martini is watered down, and she wants her money back," the bartender said.

"Ma'am, my name is Pedro, I'm the boss here. If you say your drink was watered down, we'll open another bottle and sell you another drink for half price," Pedro said, looking at the bartender and winking.

"That's fine," Becky said, going in her purse as Pedro walked off.

Becky made eye contact with the guy in the tan and black coat, and then nodded towards Pedro. She ordered another martini, and the bartender made sure that she paid first. After downing the martini, Becky placed a twenty-dollar bill on the counter and walked out of the club.

Pedro was on his way out of the club at 3:00 a.m., when the club phone rang.

"Club Megos, Pedro speaking."

"Have you heard any word from Spanish?" Bamena asked.

"No, no one has heard a word."

"All right, I'll see you tomorrow."

"Okay, Boss."

Pedro locked up, rushed out of the club, and headed home. He didn't notice that he was being followed. As he turned in his driveway, Lambo kept going.

"I got you Pedro." Lambo said, pulling out his phone and calling Dayself.

"It's 438 Newton St.," Lambo said.

"Come see me, I need you to do something for me."

"I'm on the way." Lambo said, feeling guilty as he hung up.

The next morning, Pedro and his family got up at nine to go shopping. On their way back home, they stopped for pizza. They returned home around one thirty. The kids went to their room to play their new games, and to try on new clothes.

"Honey, can I get some before I go to work?" Pedro asked his wife in a loving voice. "I don't have to be in 'til three."

Pedro's wife grabbed his hand and led him to their bedroom door. She pushed the door open and let out a loud scream. Pedro looked over her shoulder and screamed louder than she did. The kids came running into the room. Everybody was looking at each other and screaming. Spanish was stretched out on the bed with her head between her legs, with the dildo in her pussy and mouth. Pedro covered his kid's eyes, and pushed them out of the room. He followed and dialed 911. Before the police arrived, Pedro called Bamena.

"You ... you're not going to believe this shit!" Pedro yelled.

"Calm down, Pedro. What happened?" Bamena asked.

"I took my family out, we came back home and found Spanish in my bed!" Pedro yelled. "Her fucking head is between her legs, with a dildo in her pussy, and mouth!"

"Shit ... shit, you didn't call the cops, did you?"

"Fucking right I did!" Pedro yelled. "How could I tell my wife we're not going to call the cops? My wife and kids may have to see a shrink behind this!"

"Take the next two weeks off with pay."

"Thank you, Boss. I have to go, the cops are here."

"All right, bye."

"Hey, Boss, I don't know Spanish."

"Your pay just doubled for the next two weeks, bye."

Bamena hung up the phone and threw everything that she

could get her hands on. She sat in the corner and put her head on her knees. "I know the cops are going to think it was the same people that killed Dick and Destiny. All the heat and questions are going to come on me. What if Spanish gave my name? I'm going to wait 'til dark to clean my safe at the club, then I'll make the girls move back to the old house," Destiny said aloud to the empty room.

≈

Club Megos was just opening. Lambo and two of his little homies, Skip and Antrail from Double L, walked into Megos. Skip was dark as night, eighteen years old, 5'9", 170 pounds, with big long dreads. Antrail is light skinned, eighteen years old, 5'8", 205 pounds, with a close cut.

"Sorry, we're not set up yet," The Mexican security guard said, standing at Lambo's table.

"It's all right, we'll just wait." Lambo said, pulling out his money.

"That's fine." The security guard said and walked away from the table.

Lambo stood up, pulled out his black .45, and blew the back of the security guards head through the front of his face. Three of the Mexican security guards reached for their guns, but Antrail and Skip opened fire on them. Two of the guards dropped to the floor.

The last security guard caught two shots to the back and fell to the side. He rose up, and let off a shot, catching Antrail in the throat. Antrail grabbed his throat, and fell to the floor. The Mexican guard fell over on his stomach, and tried to slide away.

Lambo walked up on the guard and kicked his Glock .40 out of the way. The security guard turned over fast, with a two shot .38 Dillenger in his hand. He let off a shot, grazing the side of Lambo's face. Lambo let off a shot in the security guards face with the .45, blowing half of his face off.

Lambo grabbed a napkin off the bar and put it to the cut.

Lambo and Skip walked out of the club, and went to the house next door. One of the Mexican strippers opened the door in a sheer nightgown, with nothing on underneath.

"Bitch, back up!" Lambo yelled, putting the gun to her face.

"We ... money ... money there," The Spanish stripper said in very little English, pointing.

"Call the others in here!" Lambo said.

She called the other four strippers into the living room. They all came in naked, looking for a trick.

"All of you, get on the wall. I want to see your face down and ass up!" Lambo said, pointing his gun, watching them on the floor. "Homie, hold the gun on them. I'm going to check the office."

Skip shook his head, staring at the different shapes of pussy, in front of him.

Lambo walked out, laughing at Skip.

Lambo had checked everything in Bamena's office. He walked to Gormez' picture and then asked himself, *what the fuck is his picture doing still up?* He felt around the picture and it pulled open. A safe sat in the wall. Lambo pulled out a small digital device from his back pocket. He attached it to the safe, and some numbers appeared. Lambo dialed the number on the safe key pad. The little device did a count down from fifty, and the safe came open.

Approximately two hundred thousand dollars, two bags of ecstasy pills, and a stack of DVDs sat in the safe. Lambo whistled and loaded everything in a bag with one hand, catching the drop of blood with the napkin in the other hand. He turned to the computer to eject the surveillance DVD, and stepped on a little button. He turned real fast with his gun drawn. The hidden door Bamena used had opened.

Lambo smiled, turned back around, took the DVD, and walked out. He walked back into the house beside the club. Skip had the Mexican strippers in a circle eating each other.

"All right, ladies, party is over. Get back in your positions," Lambo said, making the women get back in their positions. They began to cry. "Let's go, lil homie."

"What about them?" Skip asked, pointing with his gun at the strippers.

"Kill them." Lambo said, walking out of the house.

Skip walked up behind one and shot her execution style. The other four tried to run, but he shot them down and walked out of the house.

CHAPTER 26

*N*ight came faster than Bamena wanted. She drove up in front of the club in her Dodge Shadow. There were no cars in the parking lot, and the lights were out in both the club and the house. Bamena thought the police had shut the club down. She went through the open door and hit the light switch. The safe was wide open, and everything was gone.

Bamena pulled out her gold .45 and walked lightly to the front of the club. Her whole security team was laid out dead. There were holes everywhere. Bamena ran to the bathroom and threw up. She walked out of the bathroom wiping her mouth, and went to the house beside the club.

The first thing she saw was the bodies of two of the Spanish chicks. One was in the hallway dead. Blood and brains were all over the wall. Bamena ran to the bathroom to throw up, but she didn't make it. She heard a moaning noise and pulled her gun as she looked around the corner. Two strippers lay side-by-side, holding hands. Bamena walked closer and saw that one had died. The other one lay there with a big hole in her leg and back. Bamena leaned down and squeezed her hand.

"Help ... me ... help ... me!" the stripper begged low in Spanish.

"I can't let you live," Bamena said with tears in her eyes.

Bamena pointed the gun at the stripper's chest and pulled the trigger. She stood and called the Mexican bodyguards.

"Get to the club, right now!" Bamena said as soon as guard answered.

"What's wrong, Boss?"

"Just come!"

Bamena ran to the bathroom and threw up again. She threw cold water on her face, went outside to get some fresh air and make some phone calls. Her first call was to one of the black strippers.

"Hello." Crystal answered.

"The club will be closing indefinitely," Bamena said.

"What happened, we just started?"

"The Feds are on to me."

"What will we do now?"

"For y'all loyalty, keep the drugs, and I'll turn y'all on to my connect. All y'all gotta do is pay me for rent every month."

"Okay, Boss, I'll tell the girls what's up."

"Bye, Crystal."

"Bye."

Bamena sat on the step and thought to herself, *I gotta get out while I can. First, I gotta get rid of Double L, so I can live in peace.* The bodyguards met Bamena at the back of the club.

"I'll give each one of you twenty-five thousand dollars to clean up the house and the club. It's ten bodies in there that I don't want ever to be found.

"There's a funeral home down the street, Boss. We can kill the funeral home director and cremate the bodies."

"I don't care how it's done, just do it!" Bamena said, irritated. "When y'all are done, I have another job for you."

Bamena drove back home in a daze. The Spanish stripper's voice begging for help echoed in her mind. She walked in the house and dialed Boybaby's number. After four rings, Boybaby's phone went to voicemail. Bamena's motion sensors in her driveway went off, and she ran to the screen beside the door. Bamena watched Bonito get out the back of his white Phantom and ring the doorbell.

"How the fuck he know where I live?" Bamena said to herself as she opened the door with a smile on her face.

"Are you all right?" Bonito asked.

"Besides being pregnant by a black man, I'm good."

"That's not so bad. I have a couple of mixed kids around the country myself." Bonito laughed as he sat down on the couch.

"That's not funny, Bonito. What if they need their father?"

"They and their mothers are well taken care of."

"So you give them hush money?"

"Father would kill me if he found out that I've mixed our blood! He's very strict about that."

"My father was the same way. He used to tell me all the time, to never mix our blood with outside races."

"My father wants you to join us in Texas."

"Tell Uncle Gormez that I'll be there as soon as I handle my affairs. As of today, I'm out of the game."

"Why?"

"Too many people dying, and I want my baby to be safe."

"I went by the club, and there were bullet holes everywhere. If you need help from the family, please don't be afraid to ask. Although your last name is different, you are still a part of the Gormez cartel, and we will wipe our enemies off the face of this earth."

"I'll take care of it."

"Are you sure? Because—"

"I said I'll take care of it!" Bamena almost shouted.

"You know, back in Mexico, women don't get involved in manly affairs."

"What are you trying to say?"

"You just don't seem capable of … you know, killing."

"If you don't think so, keep your TV on, because I've got a surprise for you."

Bonito stood up. "Now that I know you're all right, I gotta get going. Hey, are you interested in selling the club?"

"No, that was my father's pride and joy."

"I'll keep it in your name, and give you double the value. I just need it to handle other business, if you know what I mean."

"All right, but it stays in my name."

"Your money will be here tomorrow."

"I have enough money lying around here. I'll give you an account in Mexico to send it to."

"Where is the black stripper, Kia, that you were telling me about?"

"You are not leaving any kids around here."

"I don't think father will accept your mixed child, unless he or she looks Mexican."

"Then he won't accept me."

"I'll have a talk with him."

Bonito walked to the door and opened it, with Bamena behind him.

"Stop by my restaurant in Princeville. I have a pretty Mexican friend who works there named Sabina."

"I'll make sure that I do. Goodbye, cousin," Bonito said as he got in the back seat of his car.

Bamena watched Bonito drive off then went into the house and dialed Boybaby's number. His phone went to voicemail again. As she was about to dial Boybaby's number once more, Bamena felt herself about to throw up, and ran to the bathroom.

After brushing her teeth, Bamena lay down on her bed and cried herself to sleep.

Boybaby was in the kitchen cooking up crack, with his CD playing. He saw his phone blinking and went over to check it. Boybaby had two missed calls from Bamena and Dayself. He called Dayself back.

"What's good?" Boybaby asked, putting ice cubes in the gelled up crack.

"We're low again. Call your people and tell them we want thirty more of them thangs."

"I got you, G."

"This is my last run. I'm tired of this shit."

"You all right, bruh?" Boybaby asked, taking the hardened crack out and putting it on a napkin. "You have lost a lot of people that were close to you this year."

"Sun, I'm doing the best I can. I just concentrate on making money and revenge to block out the pain. You know Dick came to me in my dreams again."

"Day, you're tripping."

"I'm serious!" Dayself said in a serious tone. "He said, 'Dayself, you've figured out most of it, now put the final piece to the puzzle.'"

"You been drinking?"

"Naw, Sun, I'm just tired of this shit, that's all. I have come and conquered. I give the throne to you with open arms."

"I'm at peace with that. So what will you do now?"

"I'm leaving Tarboro and Princeville for sure. This is no place for a black man to raise his kids. I got a couple businesses down here, and enough money to last me the rest of my life. What good is it for me to have knowledge itself, if I'm not teaching it? I got two kids on the way, I gotta teach them, and give them the best life. I have a war to finish first, though."

CHAPTER 27

*D*ayself rode with Boybaby and Dirty to Shay-Shay's family home. He got out of the car, and felt like everyone was staring at him. He turned to get back in the car.

"Dayself, come in the house for a second. I need to talk to you," Shay-Shay's mother yelled before he got in.

Dayself walked into the house and walked straight back to Shay-Shay's mother's room. Ms. Willis was about fifty-six years old, 5'8", 165 pounds, brown skinned, light brown eyes, and long hair, with grey strings in places.

"Ma'am?" Dayself asked, walking to the door.

"Come in and close the door behind you. I think Shameka would want you to have this," Ms. Willis said and handed Dayself a photograph.

Dayself stared at the picture. It was a picture of a newborn baby girl that favored him.

"Who this?"

"It's you and Shameka's baby. You were in so much pain in the hospital, that you didn't have a chance to see her. I had the funeral home pick her up when they went to get Shameka's body. Shameka had ordered a beautiful white going home from the hospital dress for the baby, so I took it to the funeral, and then I had the picture taken. She will be buried in a little casket right beside her mother."

A tear came to Dayself's eye, and he quickly wiped it away.

It's all right to cry, child." Ms. Willis said, hugging Dayself. He couldn't hold it any longer. He broke down in tears. "Let it out baby, let it out."

"She looks so much like me," Dayself said, wiping his eyes.

Someone yelled that the family car was there.

"It's going to be all right, just take one day at a time," Ms. Willis said, getting up and walking out of the room with Dayself behind her.

"You are a part of this family. You can ride in the family car with us," Ms. Willis said.

"Thank you, Ms. Willis, but I rode here with two of my friends."

The church was packed. Many of Shay-Shay's co-workers and classmates had showed up to pay their respect. The singing from the choir caused many people to cry worse.

The preacher walked in and surveyed the room before he spoke.

"Good evening friends and loved ones. Today, we celebrate the homegoing of our dear Shameka. Earth has no sorrow that heaven can't heal, and today, Shameka is all right. She is in a better place, so don't cry for Shameka. Yes, we are hurt by her loss, and we will surely miss her. But, if you knew Shameka, you know that she would not want us in here crying. That little girl loved to laugh and make people laugh." The minister paused as the congregation chuckled, because he was right.

"Shameka and my daughter were very close growing up. I remember one day, I took Shameka and my daughter skating. On the way home, my daughter said, 'I want them to sing, "Walk Around Heaven" at my funeral before I go to heaven.' Shameka said, 'I want them to sing, "I Miss You," by Aaron Hall at my funeral before I go to heaven.'

"I hadn't ever heard that song sang in church before, so I went home, got on iTunes and pulled it up. I hit play, and as the song flowed from the speakers, I said, 'man, he should've sold me that song." Everyone laughed.

"So today, we will honor Shameka's wishes. Please welcome, Aaron Hall."

Aaron Hall walked up to the front of the church. The pastor handed him a cordless microphone and he began to sing. Tears and cries of sorrow filled the building as Aaron stood between the two caskets and sang one of Shameka's favorite songs.

As Aaron continued to sing, the minister called everyone up for the final viewing.

Dayself stood in front of Shay-Shay's casket and spoke his heart.

"Shay-Shay, baby, you should see our daughter. She looks just like me, her nose, and even her hands. Baby, I miss you joking around and walking around in those Tweety Bird slippers. I will always love you," Dayself said.

"Hey daddy's princess, you know I would have spoiled you, and made your momma jealous. Daddy has a picture of you. I'll always keep it close to me. I already know that you would have been daddy's little girl. I love you, princess."

Tears ran down his face as Dayself touched his baby's hair, and then her face. He couldn't move, his hand was stuck. Boybaby and Dirty came to the front of the church.

"Partner, come on. It's going to work itself out, come with us," Dirty said.

Dayself shook his head, turned around with his friends, and walked out of the church.

At the burial, Dayself stood over Shay-Shay and his baby's caskets, with Ms. Willis, and some of her family, dropping flowers on top of the caskets.

Dirty kept seeing a black Yukon ride by. He walked closer to the road and watched the Yukon go down the street and park. Dirty walked back to the burial, where Dayself was.

"Yo, walk with me real quick, this is important." Dirty whispered in Dayself ear.

Dayself walked from the family, behind Dirty, until they got to the road.

"Look down there. Either it's the feds, or a hit."

"Go check it …"

Boom! Boom!

Dayself and Dirty dropped to the ground. The Yukon took off down the street. Dayself jumped up off the ground, and ran back down the hill. The two caskets were gone. There were small pieces in car windshields, on top of cars, and people. Shay-Shay's mother and sister laid out dead, missing limbs. Dayself stood there shocked.

"We gotta get the fuck out of here before the police come!" Dirty yelled, pulling Dayself's arm. He wouldn't budge. "Come on, Partner, we gotta go!"

"Y'all get in!" Boybaby yelled, pulling up beside them.

They ran to the car, jumped in, and took off.

Bamena waited in her room, listening to Beyonce's Spanish CD. Her phone rang, and she ran to it.

"Hello!" she answered.

"Boss, it's done," one of the guards said.

Bamena turned the TV to the news station.

"Good job, I'm watching it right now!" Bamena smiled. "Y'all need a break for this!"

"No, Boss, we have to make sure that you're protected. We'll be on call until all of this is over. We thank you for bringing our family to America."

"You're welcome. I guess I'll go to the outlet in Smithfield, and do a little shopping.

"Do you need us there with you?"

"No, they don't have a plan yet, or who's behind it. If they did, I would've been in the dirt," Bamena said, getting into her Porsche truck.

"All right, Boss, be safe."

"All right."

Boybaby, Dirty, and Dayself arrived at the hiding spot. Boybaby and Dirty got out of the car, but Dayself stayed in. He seemed to be stuck to the seat.

"Come on, Partner, get out." Dirty said, coming back to the car.

"They killed Shay-Shay and my baby twice, Dirty, man!"

"Sitting in this damn car is not going to get the people responsible back!" Dirty yelled.

Dayself got out of the car slowly, and walked into the house with his head down.

"Call Eugene and Big Buddy, tell them to bring Pedro here to me, even if they have to kill his whole family!" Dayself yelled.

"You know they don't do the murder thing anymore," Dirty said.

"Call Lambo, and tell him to do it!" Dayself said.

"I got you, just sit down and think first," Dirty said.

Boybaby handed Dayself a cup of Hennessey.

"Give me the whole bottle, G." Dayself said, reaching for the cup.

Dayself rolled up a blunt and gulped the liquor down.

Later that night, Lambo pulled up in front of Pedro's new house. He crept to the side of the house and looked in the window and saw Pedro at the table snorting powder. Lambo went back to the car, put on a Domino's pizza hat and coat. He took an empty pizza box out of the back seat, and walked back to the house.

"Domino's pizza!" Lambo said, knocking on Pedro's door.

Pedro looked through the peephole, disarmed the alarm, and opened the door.

"I'm sorry, I didn't order a pi—"

"Back up, bitch, before I make your brain explode," Lambo said, pointing the gun in Pedro's face, making him back up into the house. "Put these on before I cut your fucking head off!"

Lambo tossed Pedro the handcuffs.

"Please, I don't have any cash here!" Pedro begged.

"I made enough off the DVDs of you letting Spanish shit and piss on you. Turn your sick ass around, bitch!"

Lambo turned Pedro around, squeezed the handcuffs, picked Pedro's dress socks up off the floor and stuffed them in his mouth.

Pedro walked into the hiding spot with Lambo behind him. His eyes were glassy and his nose was runny, from the cocaine.

"Mr. Pedro, it's nice to finally get to meet you," Dayself said. "Sit him in the basement."

Lambo took Pedro to the basement and tied him down. Dayself sat across from Pedro, and stared at him for about two minutes before he spoke. "Why are you killing my family?" Dayself asked, snatching the tape off his mouth.

"I don't have any idea what you're talking about!" Pedro said in a scared voice.

"You are the boss at Megos, right?" Dayself asked.

"Yes, I mean no!" Pedro said.

"Maybe this will help you remember," Dayself said.

Dayself took the axe out of the corner, walked up to Pedro, lifted the axe, and came down hard on his foot, chopping half of it off. Pedro screamed out in pain as blood sprayed from his foot.

"Now, I want to know two things. If you're not the boss of Megos, who is, and where are the people that's been killing my family?" Dayself asked.

"I have no idea what people you're talking about!" Pedro yelled.

Dayself raised the axe up high, and came down hard on Pedro's other foot, chopping half off. Pedro begin to hiccup.

"Who are they?" Dayself screamed.

"I'm not the boss, please!" Pedro begged.

"Who is, Pedro?" Dayself asked, raising the axe again.

"Bamena!" Pedro yelled.

"Describe her." Dayself demanded.

"She's Spanish, in her early twenties, black hair, a mole on her top lip. I think her father left her the club," Pedro said, bleeding badly.

"That sounds like Gormez' daughter!" Dirty said.

"Do you know where she lives?" Dayself asked.

"No, I swear I don't! She never told us where she lived. I have her phone number."

"Why did you say you was the boss?" Dayself asked, leaning on the axe.

"She … she said that if anybody asked, say I was the boss. She was hardly there!" Pedro was getting cold as blood poured from his body.

"She used you, she knew if the heat ever fell on the club, that you would take the fall," Dayself said.

"I've told you what you wanted to know, could you please get me to a hospital before I bleed to death! Don't let me die like this. Please, I have kids!" Pedro cried.

"So did Trent, Shay-Shay, and the rest of my people!" Dayself yelled. "You put yourself in a bad situation. What's Bamena's number?"

"907-8126," Pedro said.

Boybaby looked at Pedro with a shocked expression.

"What number did you say?" Boybaby asked.

"907-8126." Pedro repeated.

Boybaby was devastated and it was written all over his face. Dayself looked at him, and he quickly straighten his face.

"Do you know that number, Boybaby?" Dayself asked.

"Naw man, I thought I did."

"I can get my people at Sprint to run the number. It'll take a day or two," Lambo said.

"Handle that for me, Lambo. As for you, Pedro, your time is up." Dayself said. He walked up behind Pedro, and put the tip of his knife at the top of Pedro's head. Dayself then hit the handle, sending it into Pedro's brain. "Get rid of the body, your money is on the table."

"I'll get with you on that address in a couple of days," Lambo said, rolling out plastic for the body.

After helping Lambo load the body, Dayself, Dirty, and Boybaby stood on the porch. Castro pulled up and jumped out of the car with a Mac-11 in his hand.

"What the fuck happened after I left the funeral?" Castro yelled.

"Gormez' daughter blew them up, bruh," Dayself said, almost in tears.

"Why the hell you didn't call me!" Castro said.

"My mind was going one hundred miles, a minute," Dayself said.

"Do you need me to do anything?" Castro asked.

"Yeah, let me speak with you in the house." Dayself said.

Dayself and Castro walked to the back room so no one could hear them.

"When Pedro gave us Bamenas phone number, Boybaby got this funny look on his face. I asked him did he know the number, he said no, but it's the way that he said it that makes me feel like he knows more."

"You want me to kill him?" Castro asked.

"No, not yet, anyway. I want you to follow him. If he goes anywhere strange, call me right away."

"That's peace, bruh." Castro said, walking back to the porch.

Boybaby sat quietly on the steps. He usually had a rap for them to hear, but tonight, he had no words.

"I'm out, y'all, if y'all need me, give me a call." Boybaby said. He gave everyone dap, and the brotherly hug before leaving.

Castro waited until he saw the back of Boybaby's taillights, then he got in his car, and left behind him.

"I'm already on it, partner," Dayself said when Dirty looked at him.

"Go home and get some sleep," Dirty said.

"I can't, I gotta end this before she hurts somebody else. We okayed for her to live. Now we have to accept what's come and gone, and deal with her."

"You want me to take you to Muffin?"

"She's at her grandfather house until this is over. Just drop me off at the chill spot."

"That's what's up, come on."

Chapter 28

$\mathcal{B}$oybaby sat at the red light, thinking, "How could I let her play me like that? Damn, I should've seen that shit!" He reached in the passenger seat, picked up his phone, and called Bamena.

"Hello." Bamena answered.

"Where are you?" Boybaby asked.

"I just pulled up from shopping. I bought you something."

"Word, I'm on my way there now."

"I thought you wasn't coming 'til tomorrow."

"A lot of crazy shit has happened today. I need you to hold me, and let me know everything will be all right."

"Come on, baby, I'll be waiting."

Boybaby made it to Bamena's house in ten minutes. He got out of the car and walked up to the cracked door. Reaching for his gun, Boybaby pushed the door open slowly. Bamena stood there in a purple negligée, purple open toe heels, with her toenails done in purple, and her hair hanging down. She wrapped her arms around Boybaby's neck and tongue kissed him.

"You never called to teach me how to play in my cake," Bamena said in a sexy tone. "It looks like you're gonna have to sit in the chair and I lay on the bed, while you coach me."

"Not now, Salita!" Boybaby almost yelled.

"Come on, baby," Bamena said and hooked her fingers through his.

As she led Boybaby to the bedroom, Bamena noticed that he didn't hold her hand back. She walked in the room and reached for the straps on her negligée.

"Keep it on, Bamena!" Boybaby yelled.

"Why are you calling me somebody else?"

"Pedro is dead, he told us everything."

"I can explain!" Bamena said, reaching for Boybaby's hand.

"What the fuck is there to explain?" Boybaby yelled. "You had my people, my man's baby and his baby mama killed! Then you went all out and blew them up!"

Bamena tried to think quickly. Her gun was in the drawer.

"You used me to get to my friends!" Boybaby continued to yell. "Our relationship was a big lie!"

"I didn't use you!" Bamena cried. "Do you think I would've given you my virginity if I wasn't feeling you?"

"Tell me why you did it, and don't leave shit out!"

"All right! My name is Bamena Salita Chanchez, so I didn't lie to you about my name. I only gave you my middle name because I didn't know you. For the record, you came up to me. I didn't even know you had any dealings with Double L until I heard your CD," she said, wiping her eyes with the back of her hand.

"You still have not told me why you killed my people!"

"I was kidnapped by your people! That was the only way my father, Gormez, would give them the money and drugs! Destiny raped me in front of my father and your crew!"

"But you was a —"

"She raped me in my ass with a strap on dildo! They burned my father's feet to the bone, beat nails in his knees with a hammer, then snatched them back out!" Bamena said, rocking back and forth with her arms wrapped around her stomach, replaying the scene over in her mind.

"My father was all the family I knew, until I met Bonito. He's my cousin. I was going through him to get the drugs."

"So it was you who was selling us the drugs?"

"Yes."

"Damn, them my people you killed!"

"What was I supposed to do?" Bamena asked, hands trembling. "How did your mother feel when they killed your father? I felt the same way about my father, and I do love you, with all my heart!"

"Salita ... Bamena, or whatever your name is, I could never trust you again."

"Please don't say that!" Bamena said and reached for Boybaby.

"Dayself and them know you're responsible." Boybaby said as he stepped out of her reach. "If they find out I had any dealings with you, they'll probably kill both of us. Dayself has been a father to me for many years. I can't let you live, Salita!"

"I have something to show you," Bamena said and leaned over to reach under her pillow.

"If your hand slide any further under that pillow, I'll blow your fucking head off!" Boybaby yelled, quickly pulling out his .9mm and gritting his teeth.

Bamena froze, nearly pissing on herself. Boybaby walked around the bed with his gun pointed at Bamena's head and threw the pillow to the floor. A plastic object sat there.

"What the fuck is this?"

"It's my pregnancy test!" Bamena cried. "I'm a month and two weeks!"

Boybaby looked like he was on the verge of crying.

"What the fuck?" Boybaby screamed. "What have I got myself into? What the fuck!"

"We could go to Mexico and never come back!"

"I'm not going to Mexico, do you read the newspapers? Them motherfuckers over there killing each other faster than plants with no water. I'm not fucking with Mexico!"

"We can go anywhere you want to go."

Boybaby dropped his gun on the bed, sat down, and put his hands over his face.

"I'm sorry ... Please don't kill me and our child." Bamena laid her head on his back.

"I can't kill you, not with my child growing inside of you. I can't let anyone else kill you either."

"So you're leaving with me?"

"I can't leave like that, I gotta talk to Dayself."

"He will kill both of us!" Bamena yelled.

"You won't be here. You're leaving this house first thing in the morning."

"I won't leave without you!" Bamena screamed.

"He may kill me! I'm sacrificing my life, so our baby can live. If it's a boy, name him after me and my father," Boybaby pleaded with Bamena as tears flowed from his eyes.

Bamena started to cry. She grabbed Boybaby's face, and kissed his tears. They looked in each other's eyes as Boybaby slid her straps off her shoulder. Bamena lay back and pulled her negligée down her legs. Boybaby looked at her naked body, and began to undress. He laid on top of Bamena, feeling her naked body one last time. Boybaby kissed her lips while staring in her eyes, and then he kissed a trail down to her breasts. He sucked each one, until Bamena's back raised up off the bed.

Boybaby continued his trail of kisses down to Bamena's navel and planted soft kisses as tears dropped on her stomach. Bamena pulled Boybaby up, back on top of her. They looked at each other with tears running down their cheeks. Bamena reached between them, grabbed Boybaby's dick, and slid it in her pussy. Boybaby moved in and out slowly as Bamena reached over and turned the night light off.

The room light went out. Castro waited about thirty minutes and called Dayself.

"Hello." Dayself answered in a stressed tone.

"He's at some big ass house in Wilson," Castro said.

"How long has he been there?"

"About two hours. The last light went out thirty minutes ago."

"Go to the nearest hotel, get some sleep, get up in the morning, and watch the house."

"I can handle that. When we handle this, we're going to Asia and Amaka's crib for a week."

"Damn, nigga, all you think about is pussy. I'm out, man, peace."

"Peace."

Castro pulled up in front of Bamena's house in his 2013 white Toyota Camry early the next morning. The police rode through every hour. The last time he rode through, he called Castro's tag number in. Castro drove off to a crack smoker's house who drove a United Nationa cable truck. About fifteen minutes later, he pulled back up in front of Bamena's house in the cable truck.

Boybaby woke up to Bamena standing over him with a tray of eggs, grits, sausage, toast, and orange juice.

"I'm not hungry, I don't have an appetite." Boybaby said.

"You have to eat something," Bamena said, watching him jump up and put his clothes on. "Where are you going?"

"I have to go talk to Dayself before they find you!" Boybaby said as he put his shoes on.

"Please don't go!" Bamena cried.

Boybaby grabbed the fifty thousand dollars and walked out the bedroom. Bamena ran behind him, and grabbed his arm. Boybaby's face was full of tears as Bamena silently pleaded with him to stay.

"I have to go, Salita!" Boybaby yelled, pulling her arms from around him. "Get yourself together, and get out of this house! This is not a game! I have to do this for our baby!" Boybaby walked out the door quickly before his emotions took over again.

Bamena watched through the window as Boybaby drove away, until he was out of sight. She dropped to the floor in tears.

"I have to save him!" Bamena said and jumped up. She grabbed her cell phone and dialed one of the guards.

"Hello," one of the Mexican guards answered sleepily in Spanish.

"I need y'all to the stash house right now!" Bamena yelled.

"Boss, soon as I get in touch with the others, we'll be there. You know it's eight thirty in the morning."

"I don't care, I want y'all there!" Bamena yelled and hung up.

Bamena ran up the stairs and put on a pair of sweats over her negligée.

On Boybaby's way back to Tarboro, many thoughts ambushed his brain. His mind flashed to his father in a casket, then his mother. Then it rewound to when all three of them were happy together, then back to them in the caskets. He thought to himself, *they died for love.* Boybaby wiped the tears, before they could leave his eyes, picked up his phone, and called Dayself.

"Hello." Dayself answered on his way to the shower.

"I need to talk to you about something important," Boybaby said.

"Meet me at the hiding spot in twenty minutes."

"I gotta stop by and see my grandmother first."

"That's peace."

"Peace."

Castro sat in front of Bamena's house chatting with a girl he met on Facebook. He looked up, and saw Boybaby leave. Just then, he got a picture text. It was a picture of some fat pussy lips. Castro shook his head and dialed Dayself's number.

"Hello." Dayself answered.

"Pretty boy just left."

"He just called me and said he needs to talk to me about something important."

"You need some back up?"

"I'm good, I feel like I can trust him. I don't trust many people, but he reminds me so much of myself."

"I feel you on that. Do you want me to come to Tarboro?"

"Hang around 'til about three."

"Hold on, somebody's coming out of the house in a hurry! You're not going to believe this shit. It looks like your girl!"

"My girl, who?"

"Bamena!"

"You're bullshitting, nigga!"

"You still trust pretty boy?"

"Bring her to me alive!"

"Alive?"

"Yes, alive. Peace."

"Peace."

CHAPTER 29

Boybaby pulled up at his grandmother's house, knowing it would be his last time seeing her. She was almost sixty-eight years old, with long wavy grey hair.

"Boybaby, is that you?" his grandmother asked

"Yeah, Grandma," Boybaby said sadly, watching her come out of the kitchen, wiping her hands on her apron.

"Where have you been? I haven't seen you in a whole week."

"To my friend girl's house. Did Uncle Buddy give you the money I sent?"

"Yeah, I got it. What's the matter, baby?"

"Nothing, Grandma."

"Boy, you can't lie to me, I raised you."

"Grandma, I got a baby on the way."

"By who?"

"This girl named Salita."

"Why haven't you brought her to see me?"

"She's not black, and I know how you are."

"She's not a skinny white girl, is she?"

"No Grandma, she's Mexican."

"Can she speak English?"

"Yes, I was going to bring her by, but something came up."

"That's fine. Bring her by to eat Sunday dinner with me."

"If I'm not in town, call her over to eat with you." Boybaby said and handed his grandmother the number.

"Okay, baby, are you going to eat before you go?"

"I'm not hungry. Here, put this money up." He handed her the fifty thousand dollars in a bag.

"I don't know what you're out there doing, but it's time to stop. You're following in your father's footsteps."

"I know, Grandma, and I will."

"Why do you have short answers for me today?"

"It's nothing, Grandma."

"Something is bothering you. This is the first time you've been around me and haven't smiled. The only time you ever refused my food is when I used to cook them pig feet."

"It's nothing, I'll be all right."

"Baby, always remember, you can come to me for anything."

"That's one reason why I love you."

"I love you too, baby."

Boybaby kissed his grandmother on her cheek and hugged her tight. He turned with tears in his eyes, and walked out of the house.

Bamena paced back and forth until she heard the black Yukon pull up. She ran to the window and peeped out. One of the body-guards got out and came into the stash house.

"Where are the others?" Bamena asked.

"They said that they'll be here in ten minutes," the guard said in Spanish.

"We don't have ten minutes!" Bamena yelled.

"Calm down, Boss, what's going on?"

"My baby's father —"

"Baby father!"

"Just listen, he went to the Double L guys to give them his life for mine. We have to save him!"

"When the others get here, we'll try to figure this all out. In the meantime, have a seat, and relax!"

"I can't at time like this!"

"Stressing is not good for the baby."

Castro sat in front of Bamena's stash house in the cable truck. He pulled out his phone and called Dayself.

"Hello," Dayself answered on his way to the hiding spot.

"She just stopped at the house I snatched Gormez up at. I was about to snatch her up, but a black Yukon pulled up."

"Does it have tinted windows?"

"Yeah."

"Don't let them out of your sight. I'll call Lambo to help you out. Give me the address."

"515 Dale Street."

"All right, peace."

Dayself hung up and called Lambo.

"Hello." Lambo answered, with Rick Ross playing in the background.

"How fast can you get to Wilson?"

"I live up here. You know I bought the house from Muffin."

"Castro needs some help. Go to 515 Dale Street."

"Me and my little homie walking out the door now."

"Castro will fill you in when you get there."

"All right, peace."

"Peace."

Boybaby pulled up at the hiding spot and let out a deep breath as he took his gun out and put it in the secret compartment. He got out of his car and walked to the house slowly, with his head down.

"Yo, Dayself," Boybaby yelled, walking into the house.

"Hold on." Dayself said, coming from the back room, answering his ringing phone.

"Hello." Dayself answered.

"What do you want us to do?" Lambo asked.

"Are you with Castro?"

"Yeah, I got Skip with me too."

Dayself walked off so Boybaby couldn't hear his conversation.

"These are the people that killed our family. Call me when you get them tied up."

"Say no more."

"No gun play."

"All right, peace."

"Peace."

"What's up Boybaby?" Dayself asked, walking back into the front room.

"I fucked up, man. You remember the shorty I told you I met at the mall?"

"Yeah, I remember that."

"She told me her name was Salita. I hollered at her, and we hooked up."

"That's who you were going through to get the dope, right?"

"Yeah, I didn't really know who she was until Pedro said her phone number. If I would've known she was behind killing our people, I would've killed her myself. What type of leader would I have looked like to you, fucking the enemy? That's why I didn't tell you last night. I went to go kill her last night, and found a pregnancy test under her pillow. She's pregnant by me, Dayself. Now I'm stuck in a bad situation."

"Didn't I tell you to learn from my mistakes, not to mix business with pleasure?" Dayself yelled.

"Yeah, you did, but you know how shit is."

"How do you know it's yours?"

"She was a virgin when I first hit."

"What do you expect me to do?" Dayself yelled. "She killed my baby, her mother, and our friends, not including blowing them up. That bitch gotta die for that."

"I know, Day, but she has my child!"

"What about my child?"

"You know I would do anything to bring them back if I could, but I can't."

"So what the fuck am I supposed to do, Boybaby?"

"I'm begging you, on the strength of my seed, please let her live, and take my life in place of hers."

"So you're willing to die for her?"

"No, I'm willing to die for my seed in her stomach."

"Damn, Boybaby, are you sure this is what you want?"

"It's not what I want. It's what I have to do to make sure my seed is born. As you know, my dad died to protect me. Before he left, he said, 'Son, either I'm going to die in the streets, or die for my family. I would rather die for my family.' That was the last time I ever saw him alive. Then Mom died from the sadness and hurt it caused us. Putting my seed first was implanted in me."

"Let me use the bathroom, I'll be back."

Dayself walked into the bathroom, pulled the .357 out of the cabinet, and waited for five minutes.

"Have you thought about it?" Dayself asked, walking out of the bathroom with the gun in his hands.

"Yeah, I have to do it this way."

"I'll let her live, and kill you, on one condition."

"I'll do whatever I have to do."

"You have to kill yourself." Dayself said and held the gun out.

Boybaby stared Dayself in the eyes and took the gun out of his hands.

"Before I do this, I want to thank you for all you've done for me. I have mad love and respect for you, even more for letting my seed live."

Boybaby put the gun to his head, closed his eyes, and pulled the trigger. The gun clicked. He pulled the trigger two more times. Boybaby lowered the gun and began to cry, then he jumped up and hugged Dayself.

"Any man with Double L that's willing to blow their own brains out so his seed can live, I have the upmost respect for. You bring forth a lot of understanding to the black man. I had to give you the gun to test your realness. Now I see what you're about."

"What about Salita?"

"Who."

"Bamena."

"I won't kill her, but we have to come to an understanding. If you would've died, who would've led your seed to become a true queen or king?"

"You taught me that we're born kings and queens."

Dayself looked at Boybaby and smiled.

Lambo, Castro, and Skip snuck up behind the black Yukon. As they were getting ready to run and kick the door in, another truck pulled up. They quickly hid under the Yukon. The two Mexican guards got out of the truck, and walked past. Lambo, Castro, and Skip rolled from under the truck, crept up behind the two Mexicans going up the steps. They turned around to five guns in their faces.

"Put your hands up motherfuckers!" Castro said.

Lambo and Skip took the guns from the bodyguards.

"Walk slowly, and open the door," Lambo said.

The two guards immediately complied.

"What took y'all—" Bamena yelled until she saw the other men behind them with guns.

The bodyguard in the house pushed Bamena to the floor and pulled his gun out. Before he could get a shot off, he was shot seven times. The vest that he was wearing stopped most of the bullets. On his way to the floor, he let off a shot, hitting Skip in the middle of his forehead. He dropped to the floor, with his body jumping.

The guard that was shooting ran out of bullets and reached into his cowboy boot for his .32 revolver. Castro and Lambo shot the guard in the face so many times, it looked like his head was blown off.

"Start tying their asses up. Let me call Dayself," Castro said, dialing the number.

"Hello," Dayself answered.

"We had to shoot. One Mexican guard is dead," Castro said.

"Tell Dayself I found twenty keys and a small trash bag of E-pills." Lambo said.

"Tell Lambo to keep five, you keep five, and bring me ten. Y'all take most of the pills and bring the rest."

"What about the dolls?"

"Throw the men dolls in the trash, and bring the Barbie doll to me."

"I got you, peace."

"Peace."

"Y'all done fucked up!" Castro said to the Mexican guards.

He pulled out his gun and shot one in the head twice. Castro aimed his gun at the other one as Lambo ran in from the other room with his gun pointed.

"What are you doing?" Lambo asked.

"Killing these two." Castro said.

"Fuck that!" Lambo yelled and pointed his gun at the other guard's head. He pulled the trigger twice. "I came to kill too!" Lambo let out a crazy laugh.

Castro thought to himself, *something is wrong with this dude.*

Bamena lay still on the floor with her eyes tightly closed. She knew that she was next. Opening her eyes, she saw all three guards dead around her. She felt Castro standing over her, so she closed her eyes and waited. To her surprise, Castro pulled her off the floor, put handcuffs on her, and led her out to the cable truck.

Castro drove up to the hiding spot and took Bamena in the house. Boybaby looked from Dayself to Bamena.

"Yo, Dayself, what's going on?" Boybaby asked, watching

Dayself take the cuffs off Bamena.

She ran to Boybaby and hugged him. "Don't kill him, he had nothing to do with it, kill me!" Bamena cried.

"Calm down, Salita, it's going to be all right," Boybaby said, rubbing her back.

"Not it's not. I shouldn't have put you in the middle of this!" Bamena continued to cry.

"I'm not going to hurt you. I just want to talk to you. I had to have that done to your people. I know they were the hands on guys. We have to come to an understanding and stop this beef. We both have lost family and people we care for. I'm letting you live, only because you're carrying my man's baby. He's like family to me. If he can put a gun to his head and pull the trigger to save his seed, then I got enough love for him to let you live for his seed. Do we have a deal to squash all of this beef?"

Bamena was quiet for a minute as she thought about her and Boybaby being a family.

"We have a deal." Bamena said, rubbing her stomach.

"How do I know you won't renege on your word?" Dayself asked.

"My word is my bond. I'll die trying to make my bond complete."

"That's good. You're teaching her, Boybaby." Dayself said.

Bamena turned and hugged Boybaby.

"It's ten keys in here. Five for you, and sell the other five for me. I'm out of the game," Dayself said and handed Boybaby the bags with the keys in them. "Stro, let's go to New York."

"You ain't said nothing. Plane or car?" Castro asked.

"Plane," Dayself said. "Let me call Muffin. I need another vacation."

"Hello." Muffin answered, breathing hard.

"Hey, baby mama. You can come home now. I'll be gone for five days."

"No the hell you won't!" Muffin screamed. "I'll have this big ass … o shit!" Muffin yelled as liquid ran down her leg.

"What's wrong?" Dayself asked.

"My water just broke!"

"Breathe, Muffin!" Dayself said.

"Just get your ass here!" Muffin yelled in pain.

"All right."

"Castro, there's been a change of plans. My baby, Muffin, is in labor, partner. My seed is on his way!" Dayself yelled.

SNEAK PEEK OF DOUBLE L VS THE CARTEL II

Coming Soon!

CHAPTER 1

"Papa, I told Bamena that you wouldn't accept her having a mixed kid the way I could. She wouldn't listen to me. I called Lambo back, but he wouldn't tell me exactly where Bamena is now living."

"I paid that fucking monkey one million dollars to shoot me with blanks after he burnt my feet and put nails in my knees. We paid him to make sure Bamena was safe, and to keep an eye out on Yellow. He let Dayself's people kill three of your uncles. I told them not to be Bamena's bodyguards, but they insisted. Yellow killed your grandpa, Big Gormez. He think he got away, but I have somebody closer to him than he thinks. Asia knows it was he who set her mother and step father up to be killed. I'm just waiting for the right time to clip him. We'll take Dayself down with him. Don't forget to send the doctor the million dollars for killing Dayself's wife and baby mother. Bonito, go ahead and kill Lambo. He's useless to us now. Also, get in touch with Bamena, tell her to leave that black baby and come home, or die!"

"Papa, don't speak of killing your daughter, my only sibling."

"Well, either you do it, or I'll turn my back on you and kill you in her place."

"Papa, don't speak of killing your kids. You can't be serious."

Gormez' two bodyguards pulled out guns. One put a gun to Bonito's head, and the other one put a gun to his heart.

"I'm with you, Papa, you know that!"

"Then do as I say!"

"I'll do it now, Papa."

Bonito went to the phone,

"Hello."

"Lambo rest."

"It'll be taken care of as soon as possible."

The three black strippers who worked for Bamena had become the ecstasy pill queens. They were getting the pills from Bonito for three dollars and fifty cents a pill. Lambo happened to be fucking one of them and she would do anything Bonito asked for the right price.

Gormez picked up the phone and called the four Mexican killers he had sent to North Carolina.

"Hello."

"I want Dayself, Boybaby, Dirty, and Castro dead! Do you hear me?"

"Si, si, si Boss."